Praise for the

"Fresh and exciting, humo
fantasy at its best."

–Ilona Andrews, #1 New York Times *bestselling author of the Kate Daniels series*

"Makenna Fraser brings Southern sass, smarts, and charm to the mean streets of Manhattan as she battles monsters and other magical beings."

–Jennifer Estep, New York Times *bestselling author of the Elemental Assassin novels*

"Plenty more gasp- and laughter-inducing adventures…this is a thrilling series, so hang on tight, for things are going to get seriously bumpy!"

–RT Book Reviews

"A word of warning, don't start this book unless you have a solid block set aside as you simply will not be able to put it down."

–A Book Obsession

"Shearin has been on my auto-buy list for years. She is able to combine humor, mystery, suspense, slow-burn romance, high stakes, and her own spin on the supernatural into a cohesive whole. I'm addicted to finding out what will happen next in the SPI Files."

–Bookpushers

"There is so much action that you can't put this book down… fun and truly great adventure stories."

–Night Owl Romance

"There are twists, turns, danger, romance, action, but more importantly—lots of fun… Laugh out loud funny… A brilliantly addictive urban fantasy series."

–Terror Tree

Praise for the Raine Benares Novels

"Exceptional...Shearin has proven herself to be an expert storyteller with the enviable ability to provide both humor and jaw-dropping action."

–*RT Book Reviews*

"The kind of book you hope to find when you go to the bookstore. It takes you away to a world of danger, magic, and adventure, and it does so with dazzling wit and clever humor. It's gritty, funny, and sexy—a wonderful addition to the urban fantasy genre. I absolutely loved it. From now on Lisa Shearin is on my auto-buy list!"

–*Ilona Andrews, #1* New York Times *bestselling author*

"A wonderful fantasy tale full of different races and myths and legends [that] are drawn so perfectly readers will believe they actually exist. Raine is a strong female, a leader who wants to do the right thing even when she isn't sure what that is...Lisa Shearin has the magic touch."

–*Midwest Book Review*

"Tons of action and adventure but it also has a bit of romance and humor...All of the characters are excellent...The complexities of the world that Ms. Shearin has developed are fabulous."

–*Night Owl Reviews*

"If you're new to Shearin's work, and you enjoy fantasy interspersed with an enticing romance, a little bit of humor, and a whole lot of grade-A action, this is the series for you."

–*Lurv a la Mode*

"The book reads more like an urban fantasy with pirates and sharp wit and humor. I found the mix quite refreshing. Lisa Shearin's fun, action-packed writing style gives this world life and vibrancy."

–*Fresh Fiction*

"Lisa Shearin represents that much needed voice in fantasy that combines practiced craft and a wicked sense of humor."

–*Bitten by Books*

"The brisk pace and increasingly complex character development propel the story on a roller-coaster ride through demons, goblins, elves, and mages while maintaining a satisfying level of romantic attention…that will leave readers chomping at the bit for more."

–*Monsters and Critics*

This book is a work of fiction. The characters, incidents, and dialogue are drawn from the author's imagination and are not to be construed as real. Any resemblance to actual events or persons, living or dead, is entirely coincidental.

Published by Murwood Media, LLC

Editor: Betsy Mitchell
Copyeditor: Martha Trachtenberg
Cover artist: Elizabeth Peiró
Book designer: Angie Hodapp

ISBN 978-1-7327226-7-5

THE GORGON AGENDA

A SPI FILES NOVEL

LISA SHEARIN

1

Did you ever get the feeling you were being watched?

I glanced over at my dad. Yes, he was watching me. But not in a bad way.

It was a statue, a desktop version of my dad.

Cernunnos. The Master of the Wild Hunt.

I'm good friends with a dryad, a witch, and a werewolf. My manager is a vampire. My boss is a dragon. And I'm in a serious relationship with a goblin. Now I had something new for the list. My dad is the Master of the Wild Hunt.

When I'd come back to work after Christmas, the statue had been waiting for me on my desk.

At SPI (Supernatural Protection and Investigations), it was known as desk flair, mementos of particularly memorable missions. When your coworkers deemed your actions deserving, they'd gift you with desk flair.

It was from everyone. They'd all chipped in.

It was about twenty inches tall and looked like it belonged in a museum—or on an ancient altar.

It was carved from exotic wood. At first I thought it'd been painted, but it was masterfully carved to reveal the grain. Tan where the skin was, blond for the hair, ebony shadings for the armor. All from a single block of wood.

Kylie O'Hara, our director of Media and Public Relations, had reacted with wide eyes and no words when she'd seen it. If a wooden carving impressed a dryad, it didn't just look flawless, it was flawless.

It was as if my dad had been miniaturized and taken up residence on my desk, complete with secretive smile and perpetually amused expression.

Whenever I was at my desk doing paperwork, I'd steal quick glances to try to catch him winking at me.

I had maybe a dozen pieces of desk flair. My partner Ian Byrne, aka SPI's version of 007 meets Rambo, had shelves of the stuff. From action figures out of an assortment of horror and fantasy movies to shell casings from impossibly large guns. More than a few of the monster action figures were missing their heads, or had sharp, pointy objects sticking out of them.

Fairy tales are fairy fact.

Magic exists. Monsters are real. Fighting the forces of evil is a full-time job.

At least there's hazard pay.

SPI was founded in 1647 to fight the forces of supernatural evil. We're headquartered here in New York but have offices and agents worldwide.

My name is Makenna Fraser. I'm a seer. I can see through any kind of ward, shield, or spell a supernatural criminal can use to disguise itself from the human population. My abilities also apply to cloaks and veils that render their wearers invisible. You can't apprehend what you can't see. I do the seeing. Agents like my partner do the apprehending.

Ian and I had been hit over the heads in the past year with our pasts. Not pasts as in what we'd done, but in who we were.

We were still human, but the kind that came with significant upgrades.

Ian was the direct descendant of Lugh Lámhfhada, a king of the Tuatha Dé Danann, a supernatural race considered heroes and deities by the ancient Celtic people. Lugh's claim to fame was killing his grandfather Balor, the last king of the evil race of sea monsters called the Fomorians. Balor's death in an ancient battle broke the Fomorians, and the Tuatha Dé drove them into the sea and kept them there for thousands of years with a curse. Recently, the Fomorians had tried to stage a comeback led by a megamage and demigod wannabe named Janus, who'd been stalking Ian for years.

Now we knew why. Ian was the last of Lugh's direct line. His death would have released the Fomorians from the curse and their exile. Janus had been the captain of Balor's personal guard and had been tasked with finding Lugh's descendant and sacrificing him so the Fomorians could once again emerge from the oceans and walk the earth.

SPI and our allies had collectively rained on the Fomorians' return tour, banished Janus, and sent the Fomorians back where they came from.

And me? I got a special surprise during Christmas vacation

with my family. My father hadn't died before I'd been born, as I'd always been told.

I was the daughter of Cernunnos, the Master of the Wild Hunt. When my mom had sowed her collegiate wild oats, she hadn't messed around.

I was the daughter of one of the supernatural world's apex predators. My dad, as leader of the Wild Hunt, commanded a raging, unpredictable, and unspeakably ancient force of nature. Dad himself was one of the most powerful supernatural entities in existence.

And I was his little girl.

Two months ago, Janus tried to break the curse that kept the Fomorians in exile, this time by becoming a god himself. He'd used me and my mom as bait to lure Cernunnos into a trap—and his plan for taking my father's power had come entirely too close to succeeding. Dad and I had orchestrated Janus's final and permanent demise by tag teaming with a couple million really pissed-off souls that Janus had imprisoned.

I was still coming to grips with what being Cernunnos's daughter meant in terms of who and what I was. Mostly I was still the me I'd always believed myself to be. Over the past few years, I'd acquired a few new—and quite frankly, disturbing—abilities. I now realized they'd come from my dad and not through a brief mind-to-mind contact with a psychotic, megalomaniacal Russian oligarch/dragon.

That was a huge relief.

If any new talent popped up that I didn't understand, I could call Dad and ask him about it. Not call in the speed-dial sense, but via a gold wrist cuff covered in Celtic scrollwork he'd given me when I'd last seen him in the wee dark hours of Christmas Day.

Since then, I'd occasionally sensed his presence, psychically checking in on me, or however it was that Celtic gods kept tabs on their progeny.

I hadn't called him directly. I knew he was busy hunting the wicked and gathering the souls of the dead and all that. And being well-nigh immortal, time passed differently for him. A year to me was a few minutes for him, and no one wanted their kid constantly tugging on their sleeve. I'd just gotten a father and wasn't about to annoy him by being one of those "Dad, Dad, Dad, watch this" kind of kids. He'd told me to call if I needed him. However, there might be rare times that he wouldn't be reachable, but those would be few and far between.

When he reached out to me, I reached back, and we exchanged a quick hand-squeeze kind of thing. He knew I loved him. And yes, I did love him, even though we'd spent only a few hours together.

For the first time in my life, I had a dad.

Best Christmas present ever.

Though I did get another present from my family that was equally awesome.

I took my boyfriend, goblin dark mage Rake Danescu, home with me for Christmas. Turned out me being a nervous wreck about the whole experience had been completely unnecessary. He not only won over my family, but also the entire population of my hometown. Helping to save said town from an awakening primordial evil had earned him some serious points.

When I'd come back to the office after the holidays, no one had asked what I'd done on vacation. Juicy news like that had already arrived and spread like wildfire. My stock had risen in the eyes of some of our senior-most agents as well as those of our not-easy-to-impress department directors.

SPI was one of the few places you could work and have "daughter of the Celtic god of death" not only be widely known, but also be the crowning glory of your resume.

However, other than seeing portals, talking telepathically to dragons, and being able to ride a horse without falling off, I still felt like the same Makenna Fraser. I'd been tempted to tell everyone as much, but our boss, Vivienne Sagadraco, had instructed me to simply say nothing, or "thank you" if the comment was congratulatory, and move on. That's what SPI's boss lady had said, so that's what I had done. After all, I *was* Cernunnos's daughter. No stretching the truth there. I wasn't claiming to be anything more. Ms. Sagadraco had added that if people believed otherwise, that was on them, not me.

In addition to now having ties to legendary bloodlines, Ian and I had come into possession of some legendary weapons.

Ian had his ancestor's spearhead. Being a famous mythological weapon, it had more than one name, but it was most often known as Lugh's Spear. Fortunately, it didn't need to be attached to a shaft to do its thing. Ian couldn't exactly walk around town with a seven-foot spear; even jaded New Yorkers would have a problem with that.

Probably.

That didn't mean Ian wouldn't have easy access to his ancestor's weapon. All the power was contained in the spearhead, so Ian did the concealed-carry thing under his jacket.

The spearhead no longer glowed when Ian touched it, but I sensed a thrum coming from it now. Maybe since the blade now knew Ian better, it didn't feel the need for extreme PDA, just a quiet acknowledgment of affection.

In addition to the aforementioned wrist cuff, which took up half my forearm, Dad had given me his hunting knife. In my hands it was more of a short sword.

Dad hadn't told me what the cuff did. Initially I'd thought it was just a museum-quality piece of jewelry. He'd given one to me and one to my mom. After I'd discovered that Dad was able to check in with me, I'd called Mom. Yep, he was doing the same with her. I figured that was what the cuff did, except it was gold and gorgeous.

Our R&D folks had created a chip that could be mounted on the cuff's underside that hid it from view, kind of like its own little cloaking device. During cold weather, it'd been easy enough to conceal under long sleeves, but it was early spring, and soon it'd be short-sleeves weather with no way to hide it. Not to mention every time the sun hit it, the reflection off the gold nearly fried my retinas.

I didn't think the cuff did anything else until my first mission in early January. We'd been searching an abandoned warehouse in Brooklyn when Dad's gift warned me that our suspect was closer than we thought. Like right above our heads close. The cuff had given me a mild electric zap. Having my skin try to crawl up my arm had a way of getting my attention. I'd looked up and there was our spider monster.

It made sense. Dad wanted to protect me and Mom, but he couldn't be here himself, so he'd given us each a cuff.

So far, it hadn't done anything else, though that was plenty. It could deflect bullets like Wonder Woman's bracelets for all I knew. The chance to test that theory hadn't come up, and I'd be just fine if it never did.

Zap.

My entire body shivered in response.

Speak of the devil.

Ian looked up from his laptop at the desk next to mine. "Cuff?"

I tried to look everywhere at once. "Uh-huh." Nothing but SPI's bullpen as far as the eye could see, with agents working and going about their business.

The cuff gave me another zap, as if it knew I was still clueless.

This was SPI's world headquarters, the safest place on the planet. Well, one of the safest. There was that time when my evil doppelganger had walked in with a bowling bag full of hatching grendel eggs.

We'd made significant security improvements since then.

My eyes flicked to the ceiling above my head.

Nope, no spider monster.

The cuff gave me a seriously sharp zap. I yelped.

Ian stood. "That wasn't nothing."

Then I heard it, but not with my ears. It was Vivienne Sagadraco, SPI's draconic founder. Ms. Sagadraco was British born, or hatched as the case may be, and was proud of her unflappable reserve. She got angry, but she did not show it.

She was showing it now.

I felt her outrage, along with disbelief and fear. Vivienne Sagadraco was afraid. I didn't know it was possible for her to be afraid of anything.

The floor vibrated beneath my feet, as did Dad's statue on my desk, and I knew it wasn't an earthquake.

Our boss, the dragon lady, was growling. We all heard and felt it. The bullpen went silent as every agent stopped what they were doing and looked up to the source of that growl.

The fifth floor was home to the executive suites and Ms. Sagadraco's office. The outer walls of her office were glass and overlooked the bullpen. The boss's rumbling growl was now shaking the five stories of steel catwalks connecting offices, labs, and conference rooms.

Suddenly that growl erupted into a full-throated, enraged roar, and the glass spiderwebbed with what sounded like multiple shotgun blasts. The glass didn't fall, but the agents directly below weren't taking any chances and scrambled clear.

The silence that followed was absolute.

My phone buzzed with an incoming text, as did Ian's.

All eyes were instantly on us.

We picked up our phones and read the message.

It was from Alain Moreau, ancient French vampire, the boss's right-hand legal eagle—and our manager.

Madame wants to see you both. Now.

2

Getting called into the boss's office had never marked the beginning of fun times. That said boss had just roared loudly enough to break glass that was bulletproof, explosion-proof, and everything-else-proof, guaranteed this wasn't going to be good news.

The elevator doors closed, and Ian pushed the button for the fifth-floor executive suite.

Curiosity may have killed a few cats, and it'd gotten me in trouble more than once. Regardless, I wasn't the shy sort.

"Did we do anything wrong?" I asked my annoyingly calm partner.

"What do you think?"

"If I'd done something that bad, I'd know."

"Exactly."

"Then why does she want to see us?"

"In a few minutes, we'll find out."

"I'd rather know going in."

The elevator dinged as we reached our destination.

"Well, that's not going to happen, is it?"

The doors slid open, and Ian politely indicated that I go first.

"Gee, thanks."

"My mom taught me to be polite." He flashed a grin. "And not stupid."

My partner had known Vivienne Sagadraco much longer than I had. If he wasn't worried, I'd at least try not to be. I wouldn't succeed, but I'd try.

The elevator door opened into Ms. Sagadraco's reception area, and I saw we weren't the only ones who'd been summoned, though I was still plenty confused as to why.

Alain Moreau's presence was expected. The other two men I knew, but why they were here was a mystery.

Martin DiMatteo, director of SPI's demonology department, was our resident expert on Hell and all that lived there. Martin was a nice guy but was best described as quirky. Though if it hadn't been for his knowledge, we'd never have escaped a pocket dimension with a pit that led straight to Hell.

I'd only heard about Mortimer Winters, who was the director of SPI's sorcery division. He wasn't as old as Vivienne Sagadraco. No one at SPI was, but office rumor had it he came closest. Ms. Sagadraco was already enraged. The worst she could do was go dragon and stomp on the offending party like a ketchup packet. Mortimer Winters could turn them into one.

Finding these two men cooling their heels outside the

boss's office meant what had happened was catastrophically huge.

Ian greeted both men with a solemn nod. Director Winters and I had never been introduced and I didn't anticipate that happening now, so I followed my senior partner's lead with a nod of my own. I knew Martin well enough to go with a smile and a little finger wave, though considering the tenseness of the situation, I kept my smile and fingers to myself.

Mr. Moreau made no move to open the door to the inner office or otherwise announce our arrival. Our manager was at least three hundred years old, but looked like he could be Anderson Cooper's vampiric twin brother.

"Are you saying I don't know when my vault has been breached?" Ms. Sagadraco snapped from inside her office. On a normal day, her upper-class British accent could cut glass. Right now, any diamond in her immediate vicinity was in danger.

And some poor unfortunate in there with her was on the receiving end.

"You must be mistaken, Madam Sagadraco," said a tinny voice.

Ah, speakerphone. Lucky for the owner of that voice.

"You're implying I do not know when an item from my vault is missing?"

"No, no. That is not what I meant at all. I merely—"

"So, the link I personally have to each artifact in that vault is faulty?"

"Not at all, ma'am."

"Then what *do* you mean?"

"That when you arrive, I will be waiting to escort you to your vault to assess the loss."

"Loss?"

"Theft, ma'am. If you said your hoard has been robbed, then that is precisely what has happened."

"I will be there within the half hour."

Holy crap.

"Some suicidal idiot robbed the boss's hoard?" I blurted.

The door to the inner office swept open.

"Yes, Agent Fraser." Vivienne Sagadraco's voice was crisp with righteous indignation. "Some suicidal idiot has done just that." She stepped back from the doorway. "Please, everyone come in."

The design of the agent bullpen was the epitome of a modern office. Vivienne Sagadraco's office looked like something out of Hogwarts—with the exception of the wall of now-cracked glass overlooking said bullpen. The furniture was dark wood upholstered in rich fabrics. There was an actual fireplace on the far wall. The fireplace was real, but the fire crackling in it was magically generated. The air in the office was thick with suppressed rage, and it didn't take my seer senses to know it was all too real.

The boss's hoard had been robbed.

Now I understood the roar that'd spider-webbed the glass and sent veteran agents scurrying for cover. Vivienne Sagadraco valued two things above all else.

Her employees, and her hoard.

You messed with either one at your extreme peril.

Dragons, especially the ancients, were highly territorial. In the old days, it probably had to do with carving out a sufficiently large hunting ground. It took a lot to top off a dragon's tank. Then there was their hoard to consider. Nothing stoked a dragon's fire faster than someone getting within stealing distance of their sparklies.

I'd been in Vivienne Sagadraco's office many times before, but what had always been a wall of Tudor-style oak paneling was now open, revealing what had to be at least twenty flat-screen TVs. A control panel ran the length of the screens and was nearly identical to the surveillance setup our IT guru Kenji Hayashi had downstairs in the bullpen. We called it his command center.

I wondered what else was concealed behind the boss's office walls.

Ms. Sagadraco went directly to the monitors and gestured that we all join her. "Agent Fraser, I need your opinion in particular as to what happened."

Suddenly, all eyes were on me.

"Me, ma'am?"

"Yes, you. Last year at the Regor Regency, you were able to see the cloaked intruder on the hotel's security cameras. I need you to do the same here."

No pressure.

When I got close enough to see what was on all those monitors, it was all I could do to keep my jaw from dropping.

So this was how tech-savvy dragons kept watch over their hoards.

Each screen was split into sections and displayed treasures and wealth I could only imagine. Actually, my brain was having trouble believing what it was seeing.

Some of the screens showed what looked like bank vaults, others appeared to be rooms in castles, still others were caves, or judging from the wide-angle views, caverns. And each and every one was filled with treasure and art. Piles of coins, jewels, gem-encrusted weapons, plus paintings, statues, and anything else considered beautiful and valuable on the planet Earth. And I swear, one of the caverns looked just like the treasure room under Hamunaptra in *The Mummy.* Actually, quite a few of them did, but were filled with treasures from different time periods.

Martin gave an impressed whistle. Coming from a man who took regular field trips to Hell, that said a lot.

"Do pardon the mess," Ms. Sagadraco told us. "It is difficult to get reliable help these days, or any other days for that matter."

Ian's eyes scanned each and every screen. I guessed what he wanted to know, and I'll admit I was curious myself, but some questions you simply didn't ask. One was asking a woman of a certain age how old she was. Even more dangerous was asking a dragon how many hoards they had. Vivienne Sagadraco qualified for both.

"The vault that was compromised contains twelve artifacts requiring special precautions," she told us. "It is secured with the latest technology and the most ancient of magics. It makes Fort Knox look like a child's piggy bank—at least it did. Someone has been inside."

The ancient-magics part explained why Mortimer Winters was here. Martin's presence was still a mystery.

"The vault is beneath the Gotham Bank and Trust Company." Ms. Sagadraco took a seat at the console and her fingers flew over the keyboard. All the screens went dark except for the one in the lower right corner. Then that one winked out and reappeared, with each camera angle given its own screen in the center of the wall of TVs.

It looked more like a temple than a vault to me. Judging from the curvature, the room was circular. Niches were set into the stone walls at regular intervals, and each niche was framed by columns. There was one object in each niche, but the lighting was too dim to see what they were.

"I copied the design of a Greek temple I was especially fond of in my youth," Ms. Sagadraco said in response to my thoughts. She could hear mine, and on occasion, I could hear hers. I'd been able to do this for a few years, but only over Christmas did I discover I'd inherited the ability from my father. "The twelve artifacts I keep there are each worthy of the reverence of a temple. The lighting is kept dim for safety. A few of the artifacts react poorly to bright light."

Okay then. Artifacts with attitude. Duly noted.

"A break-in should have been impossible," she continued, "but as at least one of the artifacts is no longer there, it obviously is possible. I believe I know what has been stolen, but I sincerely hope I am wrong. The thief came, stole, and fled in a matter of seconds. I sensed their arrival and departure, but the cameras showed only static. I need a description of the culprit, Agent Fraser. Let me back up the recording to the time of the disturbance." She typed some more, then stood and stepped aside. "Sit here and tell me what you see."

I slid into the seat she had vacated.

Disturbance was right.

Dust began falling from a section of the vault's wall between two of the niches. Then the entire wall simply collapsed into a pile of dust.

Ian leaned over my shoulder. "What the hell?"

Ms. Sagadraco reached around me and stopped the video.

"I excavated the chamber out of solid bedrock when I first arrived in New York," she said. "The thief would have needed mining equipment and weeks to get near it. Access should have been impossible. The vault and the bedrock beneath and around it are surrounded by ley lines."

It was my turn to whistle.

Impossible indeed.

Nothing can survive inside a ley line tube. Ley lines are rivers of energy that cut through rock much like lava. Raw energy is not kind to any being with a physical body—though I'd personally witnessed an exception on my most recent trip home. The remains of the First Master of the Wild Hunt, who rode and hunted when the world was young, were being regenerated by being suspended over an exposed ley line river.

There had to have been another explanation for how the thief got into the boss's vault.

Director Winters shook his head in disbelief at the pile of dust. "Vivienne, my wards *were* there."

"And they disintegrated along with that wall," Ms. Sagadraco said.

"But the—"

"I'm not assigning blame, Mortimer. I want answers. Help me find them."

"Of course."

She pressed a key and restarted the video.

There was movement in the shadows just beyond the opening, then the screen went to static.

At least it did for everyone else. I could see more. Not much, but there was something.

I leaned closer to get a better look.

There was a patch of transparent wavy lines, taller than a human, moving smoothly through the static. It was what I'd experienced at the Regor Regency. I could see through glamours and cloaks in person, no problem. A glamour was a disguise. A cloak was complete coverage. With a cloak, to anyone but a seer, there appeared to be no one there. On TV or surveillance camera footage, it wasn't easy, but I could at least see a presence. It would appear as wavy lines.

That's exactly what I was seeing here.

So, whatever this thing was, it clearly had a physical body.

The figure crossed out of one camera's range and into the next, then that screen also went to static. The figure then slowed and stopped.

You know how when you stare at something long enough, you begin to see recognizable shapes? That's what I was getting.

Lashing movements around the top of the figure reminded me of the arms on one of those inflatable-tube-monster thingies they have at car dealerships.

I blinked and leaned even closer.

Pain exploded behind my eyes. I fell forward, my head slamming into the keyboard. I dimly heard Ian shout as everything went black.

3

"For the last time, I'm fine."

I was on a couch in the boss's office, and there were entirely too many people in white lab coats fussing over me. I had the mother of all migraines, and if Mike Stephens didn't stop shining that penlight in my eyes, I was gonna haul off and smack him. I didn't care if he was SPI's chief medical doctor.

On the other side of the room, Kenji Hayashi and two of his techie geeks were analyzing the heck out of the video that'd caused the brouhaha. None of them had passed out, but I felt like I'd taken an icepick to both eyes. I was happy for them, but still confused for me. It was only a video. It wasn't even live. Plus, I'd only seen wavy lines. It wasn't like I'd even gotten a good look at the whatever-it-was.

I'd told everyone that multiple times, but they were still insistent on poking and prodding yours truly.

According to Ian, I'd been out for less than three minutes.

The headache was bad enough, but after waking up, I'd reached up and felt the imprint of computer keys on my forehead. The headache was staying, but my dignity was long gone.

"We're wasting time," I said. "It's not like the thief is gonna wait for us to catch up."

"I gave Mortimer access codes to get into the vault," Ms. Sagadraco told me. "He and two of his battlemages are there now. Martin has gone to get Ruby. They'll be going with us." The boss came around into my field of vision. I was grateful. It still hurt to move my eyes. Though whatever was in the eyedrops Dr. Stephens kept putting in there had helped. A little. It felt like a migraine, but with the addition of dry and gritty eyes.

"Does 'us' include me?" I asked her.

"I think it best that you remain here."

Dang it.

Ian passed me another cold compress.

"Close your eyes and rest," he told me. It wasn't exactly an order; he knew I didn't take those well, so he went with a strongly worded request. Closing my eyes with an ice-cold washcloth on top felt too good for words, so for once I shut up and did as told. For now.

So that was why Martin had been included in the meeting.

A couple of months ago, he'd brought back a pet from one of his field trips to Hell.

An actual hellhound.

Ruby had been a puppy that'd apparently wandered off from her momma and gotten herself stranded on a rock out in a river of brimstone. According to Martin, an adult hellhound could've jumped off that rock and swum to shore just fine, but Ruby was a little thing, probably the runt of the litter, and her skin wasn't thick enough yet, and she would've gone up in an itty-bitty puff of smoke. Long story short, Martin had rescued the little fluff-nugget and brought her home with him.

Ruby was all grown up now and while still small for a hellhound, she was plenty big compared to a regular dog—kinda like a cross between a Tibetan mastiff and a Great Dane. She reminded me of the hounds that ran with my dad's Wild Hunt.

While Ruby was a hellhound, she was as sweet as could be, and had become the office mascot. She especially liked being in the bullpen, where everyone kept treats and toys for her at their desks. There was nothing cuter than watching a hellhound bounce and pounce on a squeaky bunny rabbit. It shook the floor under our desks, but that didn't lessen the cute. Someone had recently given her a bright blue, plush dragon toy. The color was identical to the boss's scales. Fortunately, she hadn't seen it yet. No one would admit to having bought it.

Ruby had big, brown eyes—unless she was tracking something. Then they glowed ruby red, like those humongous temple dogs in *Ghostbusters*. Hence, her name. Our girl was an excellent tracker.

As a seer, I knew when magic was in use or had been used, and I could track its user. The vault thief had been shielded with magic. I was the only seer in the New York office, and I needed to be there.

I took the cloth off my eyes and sat up. That went well. No woozies. "I have a proposal," I told Ms. Sagadraco. "Can I go to the vault if Dr. Stephens goes with us?"

Silence met my suggestion. I took that as a positive sign and kept going. "Ruby's nose is world-class, but scents can be masked. My seer vision can't be tricked."

Dr. Stephens's eager expression said he was all for it. Bless his heart, he didn't get out much. I got an eye roll from Ian, and a resigned sigh from the boss. It wasn't enthusiastic agreement, but I'd take it.

The Gotham Bank & Trust Company in midtown Manhattan mostly looked like the buildings around it, with one notable exception. No windows, at least not real ones. Smart design feature for a bank. Fewer windows meant fewer ways in. Though the last time we'd been here on a case, the bank robbers hadn't used any of the bank's few doors to gain access to the main vault.

They'd made their own. Namely a portal.

Disguised as ghouls, Janus and his Fomorian thugs had come back to the scene of the crime, because they hadn't been able to take all they'd wanted the first time. What they'd wanted most was Ian, and they'd used the vice president of customer relations as bait to get him into that vault.

Ian. My partner. My brother from another mother.

It felt creepy to be here again. I kept my eyes straight ahead as we walked past the place where Janus's ghouls had fed on one of the bank guards while he was still alive. I was creeped out, but Ian had to be feeling about a hundred times worse.

Ms. Sagadraco had offered him an out, but my partner hadn't taken it. Ian preferred to confront his fears. He hadn't been back here since that day, and I knew it was on his confrontational bucket list. If I was going, he was going.

Yes, Janus was dead; and yes, Ian had gotten to watch it himself thanks to SPI's resident psychiatrist Dr. Noel Tierney. Noel could do dream links. He'd done one with Ian before. Ian had dreamed of a battle his ancestor had been in with Janus thousands of years ago. Noel had seen it as Ian had dreamed and had drawn what he'd seen.

To see what'd happened on Christmas Eve, when Janus had been ripped to shreds by the millions of souls he'd imprisoned, Noel functioned as the go-between with me and Ian. I'd been there for Janus's death and could recall it in detail. Noel transferred my memories as a waking dream to Ian. Ian had said it was the best present he'd ever gotten. Getting to see it himself, even after the fact, had given my partner much-needed closure. He wanted to thank my dad personally. I hoped he'd get the chance soon.

Gotham Bank & Trust existed exclusively for the supernatural one percent of the one percent. Aside from dragons, only vampires and gorgons lived long enough to amass that kind of wealth. A dragon's valuables didn't exactly fit into safe deposit boxes. They hid their hoards themselves and provided their own security. Vivienne Sagadraco had founded the bank in 1754 and had it built on top of her artifact hoard as added protection. It'd worked just fine, until today.

I wouldn't want to be the Gotham Bank president right now or any other time. He'd been the one on the phone with Ms. Sagadraco back at the office. He had to be the abnormally pale man in the dark suit who was waiting by the elevators with a group of what were probably bank officers. He wasn't vampiric pale; he was terrified-human pale.

The bank president took a breath to steel himself and made a beeline for us. Vivienne Sagadraco simply held up a hand and shook her head. He froze where he was as she swept past with me, Ian, Dr. Stephens, Martin DiMatteo, and Ruby in her wake.

She walked right past the bank of elevators and down a narrow hallway. At the end was an elevator door with a keypad. Ms. Sagadraco's fingers flew over the keypad for nearly a minute. Now *that* was a strong password. The door opened and we got on. There were no buttons on the inside and no way to know where we were going other than down.

The elevator doors closed, and we started down to Vivienne Sagadraco's private vault and hoard.

I'd been with SPI for five years, and I was now part of a very select group. Ms. Sagadraco trusted me with one of her most valuable secrets, and I was honored.

I didn't know how many minutes had passed, but the elevator was still going, and it wasn't going slowly. My ears were popping, and I wished I had some gum. In addition, my stomach was getting confused as to what was up or down. It wasn't as bad as airplane turbulence, but I was starting to need some Dramamine to go with that gum.

Ms. Sagadraco's eyes were straight ahead. "My apologies for your discomfort, Agent Fraser. We will reach our destination shortly."

Shortly couldn't come soon enough for me.

At least the headache was going away. I'd worn sunglasses all the way here. I squeezed my eyes shut and opened them.

They were dry again. I wiped more grit out of the corners of both eyes. Mike passed me the miracle eyedrops and I made use of them. Hopefully, that'd hold me for a while.

When the elevator finally stopped and the doors opened, we were in a small room of about ten by ten with a vault door that took up half the opposite wall. I say vault, even though it had no lever, handle, or wheel that I'd normally associate with the entrance to a bank vault. The only indicator that there was a way to open the door was a phone-sized pad to the right of the door.

Ms. Sagadraco went to it and put one eye, then the other in front of the scanner. There was a thunderous click and I jumped.

The door opened on silent hinges.

Beyond was a narrow passageway leading to an identical door with another scanner. Ms. Sagadraco spoke at length into this one in a language I'd never heard, and I suspected hadn't been spoken in millennia. Beyond that was yet another hallway and a third door, with a larger scanner. The boss held up both hands that were no longer human, but small versions of her dragon front claws.

There was a third click and the door opened.

We were in.

Wow. Greek temple was right.

My eyes swept back and forth over the vault's contents.

As I'd suspected, the room was circular. I counted twelve niches, each containing an artifact. That is, all but one.

Power rolled in waves from each and every object. I reached out to the wall next to the elevator to steady myself. Ian was likewise afflicted. My cuff was glowing, as was the spearhead in the harness under Ian's jacket.

Power called to power.

Mortimer Winters was waiting near the door. On the far wall was an opening approximately the height and width of the wavy lines that'd I'd seen from the cloaked thief. It went further into the bedrock than I could see.

"You were right," he told Ms. Sagadraco. "It's the Aegis. It's gone."

4

"That opening extends through forty feet of solid bedrock," Director Winters continued. "The rock appears to have dissolved into dust."

"Acid?" Ian asked.

"If so, no trace remains. It's as if the rock turned to powder as the thief walked through. The access point was through the side of a natural tunnel. They just made a hole and kept going until they were in the vault. Two of my mages are attempting to track the thief. So far, they have found nothing."

Vivienne Sagadraco's eyes were on the solid bedrock the thief had somehow bored through to get in. Then her consciousness launched itself into the opening—inadvertently taking me along for the ride. She raced down the narrow opening and into the tunnel beyond, twisting and turning like a hunting hawk, or an ancient dragon in pursuit of the one who had dared desecrate and rob her hoard.

I had to pull my mind away to keep from being sick.

"My apologies, Agent Fraser. I did not block my thoughts. My anger distracted me."

"No, no. My fault." I knew better than to close my eyes. That'd just make it worse. I focused on my feet. At least they weren't moving.

Ms. Sagadraco suddenly stopped swooping. She must have lost the trail. It felt like the roller coaster I was on had just slammed on the brakes.

"Hoo-boy." I slowly blew out my breath. I tried to convince myself I wasn't moving, and neither was anything else. After another couple of seconds, I was again the master of my own stomach.

Which was a good thing because the entire vault was vibrating with power.

I fumbled in my purse, found my Dramamine, popped one, washing it down with what little spit I had left.

I'd recently had an up-close-and-personal experience with ley lines, so I was familiar with that sensation. I didn't like it any more now than I did then.

This wasn't only ley lines.

Yes, I felt the surging energies in the bedrock beneath my feet, but this was coming from the vault's artifacts. Vivienne Sagadraco's collectibles that needed extra protection. If what I felt coming from those niches was any indication, every artifact here could protect itself just fine.

That was the problem.

They didn't want to protect or be protected.

They wanted to be *used,* and I got the impression none of them would be too particular about who did the using.

They had been created/forged/conjured to do one job, and they wanted to do it. Badly and now.

The artifacts called out to me. To me and Ian.

We were the people who had ended up wielding objects such as these. Humans descended from gods with a small "g." Or heroes foretold by prophecy. Or just some poor schmuck in the right place at the wrong time. The artifacts didn't care who we were. They could sense *what* we were. They sensed and they were making some seriously powerful sales pitches.

Ms. Sagadraco, Martin, and Mike Stephens had stepped into the vault.

Me, Ian, and Ruby? We didn't budge.

Considering my partner's level of badassery, that said it all. Ruby was a freaking hellhound, and even though she was a small one, her bravery was unquestioned. She'd go after what we humans would take one look at and go "nope." But by not simply following Martin into that vault, Ruby was showing she also had a dog's good common sense. I wasn't saying Ms. Sagadraco and Martin didn't, but the boss was a dragon and Martin went to Hell for fun. We're talking apples and oranges here.

Dr. Stephens was just following the boss and was confused why we weren't doing the same. Like I said, he didn't get out much.

The three of us still standing on the other side of that door were in agreement—no one needed to be messing with anything in that vault, and we had no intention of giving any of them what they wanted.

Our unique ancestry enabled me and Ian to sense objects of power, but when they were packed into a small space, every square inch of my skin wanted to crawl away and hide. Ain't nobody wanting their skin doing that. I'd talked to Ian about it after getting back from my trip to North Carolina, and he'd said he had the same reaction.

From the level of power simmering just below the boiling point in that vault, my skin had the right idea. I wanted nothing more than to go back down that hall to the elevator, push the "L" button, and ride it right back up to the bank lobby.

All of the above reluctance took about five seconds.

But we were SPI agents, so Ian and I told our collective skin to stay put and stepped out into the vault.

Ruby's canine huff before doing the same said she thought we were crazy, but what the heck.

The twelve niches were equally spaced around the wall. Though "niches" implied the artifacts set inside were decorative. These were miniature vaults. Prison cells. Mortimer Winters's wards that still covered eleven of those spaces were as much to keep the artifacts' power in as they were to keep potential thieves out. Those wards were all that was keeping me and Ian from being overwhelmed by artifact-come-hither.

I took a quick glance around at what Ms. Sagadraco had felt she needed to hide deep in the bedrock of Manhattan.

The air around each artifact hummed like a small electrical substation.

In terms of high-powered magical doodads, the boss had cornered the market.

I wasn't surprised to see the Dragon Eggs there. Our

resident gem mage, Ben Sadler, had called them out from below North Brother Island. SPI could hardly leave them there for an evil gem mage to get their grubby hands on.

The Golden Fleece displayed years ago at the Mythos exhibit at the Metropolitan Museum had been fake. Ian had told me then that the real thing was safe in the boss's hoard. Here it was. The museum version had been golden and fluffy. The real thing looked more than a little worse for wear. The wool was missing in places and the gold had dulled to a dingy yellow, but the power was still there.

The usual arrangement was that people used objects. A couple of objects in the Mythos exhibition had the reputation of using people.

The same was true here in Vivienne Sagadraco's vault.

There were two swords, each in their own niche.

"Excalibur and St. George's," Vivienne Sagadraco murmured in response to my glance.

I couldn't see what was in the others. The wards covering the remaining niches were too thick to see what was inside. I had a feeling that had been intentional on Mortimer Winters's part, and I was suddenly grateful for his attention to detail.

"It's like Odin's treasure room with the Infinity Gauntlet and Tesseract," Martin whispered in awe.

Our director of demonology was a Marvel fan. Who knew?

One niche had no glowing ward and no occupant.

"What's the Aegis?" I asked.

"Zeus's shield," Director Winters said. "Forged by cyclopes under the supervision of Hephaestus, the god of blacksmiths. Zeus gave it to his daughter, Athena, and when Perseus gifted her with the head of Medusa, she placed it in the center of the shield. The Aegis protects those who wield it while causing terror or even paralysis in those who look upon it."

"Zeus's shield," Martin said. "This *is* like Odin's stash."

The twelfth niche may have been emptied of its artifact, but the magical imprint of what it had contained was still there.

I knew what Ms. Sagadraco needed me to do. I crossed the vault to stand before the empty niche to get a psychic sniff. Since the Aegis was gone, most of the danger should've gone with it.

Ruby came with me. She took one actual sniff with her super-sensitive hellhound nose and growled. Low, rumbling, filling the vault.

Under normal circumstances, I'd have listened to the dog, but I had a job to do.

Clearing my mind was easier said than done with the other eleven artifacts trying to get my attention.

Ian had a job, too. He'd recently found that his ability to use certain objects of power extended to essentially telling them to be quiet. He could do that, I couldn't. However, he was still learning, and with objects at this level of power, he'd have his work cut out for him. He needed me to hurry up and do my thing.

It took a nearly a minute to block out the vault, artifacts, and ley lines, and narrow my focus onto the residuals left by the Aegis.

A shield forged by a god and wielded by the father of the gods. Used against gods and mortals.

It swept me away like a tsunami.

The Aegis wasn't even here, but the fear it could cause

remained. Not just fear, mad unreasoning terror. The kind that froze you where you stood, or caused you to turn and run, and keep running until you couldn't run any more, screaming the entire time. If the Aegis had still been here, its power would've eclipsed all the others. The terror's source was whatever formed the artifact's core. I felt the actual head of Medusa being forced into the metal of the shield. Now, after all this time, the blood was still fresh, still powerful. The dead eyes retained their lethal, paralyzing power. The mouth was forever open in a silent scream.

No. Not silent. I could hear it.

But it was a man's scream. Then another joined it. Screams that shouldn't have been able to have come from human throats.

Our mages.

Director Winters pushed past us, ran through the opening the thief had bored through solid rock, and into the darkness beyond. We were right behind him.

Under New York City were eight hundred miles of subway tracks and thousands of miles of sewer tunnels. Then there were the tunnels that had been here before the first human set foot on the island.

This had to be one of those.

The glow from Director Winters's hands illuminated a tunnel just high and wide enough to squeeze in a minivan. The walls were dark and the air dank.

The screams had stopped, meaning the men no longer needed to scream.

Or they were no longer able.

A quick glance at Ian's face confirmed what I knew in my gut. Something out there in the pitch dark had just killed two of our battlemages, and the only thing we'd get from rushing headlong down that tunnel would be matching body bags.

Caution was called for.

What had killed them and had bored a tunnel into a vault through solid rock was still out there. Waiting. Ms. Sagadraco's quiet growl vibrating the air around us confirmed it. Her normally blue eyes now glowed with reptilian slit pupils. This was no longer about her hoard. Two of her agents were dead, and she would have who or whatever was responsible.

I shifted and Ian put out his arm out to stop me from running off into the dark.

"I ain't crazy," I whispered.

As far as I knew, Mortimer Winters wasn't crazy or suicidal either. Right now, he was homicidal. Flames erupted around his clenched fists as he took off in the direction of those silenced screams.

Vivienne Sagadraco was right behind him. Martin made a grab for Ruby and missed.

Ian and I turned on our flashlights and quickly led Martin and Dr. Stephens after them.

The tunnel curved and turned and curved again. Ms. Sagadraco and Director Winters had stopped just ahead. He was crouched over a pair of bodies. The boss was standing guard over them, staring into the darkness beyond. Ruby wasn't with them. She was probably still in pursuit.

Dr. Stephens caught up to us, his breathing ragged from the sprint. His shoulders sagged when he saw the mages.

It was obvious they were beyond all medical help.

We knew what had killed them.

Ian and I had seen previous cases in Sebastian du Beckett's brownstone office and again in Central Park and North Brother Island. Human flesh instantly turned to stone.

By a gorgon.

The men's skin looked more like marble than the flesh it had been only minutes before. There was no blood, just dust from where one man's arm had broken when he'd fallen. Their eyes were open and staring, mouths agape as they'd died mid-scream, faces contorted in terror.

Carlos Escarra and Quinn Walsh. I hadn't known them well, but we'd spoken in passing in the halls at headquarters. Carlos was a vampire, a decade older than Alain Moreau, who was immune to a gorgon's glare due to his age. Carlos should've been as well. Quinn was human and was younger than Director Winters, but not by much.

An ancient vampire and an even more ancient human. Both should have been immune. Neither had been. Why?

This was way more than theft and murder.

Dr. Stephens laid a hand on Quinn's forehead. "What's happening here?"

A warning hiss came from under the mage's stone neck. The doc jerked his hand back and scrambled to his feet.

A forked tongue tested the air, followed by the triangular head of a viper. The head was only the size of a quarter, but that didn't make it any less poisonous.

Ian's voice was calm and even. "I've got it."

And I knew how he'd get it. Ian's boots were made for stomping.

"No." Vivienne Sagadraco knelt, reached under Quinn's neck with her bare hand, and pulled the little viper out of its hiding place. It was dark red all over, with no markings. I had to admit it was beautiful.

It thanked her for saving its life by biting her. The boss didn't so much as blink.

"It cannot harm me." She ran a finger down its less than two-foot length, and in response the snake coiled around her wrist like a bracelet and went still. "Can you track Ruby?" she asked Martin.

Martin had his phone out, app already accessed. Back home, finding a hunting dog meant going into the woods after it. Ruby had a GPS tracker on her collar. "Nearly a mile that way." He nodded in the direction of a whole heap of dark. "Then she turned right." That little hellhound could move, and she wouldn't be moving that fast unless she was hot on a trail.

Of a gorgon who could turn her to rock.

Ms. Sagadraco inhaled through her nose. When it came to sensitive schnozzes, dragons put even werewolves to shame. She glanced down at our mages, her thoughts hidden even from me. "Do not worry, Director DiMatteo. I will find her." She glanced at me and Ian. "Stay with them. Mortimer and I will continue a little further. I doubt we'll find the killer, but there may be clues as to where she went."

She.

There were male gorgons, but they usually didn't live very long. While the disease was an equal opportunity afflicter, it nearly always drove males insane, and that mental instability made them careless. Careless predators tended to be short-lived predators. Many times, those deaths came at the hands—or to be more exact, eyes—of a female gorgon. Careless feeding attracted unwanted attention, either from law enforcement or vindictive humans. Older female gorgons had no patience or mercy for those who threatened their hunting grounds.

Director Winters doused the magic that had illuminated his hands, and he and Ms. Sagadraco set off at a brisk pace into the darkness, soon vanishing from our sight.

Martin was intent on his phone screen, clearly worried. "She's not responding to recall."

"She'll be back," I assured him. It wasn't working for him or me. This was Ruby's job, and she was determined to do it.

"Sounds like another stubborn agent I know," Ian muttered.

I had avoided looking at the mages' faces. I looked now. Surprise and agony. Both men were battlemages, and their long lives had given them time to hone their skills, both offensive and defensive. None of it had saved them.

I stepped away from the others.

Ian tensed. "Where are—"

I held up a hand. "Just going a little farther down the tunnel to see what I can pick up. The air's too…busy right here. Don't worry, you'll still be able to see me."

Yes, I could sense when magic had been used, but I needed space between me and any source of disruption. Ian was the descendant of a Celtic god, making his aura seriously disruptive. Then there were his protective instincts when it came to yours truly. Those were even more disruptive.

"You can keep watch," I told him, walking away, "but don't stare a hole through my back."

I stopped about thirty feet away and opened my senses to any magic in the air, willing myself to be receptive to anything that made my skin crawl any more than it was already doing.

I faced the darkness, took a breath, and slowly exhaled, closing my eyes. The problem wasn't that I couldn't sense anything. I was sensing too much. We knew an ancient gorgon had stolen the Aegis, killed two old and powerful mages, and escaped. And if her planned escape route had been cut off, this gorgon was more than capable of making her own exit. I was far from an expert on gorgons, but I'd never heard of them being able to disintegrate solid rock.

I opened my eyes and had to blink to focus against the grit in my—

My breath caught. Oh God, that's what had happened. The gorgon had looked up at the surveillance camera, and I'd watched the recording. I'd only watched a *recording*. Just an instant and the process had started. I'd passed out, breaking the contact. That was all that'd saved me. I'd watched a recording and gotten gritty eyes—and headaches. Was there grit in my brain, too? My brain didn't feel gritty; but if it was, would I know? Carlos and Quinn had seen the real thing and their entire bodies had turned to stone.

My flashlight fell from suddenly nerveless fingers. I squatted with shaking knees to pick it up, and then I saw it, gleaming in the flashlight's beam.

"Mac, are you—"

"I'm fine," I told Ian. "Stay there."

It was flat with a rounded edge, metallic. It looked almost like a small DVD.

I reached for it.

Another red viper lunged from beneath it.

I scuttled back and landed on my butt. That did not do good things for my headache.

Then Ian was there, scooping me off the ground.

"Another damned snake." Before he could go after it, it darted into the dark, doubtless to join the other creepy things rumored to live in New York's sewer system.

Martin joined us. "What's that?" He'd spotted the DVD thing and pulled a zippy bag and tweezers out of his jacket pocket. Leave it to Martin to be prepared to collect a specimen anywhere, anytime.

I'd retrieved my flashlight, and Martin held up the whatsit in its beam. It looked like half a small DVD. Our boss was a dragon, so we'd seen these before.

It was a scale. A big one.

Ms. Sagadraco's were bigger, but then her draconic body was close to three stories tall.

Dr. Stephens joined us. "Uh, don't gorgons have the lower body of a snake? And snakes for hair?"

My mouth was as dry as the dust from Carlos's arm. "Just Medusa."

"And her two sisters," Ian added. "But they're all dead. At least according to mythology. I think."

On the surveillance recording, I'd seen writhing shapes around the thief's head.

Snakes.

Ruby ran out of the dark toward us, red eyes wide. She plowed into Martin, knocking him down in her joy to see him. Moments later, Vivienne Sagadraco and Mortimer Winters walked out of the same dark. Other than the little viper still coiled around the boss's wrist, they didn't have any trophies from their hunt, like a gorgon head.

"I take it you didn't find her?" Ian asked the boss.

"We did not."

They may not have found anything, but Ruby had. Her eyes had gone back to their normal brown, but she was shaking as she wedged herself between me and Martin. If what she'd seen terrified a hellhound, it'd give me nightmares for life.

I kept my eyes on the dark while I scratched Ruby's massive ears. "Me too, baby. Me too."

5

Dr. Stephens had called ahead to HQ and had his team warm up the MRI machine.

I was going for a spin.

Considering what'd happened to our two battlemages and to me when I'd merely watched a video of the gorgon that'd turned them to marble, I thought an MRI was about the best idea I'd ever heard.

Not only had my eyeballs—and possibly parts of my brain—nearly been turned to gravel, I'd narrowly escaped a bite from a strand of poisonous gorgon hair.

I felt like I'd used up two lives in as many hours.

"Agent Fraser, I need you to be perfectly still." The MRI technician had directed me where to lie on the table and had positioned my head. "Just breathe normally and remain calm."

Being still I could do. Calm was a long way from happening.

Though there were worse slabs to be on. Much worse.

I was here. Our two dead battlemages were in the morgue.

Different doors on the same hall.

I was grateful to be alive to get an MRI. I was only being told not to move for a minute or two. Those two men would never move again. In fact, they'd been paralyzed before they'd died.

Calm, Mac. Breathe.

Ian was here with me. I had no problem with that. Truth was, I wanted him here. Dr. Stephens had said I was fine, but considering what we now knew had caused the grit in my eyes, Ms. Sagadraco wanted to take every precaution. So did I. My logical self knew I'd successfully dodged the gorgon-glare bullet, but there was a little voice inside my head that was screaming her lungs out at what had nearly happened. My logical self had tried to chase her down and slap some sense into her, but dang, she was fast.

I could've ended up like them.

But you didn't. You're fine. You're safe.

Breathe. In. Out.

"Everything looks good, Agent Fraser," the tech said in an appallingly cheerful voice. "Just a few seconds longer."

Yes, SPI had an MRI machine, and every other fancy and expensive medical gadget that might be needed when an agent met an immovable monster object. But I hadn't been backhanded by a rabid Sasquatch. I'd merely glanced at a video of a cloaked gorgon. Two of our battlemages had been on the receiving end of more direct contact. I'd seen their tortured faces forever frozen in their last instant of horror.

To know you were turning to stone from the outside in,

to have your skin and muscles be paralyzed first, unable to move, unable to scream as the paralysis worked its way to your circulatory system, stopping your heart and lungs, leaving you aware at each stage of the process.

Had both men known what had happened? How long had they suffered? Had they still been aware as the body bags were being zipped over them? Had they screamed? Were they still screaming?

I couldn't imagine a worse way to die.

"Almost there, Agent Fraser."

Ms. Sagadraco had collected those twelve artifacts to protect them and keep them from falling into the wrong hands. She had been confident in her security, as had Mortimer Winters. Not only had the vault been violated and the Aegis taken, two of his best battlemages had gone after the thief and paid the ultimate price.

We all knew that could happen to us at any time. We had signed up to protect the world's supernaturals from themselves and from humanity. Humans had governments, agencies, armies, and police forces to protect them.

Supernaturals only had us.

The MRI had stopped whirling.

"You can sit up now, Agent Fraser. But do it slowly. Some people get dizzy."

Better dizzy than dead.

I sat up and swung my legs over the side of the table, or whatever this thing was called.

Ian offered a hand to steady me as I stood up. I took it.

"I know you won't go home and rest," he said, "but would you at least consider checking in to a sleep room for a few hours? There's nothing you can do right now."

SPI had dorm-style rooms in the complex set aside for when we were all-hands-on-deck, or if you'd pulled an extra-long shift and were too tired to get yourself safely home.

I shook my head. "I need to know what gorgon nearly gravelled my eyeballs."

"Gravelled? Is that a word?"

"If it's not, I just made it one."

"Agent Fraser, everything looks perfectly normal," the tech said. "Dr. Stephens was right. It was a severe case of dry eyes. The grit was merely crystallized saline."

"That was a *lot* of crystallized saline."

"It was outside of normal parameters," she admitted, still weirdly cheerful. "However, the brevity of the contact kept it from being anything worse."

"In other words, good thing I passed out."

"Extremely good. It broke the contact with the gorgon and kept your condition from deteriorating further. I'll see that Ms. Sagadraco and Mr. Moreau get my report."

"Uh, thank you." I didn't know what else to say.

"You're welcome. Have a nice rest of your day."

SPI. The only workplace where you'd be wished a nice rest of your day after a gorgon attack.

Ian opened the door for me.

Rake was coming down the hall. Behind Rake was Gethen Nazar, Rake's permanent and lethal shadow.

Rake was also a goblin, a dark mage, governor of the goblin colony on our world, and a lot of other things that in the past had put him at odds with SPI.

Those other things had been resolved.

Mostly.

Gethen was the chief of Rake's security team. Yep, team as in more than one member. It took seven goblin battlemages to keep my honey in one piece on a daily basis. Rake didn't just have bad guys after him. He'd taken it one step further and had pissed off said bad guys to the point that their desire to kill him in the most painful ways possible was intensely personal. My Rake didn't do anything halfway.

He was tall and lean with shoulder-length black hair, angular features, and cheekbones you could cut yourself on. Then there were the goblin elements: pale gray skin, pointed ears and a pair of fangs that he knew how to use and use well—whether for ripping out the throat of an enemy or nibbling yours truly into incoherent babbling.

Rake wasn't wearing his human glamour. Gethen had taken his cue from Rake.

While Rake could maintain his glamour 24/7, it was easier to go without. That said everything about the level of trust he now had with my coworkers. His human persona was known around the world as a billionaire, hotelier, and philanthropist. He knew the risk that came with being outed as not human. No one here would do that. He knew it, and he trusted us with his biggest secret.

Rake and Gethen strode down the hall, sending SPI's lab-coat-wearing medical types scurrying out of their path. Both men were radiating protector vibes—Rake for me and Gethen for Rake. I thought Rake's vibes were sweet, but they were sending everyone else running for cover.

Both were wearing visitor badges. Everyone knew who they were, so it wasn't like they needed badges, but they weren't SPI employees. Rake was just the boyfriend of one, namely me. SPI rules said all visitors had to be badged, so Rake and Gethen were wearing theirs on lanyards around their necks. In the past, they'd needed to be accompanied by Ms. Sagadraco or Mr. Moreau. In recent months, that precaution had been deemed no longer necessary.

Rake had definitely moved up in SPI's world.

He stopped in front of me, and an instant later, I was being crushed against his chest.

"It's been a day." My voice was muffled against his badge.

"So I heard."

"I called him," Ian said. "I told him what happened as it relates to you, so you don't have to."

I tilted my head back so I could see Rake's face. "Good. Because 'What happened?' isn't an essay question I'm up to answering right now."

Ian wouldn't have told him everything, because it was an ongoing investigation, and Ian was a stickler for rules and regs. Not to mention, this was Rake he'd talked to. The boys were getting along better, but I didn't think they'd ever be bros.

"I suspect Ms. Sagadraco will want to tell him more," Ian continued. "As the goblin governor and with his contacts, Rake is a valuable asset."

Which was a nice way of saying Rake knew a lot of supernatural underworld scum and could finagle information we couldn't.

Rake inclined his head. "Ian, that is the nicest thing you've ever called me."

Ian shrugged. "I call 'em like I see 'em."

Now that Rake and I were officially a couple, he and

Vivienne Sagadraco had an agreement that Rake would help SPI whenever he realistically could. Information was critical to our work, and Rake had helped us gain access to that information faster, and as a result, had saved lives. More than once, Rake had brokered meetings between SPI and some less-than-savory individuals. As the goblin governor, one of Rake's sworn duties was the protection of every goblin on our world. Rake took his duties seriously. Much of what we did at SPI involved preventing what could endanger not only goblins and supernaturals, but every living being on Earth.

So yes, our goals intersected with Rake's on a regular basis, hence the IDs with Rake and Gethen's photos that were kept at SPI's reception desk. My sweetie and his chief of security were becoming regulars here.

And since we had a burgled Aegis, two dead battlemages, one bitey strand of gorgon hair, and one gorgon scale from a type of gorgon presumed dead for thousands of years, I had a sneaking suspicion Ms. Sagadraco was gonna want to bring Rake in on this one.

6

The inorganics lab was on one side of the hall, organics on the other. Both were equipped to handle, contain, and analyze virtually anything. Thick glass walls along both sides of the hall provided an unobstructed view into the labs. That way, if an experiment or subject got out of control, those windows let the folks across the hall know that all hell had broken loose and to please, when they had a minute, call for help.

What we'd brought home from the tunnels under the Gotham Bank was in the organics lab. The snake was alive, and the scale had presumably come from the gorgon who was also presumably alive. Though at SPI, we knew there were all kinds of dead and undead.

A potentially undead gorgon. Sheesh.

Ian tapped his knuckle twice on the lab door, and the eyes of everyone inside were on us.

Ms. Sagadraco saw that Rake and Gethen were with us and gestured us all inside.

So much for whether she wanted Rake brought into this.

There were more than a few large fish tanks. At least that's what they looked like at first glance. A second, closer look revealed a glass thickness that'd be overkill for a pet-sized kraken. I'd been told that the glass was the same that separated the lab from the hallway.

Like I said, everything-proof.

Most of the tanks were empty. One was now the center of attention.

Vivienne Sagadraco was standing next to the tank containing the strand of gorgon hair. The little red viper was very active and looked highly pissed. Judging from the way it kept striking the glass every few seconds, its nap around the boss's wrist hadn't improved its mood any. That was one evil lock of hair. Talk about having a bad hair day.

Next to the boss was Dr. Henry Milner, SPI's crypto-zoologist. We all knew he was more comfortable studying creatures of the night than interacting with people during the day. He also felt more at home in the labs than he did in meetings, where his job was to give agent presentations on what'd just been found in a storm drain in the Bronx.

"Dr. Milner was just identifying our guest," Ms. Sagadraco told us. "Please continue."

Henry Milner glanced uneasily at his larger audience and cleared his throat. "What we have is a Milos viper. It is found only on the Greek islands of Milos, Kimolos, Sifnos, and Polyaigos."

A native Greek snake on a native Greek monster. That was confirmation we needed but didn't want.

"They're rare and endangered," he continued. "While this one is a lovely brick red, Milos vipers are usually a mixture of gray, brown, and black with red shading."

I thought of the one that'd gotten away and was now slithering under the city. "How big do they get?"

"Between eighteen and twenty-four inches."

"So, they're small. That's good news we'll gladly take."

"How much have you been told?" Ms. Sagadraco asked Rake.

"Just what directly involved Mac," Ian said.

"Good. I'll fill in the blanks. My main artifact vault has been robbed. The Aegis was stolen. And a snake-haired, serpent-bodied gorgon was responsible."

Those three short sentences landed like three large bombs.

Rake's expression froze for a few seconds as he processed the implications. "And her hair consists of rare Greek vipers."

"Just so."

Dr. Claire Cheban had joined us from the other side of the lab, where she and two of her senior staffers had been huddled over a high-powered microscope.

She was SPI's chief scientist and still didn't look old enough to be out of college, let alone have two hard-science doctorates and be in charge of a lab like SPI's.

"Ma'am, we've completed our initial analysis of the scale," she said to Ms. Sagadraco. She hesitated. "And Agent Escarra's arm." She led us over to her workstation, which consisted of a standing desk, computer, and humongous monitor.

Strange things from all over the world ended up in SPI's laboratories, but our New York lab had the latest and greatest gadgets for finding out what made supernatural stuff tick—without blowing up everything in the five boroughs.

Dr. Cheban was listing all the tests they'd run on the gorgon scale. It involved a lot of confusingly multisyllabic words describing the test, the equipment that did the testing, or pieces and parts of both.

My headache was coming back, and it wasn't due to gorgon grit.

Fortunately, she soon shifted to speaking in words I could understand.

"Based on the probability of the scale being from a gorgon, we went with the initial assumption that it was from a creature younger than fifty thousand years old, which is the extent of radiocarbon dating accuracy. Gorgons were first mentioned in Greek literature by Homer around 700 to 800 BCE. However, the Minoan civilization featured a snake goddess who was said to be a precursor or priestess to Medusa and her sisters. A figure of the goddess that was found in Knossos dated to 1650 to 1550 BCE. Using carbon dating, we estimate the gorgon who shed this scale is approximately seventy-two hundred years old."

Silence. And a second later, we heard actual crickets. Someone had brought lunch to our little viper guest.

Dr. Cheban turned to her keyboard, clicked a few keys, and the monitor displayed what looked like the layers of pastry in a piece of baklava.

"We cut a small section from the scale's edge for interior analysis," she was saying. "We were pleased to see that the cellular structure is similar to a dragon's scale—about which, thanks to Director Sagadraco, we have extensive knowledge. Both scales have strength and flexibility to an incredible degree. Think about a samurai sword, which is made by the forging and folding of thin layers of steel, each layer adding to the strength of the ones before. I feel confident in assuming that, like Director Sagadraco, the gorgon would be impervious to most weapons unless the point of entry is beneath one of the scales."

Two more clicks and the image changed.

"There was enough of a viable skin sample attached to the top of the scale for analysis." She nodded toward the microscope. "That's what we're working on now. The scale was torn from the body, giving us not only skin, but a small sample of the gorgon's blood. It wasn't a natural shedding. Thanks to that sample, we have enough for additional tests that could reveal a weakness."

"They didn't die in vain." Mortimer Winters's voice was tight with unexpressed grief.

"The scale was found near their bodies?" Claire asked.

"Yes," I said quietly.

Whatever damage Carlos and Quinn had done to the gorgon to get that scale might help us save other lives.

"What about Carlos's arm?" Director Winters asked.

"I believe both men died instantly." She made no move to show us photos of Carlos Escarra's arm, or samples that'd been sliced or diced for the microscope. I was grateful. I'd seen it, and the inside had looked just as much like marble as the outside. I didn't need to see a cellular view projected larger than life on that monitor.

"Victims of younger gorgons appear more like concrete," she said. "We know from past cases that the ossification progresses from the skin to the internal organs. How quickly that progression occurs depends on the age and strength of the gorgon. Agent Escarra's arm showed no sign of progression. From skin to bone marrow, the ossification was instantaneous. Perhaps this was due to the gorgon's great age, or the intensity of the glare due to anger or injury." She paused. "If they suffered at all, it was only for a moment."

That was the best news we'd had all day.

7

This was my third time in SPI's morgue. For me and every other SPI agent, any day we didn't end up in a drawer here was a good day.

Everything was white and stainless steel, and as sterile as an operating room. Germs didn't necessarily matter here, at least not to anyone who had been wheeled in. They were dead, and germs couldn't hurt them anymore. The pristine conditions were maintained for the gathering of evidence as to who or what had killed those who'd been brought in through the freight elevator just outside the doors. If your gurney took a right, you were headed to the medical section, where you would hopefully stay alive and be returned to health. If your gurney took a left, you were beyond the help of the folks to the right.

Ian, Rake, Gethen, and I went to the small observation room that was behind the same kind of glass found in the labs. As I'd experienced the last time I'd been here, it was also angry goblin lawyer ghost-proof. Plus, SPI's security mages had warded Bert's morgue out the wazoo. Just because a body was dead didn't mean it couldn't make trouble, and a lot of it.

Vivienne Sagadraco and Mortimer Winters were in the autopsy room with Dr. Bertram Ferguson, SPI's resident medical examiner and necromancer. Occasionally, the souls were still inside the bodies of those brought here. When that happened, Bert could contact and talk to the deceased. Murder cases were infinitely simplified when the dead could simply tell you who killed them.

Bert Ferguson looked like everybody's favorite grandpa. That is, if their grandpa was a necromancer and Vatican-trained exorcist.

Bert was big and tall, his hair and beard were white, and he gave the best bear hugs. His look was understated lumberjack, favoring jeans, work boots, and flannel shirts. He was one of those down-to-earth, nice guys that everyone liked to be around—including kids and dogs. In my opinion, kids and dogs possessed the wisdom of the ages when it came to recognizing bad people on sight. They all loved Bert, which confirmed that Bert Ferguson wasn't just good people, he was great people.

Naturally, with the white beard and hair and bright blue eyes, he played Santa for the agents' kids at SPI family holiday parties. But unlike Santa, Bert saw dead people, and he could talk to them.

Point Bert.

In a few minutes, he'd be attempting a PML—post-mortem link. All corporations had their abbreviations and acronyms, but SPI was a special snowflake.

I'd attended two PMLs. Both had been seriously freaky. In the first, Bert had found himself on the wrong end of a demon-possessed corpse and had nearly died. The next, only a day later, had been to get a statement from the aforementioned dead and extremely angry goblin lawyer. Bert had some big ones, and was the best at his craft, period.

Today's PLM would be with two of our own. This wouldn't be freaky. It would be solemn and sacred.

There was a permanent autopsy table in the center of the room. Quinn Walsh was on that one. Carlos Escarra was on a gurney that had been pulled up beside it. A little over two hours ago, both men had been living, breathing human beings. Well, Agent Walsh had been alive. Agent Escarra had been undead, which at SPI qualified you as alive. Anyone who said vampires didn't have souls had never met and gotten to know one. Most of the vampires I knew were the best people.

Now the mages more closely resembled avant-garde works of art. Bert had covered each body with a sheet, out of respect for the men and consideration for the rest of us. We'd already seen their faces frozen in terror and would probably be seeing them in our next nightmares. If we didn't have to look at them for the duration of the PML, we might at least stand a chance of remembering them as they'd looked when they'd been alive.

We knew the cause of death and had a short list of suspects. Medusa and her two sisters. We thought they were all dead, but legends were notoriously noncommittal when it came to the whole life and death thing. Medusa was dead and beheaded. I'd learned in training that if you took the head, nothing got up from that. Not to mention, I'd *felt* Medusa's head being pushed inside the Aegis. Nothing had been heard from her two sisters since soon after that beheading. They'd disappeared from the legends afterward. Ms. Sagadraco had assigned Elizabeth Wellesley, SPI's chief archivist, to find what had happened to them. The SPI Archives was the most extensive source of information on the supernatural, paranormal, legends, mythology, and occult in the world. Period.

Under normal circumstances, Bert would summon the soul of the recently departed. Some souls left their bodies at the time of death. Others remained for several hours after their heart had stopped beating and their brain had ceased to function. Unless a soul had vacated its body voluntarily at the time of death—or had been torn out—Bert should have a fifty-fifty chance of making contact.

That was under normal circumstances.

Death by gorgon petrification was not normal in anyone's book.

According to Dr. Cheban, both mages had died instantly, or almost instantly.

Depending on the age of the gorgon responsible, the victims could end up looking like cheap concrete, grainy with air pockets throughout, all the way to the finest marble, seamless and solid.

That was what we had here.

Bert had said there was a very good chance the souls were still trapped inside.

That was as horrifying a death as I could imagine. And since I'd worked at SPI for five years now, I'd seen entirely too many deaths. For this to rocket to the top of my ways I didn't want to die list, said plenty.

Unlike in the previous PML I'd witnessed from the observation room, Bert gently placed his hands on the heads of the two men, and simply and quietly said their names. These had been our people, they'd known Bert, so there was no need to use his full necromantic power. If their souls were there, they would want to talk to Bert.

I felt the sudden sting of tears in my eyes. I know I would.

In a normal PML, a silvery mist would rise from the body and hover directly above it. The form would be the size and shape of the body, but without a face. The investigating agent would ask the questions; Bert would speak for the dead person.

Nothing emerged from the bodies.

But they were trying.

Oh God. I could feel it.

They *were* trapped.

Suddenly, there wasn't enough air. I couldn't breathe. "I can feel them…hear them."

Carlos Escarra was speaking. The vampire. He'd already died once. Quinn Walsh was barely keeping his panic under control. This was his first death. Bert could hear them, and now so could I.

Ian pushed the intercom button. "Bert. Mac hears them."

Carlos and Quinn had heard us talking while we'd been standing around their bodies in that tunnel, but their souls had been trapped, locked inside their marble bodies.

Back home, I'd seen the millions of souls that'd been freed from Janus's medallion prison. I'd seen Aunt Nora's dead lover, Stephen McRae. I'd inherited the ability from my dad and thought of it as a gift. This was not a gift. Quinn's panic was my panic. His agony as his body solidified around him was my agony. His memories became my memories.

I saw what he had seen, what they had both seen.

I saw the gorgon. All of her.

But not at first.

The first thing they saw were her eyes.

Bright green. Deep. No, not deep—bottomless. So much hate blazing there. Carlos and Quinn hadn't been able to help themselves. They'd looked. If they'd seen the snake body or snakes for hair, there might have been a chance they could've kept themselves from looking into her eyes. But a pair of glowing green eyes suddenly appearing in front of you in a dark tunnel? You *would* look. It was reflex.

Her eyes had frozen them where they'd stood. Then and only then, when they were helpless to look away or even close their eyes, the gorgon slowly materialized before them, relishing their panic and helplessness.

She was holding the Aegis like the shield it was. As the men stood paralyzed before her, the shield began to glow. It started as she had, with the eyes. Only this time it was Medusa's eyes, glowing with the same green fire. Then the glow increased to a flash of blazing white light.

That was when the men screamed, mad and raw. They were trapped, drowning in Medusa's eyes. Carlos and Quinn had shown bravery time and time again in the line of duty. No one had ever doubted their courage.

The Aegis ripped their courage away.

Only once they were mindlessly screaming did the gorgon kill them with her glare. But only their bodies were dead. Their souls remained, trapped.

When I came back to myself, I was curled in Rake's lap. Apparently, he'd gathered me there, holding me tight, his lips warm against my ear, murmuring soothing, reassuring words. I was shaking so hard the muscles in my back had seized up.

With halting words, I told everyone what I'd seen, heard, and felt.

Bert could speak to and for the dead. I could see and feel their final moments.

It was a partnership made in Hell.

Mortimer Winters gazed down at the sheet-shrouded forms of his two mages. "We need to break open the bodies to release their souls."

Bert nodded in solemn agreement. "That's what they want."

In my head, I felt Carlos and Quinn's agreement and grateful anticipation.

Mortimer Winters's eyes met mine.

I had to swallow before I could speak. "They're ready. They were ready when it happened."

The mage moved to stand between the table and the gurney. He pulled the sheets down and placed a hand in the center of each man's chest. He looked from one tortured face to the other, then took a deep breath and closed his eyes. I felt him gather his power, and with a surge of his will, he shattered the bodies in place. When he lifted his hands, the bodies crumbled.

I didn't feel their souls leave, but I knew they were no longer with us.

"Are you all right?" Rake murmured against my ear.

I took a deep breath before responding. "Better now," I whispered. "Thank you, sweetie." I stood.

Kenji had once told me that the head of the sorcery department was a pompous ass who tried to take over every project he was called in on, and he thought just because he was a couple hundred years older than everyone else that made him smarter. Kenji had said all it meant was that he'd had more time to piss off more people.

In Kenji's defense, he didn't know Mortimer Winters very well. Neither did I. But in less than one day of working with him, I'd learned a lot. He was much older than everyone thought. If I'd been his age and had the knowledge he'd gained, I would've been impatient with everyone else, too. The mage had seen, heard, experienced, and done so much, and would continue to do so long after we were all gone. I could see why he wouldn't want to get close to us "mere mortals." Too little time, too painful to keep losing the people you loved while you lived on.

Right now, seeing him standing over the remains of two of his battlemages, it didn't take a seer to know that Mortimer needed a hug.

Vivienne gave him one.

"You have more than done your part," she murmured against her friend's ear—and in my mind. "Now we will do ours."

"Mac." Bert's voice was a gentle rumble from behind me.

I turned to face him, and he gathered me up in his big arms. I guess it was pretty obvious I needed a hug, too.

He lowered his head to mine. "Whenever you need to talk," he whispered, "I'm here. I can teach you how to cope with a PML. Some people are just afraid when they're newly dead, especially when it happens like this one did. They scare us, but they don't mean to." His arms gave me a gentle squeeze. "It's the worst kind to have for your first." Bert paused. "I'd say this ability came from your dad. Meeting him probably activated it, and maybe a few others you don't know about yet."

I sniffed and nodded against his chest. I knew I'd sob if I tried to say anything.

"It's a gift," he continued. "I know it doesn't feel like one right now, but it will. I promise. Carlos and Quinn don't hurt anymore. They've gone to where they need to be. They're at peace." Bert's chest rumbled with a warm chuckle. "Heck, they were worried about you. I told them you'd be just fine."

I sniffed again and looked up at him. "They were worried about me?"

"That happens a lot with the newly dead. They worry about the ones left behind. You'll be going to see Suzy now, right?"

I nodded.

"Without you seeing what Quinn saw, you wouldn't be able to show it to Suzy and have her sketch the killer. You and Quinn will be saving lives by showing the rest of us what the killer looks like. We'll find out who they are, what they are, and how to stop them from doing what they did to Quinn and Carlos to anyone else. Your daddy gave you a gift. You just need to learn how to use it." He gave me a final hug and let me go. "When you're ready, I'll teach you."

8

I'd seen the gorgon through Quinn Walsh's dying memories. SPI had a sketch artist who could get in your head, see what you saw, and draw it with photographic accuracy. Voila, instant mug shot. I'd seen the gorgon, and unlike Quinn, I was still flesh and blood; so in theory, Susan Connolly should be safe.

Last time I'd sat down with Suzy, my only source of anxiety was what the link would do to me. This time, I was worried about her.

My only other session with Suzy had been to get a sketch of a goblin dark mage and cabal member, Marek Reigory, who'd come entirely too close to vaporizing me. I hadn't had lunch that day, so you'd think I wouldn't have thrown up. Not the case. Suzy had told me that getting dizzy coming out of a link was rare. It turned out I was special. For me, Dramamine wasn't just a precaution. I used the stuff a lot. Like I should buy stock. This morning, I'd popped one of my little orange friends after the elevator ride down to the vault, so it should still be in my system. I'd know soon enough.

The process was simple. Suzy would put her fingertips on my temples, and while I remembered everything I could about what I'd seen, she'd pop into my head and watch my memory movie along with me.

Quinn's memories were now mine. But I was still alive. Our mages were not.

It's a win, Mac. Take it.

Ms. Sagadraco had called ahead, so Suzy was expecting us.

Ian and Rake knew from last time that Suzy didn't like distractions while she worked, so they waited outside her office with Gethen. I went in and closed the door behind me.

Suzy met me with a hug, and I felt myself tearing up. While helpful to my dry eyes, it didn't do much for my emotional state.

She pulled away, her hands on my upper arms. "Ms. Sagadraco told me everything. How are you?"

I smiled weakly. "Better than Quinn and Carlos."

She gave my arms a quick squeeze. "Then show me what their killer looks like, so we can make her pay."

Suzy had two chairs pulled in front of her desk, facing each other. I sat in one, and Suzy took the other, our knees nearly touching. A small trashcan was on the floor to the left of my chair, and a can of ginger ale and a couple packs of saltines was waiting for me on her desk. Just in case. Suzy was a sweetheart.

I'd only gotten a glance at Marek Reigory, so Suzy had needed to do a deep dive to get enough of a look for her to sketch. The gorgon was branded in my brain. Hopefully, this would mean Suzy could get a good look without having to make me feel like I'd been on the Scrambler.

She reached over for a remote on her desk and dimmed the lights.

I closed my eyes and took what I hoped would be a deep, calming breath. "Let's do this."

Suzy placed her fingertips on my temples. "Try to relax and remember what you saw."

Remembering I could do. Relaxing? Not gonna happen. So, I just concentrated on what I'd seen when I'd inadvertently linked with Quinn Walsh.

The eyes had been the first thing Quinn had seen, followed by the head with its unholy halo of red Milos vipers.

I took a shaky breath. "You getting this?"

Suzy swallowed with an audible gulp. "Oh yeah." Then the professional was back.

The rest of the gorgon's body followed, but like Quinn's, my focus was locked on the eyes and hair. I knew I'd seen the rest, but it hadn't registered in my conscious mind. However, it was in my subconscious, and so long as it was there, Suzy would get it.

Quinn's eyes had been focused on the gorgon's face, but now, away from the initial shock of my link with him, I noticed what he'd smelled. Water. Fishy water. And copper. A metallic scent so strong it was almost registered as a taste. Could it have been the blood from the gorgon? Had Quinn bitten his tongue? Or had the ossification caused blood vessels to burst?

I tried to slow the memory.

Suzy's fingertips tightened slightly. "Don't. Let it happen. I'll do the work."

I did, reaching and passing the point when the gorgon revealed her entire body. By then the men were already turning to stone. They only had a second or two left.

Suzy froze it there. My breath was coming quick and shallow. It might have been me or Quinn. I didn't know.

As Quinn's sight dimmed in death, Suzy abruptly broke the contact. Good. If she hadn't, I would've.

As I'd already experienced once today with Ms. Sagadraco, it was like a roller coaster had slammed on brakes. I hadn't been sick in the boss's vault, but I was now.

I made a grab for the trashcan.

Once again, Suzy appreciated my aim.

While Suzy sketched, she didn't let anyone look over her shoulder. Not that I wanted to try. I'd seen the gorgon twice today, and that was two times too many.

I was on her office couch, shakily eating a saltine while Rake held my can of ginger ale. Suzy now kept cold compresses in her small office fridge. I had one on the back of my neck. I was as comfortable as I was going to get. Thanks to the Dramamine I'd taken earlier I was feeling much less nauseous than last time.

In fact, the world had stopped moving.

There was a knock on the door.

It was Ms. Sagadraco with Amelia Chandler.

Dr. Chandler was one of SPI's historians and our resident

expert on classic Greek and Roman mythology, as well as the Nordic and Celtic varieties. Smart lady. Most folks would say that history and mythology couldn't be more different, but when you worked at SPI, you knew they were the same thing.

"I've brought what are considered the most accurate depictions of Medusa and her sisters," Dr. Chandler was saying as she opened the case on her tablet. "They appear on two vases from Crete, a tile floor from a Pompeiian home, and a wall frieze from an Athenian tomb. The colors on the tile floor and tomb are especially well preserved, as is the detail on the tomb painting. Ms. Sagadraco mentioned that two Milos vipers were found in the tunnels."

I spoke up. "Red ones. All the snakes on this gorgon's head were red. Is that what you got, Suzy?"

"Yes," she said without looking up from her drawing.

Dr. Chandler scrolled through several pages. "Then this may be our murderer."

Ms. Sagadraco was next to Amelia and could see what was on her screen. She scowled. Amelia made no move to show it to the rest of us. She was waiting on Suzy.

We all were.

Suzy's pencil stopped, and she immediately had our attention. She turned the sketchpad around and showed us her work.

Dr. Chandler showed us the photo of the tomb painting.

They were identical nightmares. Suzy's in tinted pencils, Amelia's a bringer of death in living color.

"Stheno," Vivienne Sagadraco said. "The eldest of the three gorgons, known for her viciousness. Her name means vengeance. Medusa was mortal, but Stheno and Euryale are immortal. They are the granddaughters of the Titans.

Elizabeth Wellesley can find no record of either Stheno or Euryale after Athena cursed them with gorgonism for trying to protect Medusa."

So much for how she was strong enough to turn two veteran battlemages to marble.

The little voice inside my head reminded me of what Arthur Conan Doyle had once said: *Once you eliminate the impossible, whatever remains, no matter how improbable, must be the truth.*

Medusa had been beheaded and was definitely dead. It being her was impossible. Stheno had merely been presumed dead and was therefore improbable. She was also the truth.

Arthur Conan Doyle for the win.

In Suzy's sketch, Stheno was holding the Aegis. The shield was smaller than I'd expected, though the gorgon holding it looked like an eight-footer. Her lower body was that of a snake and her hair was a writhing halo of red Milos vipers. I remembered Ms. Sagadraco's gorgon friend, Helena Thanos, saying that only Medusa and her sisters had the lower body of a snake and serpents for hair.

"Is that glow coming from the Aegis?" Rake asked.

"That's the impression I got," Suzy replied.

"She used it on them," I said. "Though not the full power. If she had, Quinn and Carlos wouldn't have had any minds left for Bert to contact. And since I felt what they did…" I leaned closer to the sketch where Suzy had drawn something new. "But I didn't see that."

"You did," Suzy told me. "Your eyes, and Quinn's, were being held by Stheno. She meant for you to see the Aegis, not the pendant."

There was a disk around Stheno's neck secured with a gold chain. Like the Aegis, it looked smaller than it was due to the gorgon's great size.

It looked like a hockey puck but only half the thickness. I knew that because I'd seen one before.

We'd all seen one before.

Our lab techs had immediately dubbed it a "cloaking device" in honor of *Star Trek* and because of what it did. It hid the wearer from view and hearing—from everyone except a seer. Based on its size and shape, some of the agents had taken to calling it the "hockey puck of hiding."

I'd seen it on the male grendel coming into SPI headquarters, and on the female grendel in Times Square.

Two monsters turned loose in our city by Vivienne Sagadraco's sister, the Babylonian goddess of chaos, Tiamat.

She was here. In New York. Again.

This time instead of grendels, she'd brought a gorgon.

9

It sucked to be the bearers of apocalyptically bad news.

The boss's hoard had been robbed by an eight-foot-tall gorgon, the big sister of Medusa, granddaughter of Titans, who was in town working with the Babylonian goddess of chaos to use a shield forged in the depths of Mount Olympus to do who knew what.

So, of course, there was going to be a staff meeting.

We were treading new ground. I, for one, would rather we didn't need to.

The main conference room at SPI HQ resembled a scaled-down version of the Security Council Room at the UN. Meetings here were hush-hush and meant that the supernatural crap had hit the fan big-time. Needless to say, not many people wanted to be called into a meeting in here.

I hadn't been in this room since my first big case. That one had involved a breeding pair of grendels. I'd ended up getting entirely too close to the female.

I'd seen Stheno twice: once on video, once via a dead man's memory. If there was a third time, I didn't want it to be in person. What was the saying? Three strikes and you're out.

A massive U-shaped table dominated the room, and in the center, the light from a pair of projectors—one mounted in the ceiling, the other in the floor—came together to form a hologram of SPI's company logo, a stylized monster eye with a slit pupil. The eye slowly spun, a placeholder for whatever visuals were going to be presented. Plush and pricey executive office chairs were spaced every few feet around the table.

Kenji was huddled over his laptop, fingers clicking away. I had a feeling he was working on said visuals. I also had a feeling I really didn't want to see them.

Sitting next to Kenji was Claire Cheban. SPI was populated by the best and brightest minds Vivienne Sagadraco could hire away from the private, academic, and government sectors. Kenji and Claire were two of them. They were also a couple. A few of us knew. Most people didn't, though it was only a matter of time until word spread. Folks at SPI were legendary at keeping secrets from the outside world. From each other? Not so much. Yet another way we were like a big family.

When you worked for a super-secret supernatural organization, it could be awkward having a relationship with the uninitiated. Kinda like Superman and Lois Lane. Some things you simply couldn't share with your significant other. As a result, office romances were quite the thing here at SPI.

Ms. Sagadraco had called in the leaders of our two commando teams: Roy Benoit and Sandra Niles. Now that we knew who and what we were dealing with, and even more importantly, who was responsible for setting her loose in the city, the boss was going straight to a lethal solution to our gorgon problem. Overwhelming magic and firepower.

Roy and Sandra's people were a mix of human and supernatural fighters who had hard-hitting magic and deadly military skills at their disposal. The last time Tiamat had brought trouble to our doorstep, asking it nicely to leave hadn't been an option. Stheno had killed two of our agents in one of the worst ways imaginable. SPI had two ways of dealing with supernatural villains: apprehend or eliminate. The boss had chosen door number two.

Roy had grown up in the swamps of southern Louisiana in a long and proud line of gator hunters. He'd done a lengthy stint in the army and had retired as a Ranger. Though according to Roy, Rangers never retired.

Sandra was a Jamaica native who'd kept me from becoming monster chow on more than one occasion. She was smart, fierce, and funny, and I was proud to call Sandra a friend.

Vivienne Sagadraco stood from her chair at the head of the table. "As all of you now know, one of my vaults was broken into this morning, and the Aegis, the shield of Zeus and Athena, has been stolen. Two of our battlemages, Carlos Escarra and Quinn Walsh, were killed in the attempt to capture the thief, a thief we have now identified as Stheno, the elder sister of Medusa."

The wide eyes and frozen expressions around the table

were entirely too similar to Carlos and Quinn's. I had to look away.

"Medusa was raped by Poseidon in the temple of Athena, where she served as a priestess," Ms. Sagadraco continued. "In retaliation for the desecration of her temple, Athena took her rage out on Medusa, not Poseidon, turning her into a gorgon. Medusa's sisters, Stheno and Euryale, attempted to protect her, and Athena turned them into gorgons as well. It's been assumed that the elder sisters were dead, since they disappeared from the historical timeline soon after. We now have evidence to the contrary."

Vivienne Sagadraco's gaze took in the reactions of her agents. "Medusa became pregnant by Poseidon and was sleeping when she was beheaded by Perseus, who used her head as a weapon to turn anyone who beheld it to stone. He later gave the head to Athena, who embedded it in her shield, the Aegis."

Ms. Sagadraco nodded to Kenji, who clicked a couple of keys, and the SPI logo was replaced by a 3D, full-size rendering of the shield.

"This is the Aegis. It contains the actual head of Medusa, so it is dangerous even without being activated." She paused. "It instills terror in any who look upon it, and with Medusa's head embedded in the shield, it instantly turns any who see the shield or its reflection to stone. We all knew Agents Escarra and Walsh, and their courage was unquestioned. Looking at the Aegis for an instant nearly broke their minds." She paused again to let that sink in. The only sound came from the humming of the overhead lights.

She continued. "We know what happened to them in their

final seconds thanks to Dr. Ferguson and Agent Fraser. During the PML, Agent Fraser experienced a link to Quinn Walsh that allowed her to see everything that happened."

All eyes were on me.

I had no problem with Ms. Sagadraco telling everyone. These people were my friends. It was a relief to have this out in the open.

"Damn, girl," Sandra muttered in sympathy.

"It wasn't my idea," I muttered right back. "Looks like I've got another 'gift' from Dad."

"I'd send that one back."

"No returns."

"You all know of my friendship with Helena Thanos," Ms. Sagadraco continued. "She is a gorgon who was turned during Greece's Golden Age, and as such is a priceless resource. Unfortunately, Helena is on vacation in a remote location, and is unreachable by normal means of contact. I have sent Alain Moreau to bring her back. I was reluctant to do so, but the situation is dire. Thanks to Agent Fraser's contact with Quinn Walsh, Susan Connolly was able to draw his and Carlos Escarra's killer." She nodded to Kenji, and Suzy's sketch was projected on the screen in the front of the room along with the tomb photo Amelia had found.

There was silence as everyone soaked in the horror double feature. I didn't need to soak. I was already saturated.

"The photograph is of a fifth-century BC Athenian tomb, provided by Dr. Chandler. This, along with two red Milos vipers found at the murder scene, gives us a positive identification of Stheno as our culprit." Ms. Sagadraco paused. "That's the good news."

Roy gave a low whistle.

"I quite agree, Commander Benoit. Ms. Connolly noticed that our killer was wearing a necklace. A pendant attached to a gold chain. A black disk that we are all too familiar with from our case involving the grendels."

Roy upgraded his whistle to his favorite cuss word.

"Again, I agree. So, unless we discover evidence to the contrary, we should proceed as if Tiamat is behind all this, and more than likely, the cabal along with her. The affair with the grendels five years ago has similarities to the situation in which we now find ourselves. Both involve a relative determined to reclaim another relative's relic and exact vengeance. Stheno has the relic, but unlike Grendel's arm, the Aegis is capable of paralyzing entire armies, both with terror and ossification."

Ms. Sagadraco nodded to Kenji, who turned off the projector. I was grateful. I didn't want to look at Stheno any more than I had to. I was sure my coworkers agreed.

"My sister had no plan for Grendel's arm," the boss continued. "It was merely a bribe to get the creatures to our shores. There were other artifacts in my vault, but I believe Tiamat wanted only the Aegis. She was unable to breach the vault's security. Director Winters and I made certain of that. Stheno, however, was somehow able to turn to dust the over forty feet of solid rock between the outer tunnels and the vault. Once she got inside, Stheno's blood link to Medusa must have enabled her to negate the wards on the niche containing the Aegis. Tiamat would not have been able to do either one."

"What's in it for Tiamat?" Sandra asked.

"Part of their deal must be that Tiamat gets the Aegis, at least temporarily. It's too powerful an artifact for her not to want and want dearly. At this moment, it may very well be in Tiamat's hands. We know nothing of her plans or her location. We must determine both, and quickly. I have people whose job it is to know my sister's whereabouts at all times. I have not received a report in four days. I have reached out to them but have yet to receive a response."

Knowing Tiamat, chances were they'd never report anything to anyone ever again.

Vivienne's expression turned even grimmer than we'd seen so far. "And we don't know what Tiamat might have promised Stheno. Stheno would've needed my sister to get to New York, but she would've demanded more for her cooperation. She has already killed two of our agents. We must consider the possibility that she could want vengeance against myself and/or SPI. Since she gained access so easily to what I considered to be an impregnable vault, she could very well do the same here. Anti-gorgon glare glasses will be distributed to those patrolling the lower levels of the complex. We don't know if they will be effective against a gorgon of Stheno's age. Alain Moreau is immune to Helena Thanos's gorgon glare, but Carlos Escarra was nearly a century older than Alain. He was completely ossified in seconds. Dr. Cheban's analysis of a scale found at the scene of the murder puts Stheno at approximately seventy-two hundred years old, which means that even those of us who are immune to older gorgons will not be immune to Stheno."

There was stunned silence at that.

Bob Fitzwilliam raised his hand to get Ms. Sagadraco's attention. Bob and Rob Stanton, who was seated beside him, were the codirectors of SPI New York's research and development department. They were the go-to guys for gadgets and gizmos our agents and commandos used to do their jobs and stay safe while doing them. They were collectively known as Bob and Rob—or, as the boss called them, "the Roberts."

"Yes, Director Fitzwilliam?"

"Ma'am, at this time, we only have fifty pairs of gorgon glasses. We will pull our technicians off all other projects to produce more, but it takes four days to make the lenses."

"We can run production round the clock," Rob Stanton added.

Ms. Sagadraco gave a nod. "Do so, but consider shortened work periods. We can't risk errors due to fatigue."

Lenscrafters could knock out a pair of glasses in an hour, though if they made a mistake, you didn't get turned to stone.

Sandra raised her hand.

"Yes, Commander Niles?"

"If Stheno is cloaked and we can't see her, can we still be ossified?"

I spoke up. "Ma'am, I may be able to answer that."

"Proceed."

"Possibly not," I told Sandra. "When I saw what happened through Agent Walsh's eyes, Stheno was less than ten feet from him. She had to have been looking at them, but they weren't paralyzed until she uncloaked and *they* saw *her*, not before." Then I summarized what had happened to me when I'd watched the surveillance video. "So, it's not safe to watch her on a surveillance tape, either. I don't have any way of knowing if she was looking at the camera, but I'm assuming she had to have been."

When there were no other questions, Ms. Sagadraco continued.

"We need to find Stheno and my sister. Now. While both

were born in caves accessed by tunnels, Tiamat would never be in one again unless she had no choice. I believe she and Stheno are comfortably ensconced somewhere nearby. The Aegis is still in New York. I have a link with each item in that hoard, and the link with the Aegis is being blocked. I know it is still in the city, and they've got to be hiding somewhere extremely private, but that is all I can determine. If Tiamat is keeping it here, this is where she means to use it. The Aegis cannot be destroyed, but it can be wielded. It is now in the worst possible hands."

Ms. Sagadraco picked up the folders on the table in front of her. "Lastly, have your people talk to *every* contact. Someone has seen something. I have spoken with Agent Kazakov. Tomorrow night is his one-hundredth birthday party at the Full Moon. The guest list includes many of those who may know something. He has given his permission to use his party for information-gathering. Right now, information is the only weapon we have."

10

There was only one thing I could do after a day like today.

Go home and go to bed.

Rake insisted on it, and I thought it was the most wonderful idea I'd ever heard.

By the way, I lived with Rake now.

Over the past year, since we'd become serious, I'd been a regular visitor to his Central Park West apartment. He'd given me a key, though I'd never used it. I'd still maintained my own apartment and had only been to Rake's place when he'd been there. Regardless, he'd made sure that I was welcomed by his staff whenever I'd visited, from the building's doormen to his butler, housekeeper, and cook.

After spending Christmas in North Carolina with my

family, and our much-needed vacation in Bora Bora afterward, I decided to accept Rake's ongoing invitation to move in with him. By then I'd spent so much time at Rake's that I already considered his stuff my stuff. Not to mention, I'd bought most of my furniture when I'd first moved to New York and had been watching every dollar. After Ms. Sagadraco had recruited me to work at SPI, I simply hadn't bothered to upgrade my worldly goods. They just hadn't been that important to me. I gave most everything away, packed my clothes, moved out, and moved in with Rake.

It was nearly seven o'clock, and my usual workday was long over. A good dinner followed by a long bath and an even longer sleep was the best thing I could do to help. I knew from experience that in the coming days, I probably wouldn't get a chance to do any of the above, and that I should get clean, fed, and rested while I could.

After dinner, Rake did that thing he did so well to ensure that my body was as relaxed as it could be and still contain bones. He followed that up with two encores.

Bravo.

A case of Red Bull wouldn't have kept me awake after that.

When I woke up, it was a little after ten the next morning.

Rake must have turned off my alarm. So much for getting to work on time.

I stumbled downstairs to find Ian and Yasha having breakfast with Rake in the kitchen.

The boys were having breakfast. Together.

I felt the urge to look out the nearest window to make sure the world hadn't ended overnight. Though considering the situation we were in, I didn't want to tempt fate.

As far as I was concerned, Ian was only one of my partners. Yasha Kazakov was the other. Ian had my back, but Yasha had both our backs and then some. Yasha liked keeping us safe. The big Russian agent was one of SPI's trackers and drivers, and Yasha drove his Suburban wherever it needed to go to bag a rampaging beastie, be it street, sidewalk, or any unpaved green space. Our buddy was an accomplished urban off-road driver. His nickname at SPI was Kamikaze Kazakov, and he'd more than earned it.

Yasha was also a werewolf.

Like most supernatural beings, Yasha used small magics to hide his werewolf form from the public. My seer vision let me see Yasha's large, furry, and red-haired aura. There were two werewolf packs in New York City: one in Manhattan and another that ranged the outer boroughs. Yasha wasn't a member of either one. He considered SPI his pack.

I considered running a hand through my hair to tame my bedhead, then decided not to bother.

"This is a pleasant surprise," I said, going over to pour myself a cup of coffee. "I think. Is there something earth-shattering I need to know?"

"It's been quiet since the meeting," Ian replied. "Whatever Tia has planned, she's not ready to do it yet."

I saluted him with my mug. "Not spectacular news, but I'll take it." I sat next to Rake and gave him a peck on the cheek. "By chance did a red-haired gorgon and a red-scaled dragon check in to the Regor Regency last night?"

Rake shook his head. "Nor have any members of the cabal. My staff has a lengthy list of undesirables committed to memory. If one of them crosses the threshold, I'm notified immediately." He glanced down at his phone. "All quiet. I also have contacts at other hotels Tia would favor, as well as the posher private rentals. Tia could pass for human, but unless she's gotten one hell of a glamour for Stheno, an eight-foot-tall, half-serpent gorgon with red vipers for hair can hardly check into a hotel or Airbnb unnoticed, even in this town."

"I need you to set up a meeting with Ollie at Barrington Galleries," Ian told me.

I tried to link that to what Rake had just said and failed miserably. "Uh, I'm going to need some more dots to connect that."

"Martin determined that Ruby was under SoHo when she turned and came running back. The coordinates from her collar put her in the tunnels directly under Ollie's place—tunnels that can be accessed through his basement."

"Consider the meeting arranged."

Barrington Galleries was a glorified pawnshop on the edge of SoHo. The owner, Oliver Barrington-Smythe, called it a collection of antiquities, artifacts, and curiosities. I called it a store full of spooky shit that only spookier people would want. Most of Ollie's merchandise looked like it'd been dug up, either from the ground, a crypt, a serial killer's basement, or a psycho's imagination. No object was too bizarre or disgusting for Ollie to try to make a buck off it.

"I'm of the opinion that Ruby stopping there wasn't a coincidence," Ian added.

"Nothing involving Ollie has ever been a coincidence."

"Exactly. Martin said Ruby approached greyhound speed coming out of SoHo. Hellhounds don't have any natural predators. When you live in Hell, that says a lot."

I reached for my phone. “When do you want to talk to him?”

“Sooner the better.”

I snagged a scone from the tray and started to stand.

“Not nearly enough,” Rake said. He started fixing me a plate. “You can take a scone to go, but you’re taking time to eat a real breakfast. I seriously doubt Stheno is still there, but any evidence she left will be.”

“Excellent point,” I told him.

“Of course, it is. Saralle is making sandwiches in a cooler to take with you. Well-fed agents are safer agents.”

“He likes us now.” Yasha smiled around a mouthful of scrambled eggs.

“I never said I didn’t like you.”

“Sometimes like is not wishing dead.” Yasha shrugged. “I’ll take it.”

Rake didn’t know what to do with that, so he turned to me. “While you speak with Mister Barrington-Smythe, I’ll talk to my contacts about where Tia and the minions are holed up.”

I grinned. “Marek won’t like being relegated to minion status.”

Rake’s eyes glittered dangerously. “I aspire to relay my opinion in person. Today. Madame Sagadraco isn’t the only one who considers New York their territory.”

Oliver Barrington-Smythe had a double-barreled last name and five aliases to go along with it. He was short, beady-eyed, balding, and resented being all the above, so it came as no surprise that he rubbed most people the wrong way. I liked his

British accent; he liked my Southern one. We'd hit it off, and Ollie had become one of my best sources.

After an international antiques broker was literally torn limb from limb in Ollie's office by a grendel, Barrington Galleries had become a museum of the macabre, and an occultist and goth tourist and shopping destination. Never one to let any source of revenue go untapped, Ollie had started selling T-shirts and mugs, and even had a source for fake voodoo dolls. Most of them had politicians' faces. Those things flew off the shelves. My little British friend made a tidy profit from the gawkers, firmly believing that today's cash-strapped tourist could become tomorrow's cash-to-burn client.

Ollie had been kidnapped during my first big case at SPI. A team of ghoul commandos had ripped the roof right off his storage unit and snatched him out on the tail end of a rope attached to a helicopter. Later I'd found Ollie hoisted over a nest of hatching grendel eggs. A couple more minutes and Ollie would've been Gerber for grendels. Our people had hauled Ollie out of that monster pit.

He owed us, and he knew it. He didn't like it, but he knew it.

Yasha was driving the Suburban. Ian was riding shotgun, and I was sitting in the second seat behind Yasha so that Ian and I could talk without my partner having to do a Linda Blair impersonation.

Right now, Ian was on the phone with Kenji, who in addition to all the other hats he wore was the grand poobah of SPI surveillance.

Ollie knew many people whom SPI considered interesting,

and we liked to know when they visited. Kenji had security cameras set up on two buildings adjacent to Barrington Galleries. As a result, on more than a few occasions, we'd intercepted trouble in time for Ollie to lock the doors.

Yet more times that SPI had prolonged Ollie's lifespan.

Ian hung up. "No unusual visitors in the past week. Though that could just mean they didn't come in through the front or back door."

I knew what that meant.

The gallery's basement had its very own entrance, and it wasn't on street level. Yasha had once told us that the bar at the end of the block had been a speakeasy in the 1920s. They'd also had a trapdoor in the basement leading to tunnels that went to the East River, and as we'd discovered a few years ago, to the Hudson River as well. Great for smuggling illegal booze.

Or for Stheno to escape with the Aegis.

The gallery also had a trapdoor in the basement. It was used by select clients and suppliers who didn't want to be seen going in or out. Some of Ollie's acquisitions weren't legal, so he liked to keep the feds and police out of his business. And as long as it didn't break supernatural laws or endanger anyone, SPI stayed out of his business, too.

I'd called Ollie and he'd agreed to meet us at the gallery at noon. He opened at one o'clock and closed at nine. His usual clientele weren't exactly morning people.

When Ollie had asked why we needed to talk, I told him it was confidential. It was our go-to reply to curious contacts. Or a contact who would go into a fit of hysterical screaming if I told him there could be an ancient Greek monster lair under his basement. Though I did tell him not to go into the basement until we got there. He assured me he wouldn't. Ollie was arrogant, greedy, and occasionally obnoxious, but he was not stupid.

11

Ollie opened the door. "Why are you here?"

Ian pushed past him. "What you don't know, you can't be tortured to tell."

That shut him up.

Once Yasha and I were inside, he closed and locked the door.

Ollie was still balding, but you wouldn't know it, thanks to a new toupee that resembled human hair and not a squirrel with Taser-styled fur. His former toupee had ended up in SPI's breakroom fridge, planted by my evil doppelganger, and tacked to a melon with a butcher knife.

It'd been a while since we'd been in Ollie's place of business, but it hadn't changed a bit, and it really should.

Ollie got his stock from who he liked to call his brokers of the bizarre.

Among the stuff for sale that packed the place from floor to ceiling were Victorian exorcism and vampire hunter kits. Antique coffins. Painted portraits of actual people who looked like Addams family relatives. Squishy things preserved in jars, dried things not in jars, funeral portraits, voodoo and séance paraphernalia, and next to the counter an actual Egyptian sarcophagus that had a fake mummy inside. It looked real, but it wasn't. The city health department had made him get rid of the real one.

Ollie kept the smaller merchandise in glass-fronted display cases that occupied most of the available wall space. These were all under lock and key. The most expensive (and dangerous) merchandise was kept in a vault in the back room. Inside were items Ollie had acquired for his special clients (i.e., people who had obscene wealth to go along with their weird).

I heard a familiar sound on the street outside, and went to Ollie's back door to let her in.

Dr. Claire Cheban rode a motorcycle.

A sweet Ducati Black Star, to be exact. She'd parked beside the Suburban in the alley that ran behind Ollie's place. We'd come in the back door, too. We had more people on the way and didn't want anyone who might be watching the shop to see a crowd arriving. Kenji was keeping an eye on things from HQ. He'd let us know if we had company.

Like many of the department directors at SPI, Claire led from the front. She wasn't about to send her people anywhere she wasn't willing to go herself.

Speaking of leading from the front, heading down the alley from the other end of the street were two familiar faces.

One human, the other canine. One looked like himself, the other was glamoured as a sleek greyhound. Just a hound and her human out for a lunchtime stroll.

Martin DiMatteo had brought Ruby and her nose to take a sniff before we went into Ollie's basement, and especially before we lifted the trapdoor to the tunnels. She'd know if Stheno had been merely passing through yesterday, or if she was now in residence. We didn't think she was, but just in case, we had people on the way to help with that, too.

The last of our team pulled up in a truck with Volta Electrical Service on the side. Sandra Niles and two of her commandos in dark coveralls got out and started unloading gear concealed in toolboxes. One of the guys pulled out an extendable ladder. Sandra was a badass. The two commandos she'd brought with her were badass battlemages.

All of our bases were now covered.

Ollie scowled. I think he knew he wouldn't be opening on time.

Sandra double-tapped the glass front door with her knuckle.

"You might want to let them in," Ian said. "The sooner your 'electrical problem' is fixed, the sooner you can open. And be grateful, Sandra was going to bring the Zap-Em Exterminator truck."

Ollie grumbled something under his breath and went to the door.

The door to the basement was in the back room.

Everyone had geared up, which included wearing weapons

and gorgon glasses. The commandos had telescoping spears, an armament addition they'd picked up from our Scandinavian team. If it worked for a grendel, it'd work for a gorgon. We hoped. Ian had telescoped Lugh's Spear, and I'd rolled back my sleeve to expose my dad's cuff. Neither Ian's spearhead nor my cuff had indicated any impending danger.

Good news was always welcome.

Ollie opened the door a smidge, and Ruby took a sniff that had to have sucked in half the air down there. Yasha's sniffer gave us a second opinion.

No gorgon in the basement.

We all went downstairs.

The trapdoor lock didn't show any sign of tampering, but Ruby's hackles went up as she snuffled around the edges. Ollie quickly gave Sandra the keys.

I tightened the strap on my yellow-lensed gorgon glasses. "Ollie, go back upstairs."

I could've saved my breath. After "go," he took off.

Ian's eyes were on the trapdoor. "Little guy can move fast when he wants to."

"How we gonna play this?" I asked anyone who might know.

"Ian's spear goes first," Sandra said. "If it doesn't glow, we're gorgon-free. Probably. Then me and my guys go."

"And if it glows?" I asked. "Plus, if she's down there, she could be cloaked. I should go first."

In response, Ian wedged the tip of Lugh's Spear under the edge of the trapdoor and pried it open a few inches.

No glow.

Sandra and her team stepped up. Ruby wedged herself

between them and stuck her nose in, sucked in all the air, then backed up, grunted, and sneezed.

We all looked to Martin for translation.

"The gorgon was there but isn't there now."

And the good news kept coming. We'd probably be going up against Stheno eventually, but I'd rather not do it in a dark hole in the ground.

Ollie kept a ladder against the wall to get into the tunnel. It was wood and looked solid enough, but he'd been known to cut corners. Though I couldn't see him risking one of his best clients falling and breaking their neck.

Still, I trusted Sandra's ladder more.

Sandra deployed the ladder, and she started down, followed by her team. Ian went next and I followed.

Ruby simply jumped down the hole, landing lightly on all fours.

Our commandos/battlemages had the tunnel lit like high noon with glow globes. They sent two of the globes down the tunnel in both directions.

No Stheno, cloaked or otherwise. But dang, had she been here.

I whistled. "Stheno had company."

Outside Vivienne Sagadraco's vault, we'd found one scale and two vipers, both very much alive.

There was a lot more here. Scales were scattered all around us, along with clumps of dead vipers. Claire had been glad to have one tiny blood sample. She was gonna be positively giddy when she got down here. Blood was sprayed all over the walls.

Ruby hadn't moved from where she'd landed, eyes wide and glowing red.

Oh yeah. Ruby had been here, seen that, and hadn't even gotten a T-shirt for her trauma.

Claire was on her way down the ladder.

"I hope you brought plenty of specimen bags," I told her.

"I have extras if you need them," Martin called over from where he was swabbing a sizeable blood sample into a test tube. He had a handful of others sticking out of his jacket pocket. I was amazed the guy didn't clink when he walked.

Claire saw the mess. "Let's turn on our bodycams. My people need to see this." She keyed her mike. "Kenji, we're all going live. Patch our cameras through to the lab—and the boss. She'll want to see this, too."

To look for further traces of our combatants, Yasha and one of the battlemages went down the tunnel that emptied into the Hudson River. Ruby, along with Martin and the second battlemage, went the other way, toward the East River.

I tried to make sense of the mess we had here.

The vipers were all dead. At least the ones still here were dead. Whatever had happened had happened yesterday. Any serpentine survivors were long gone.

I shone my flashlight on the largest group of vipers. They were a tangle of two colors: solid red, and a patterned mixture of gray and brown.

And as far as I could tell, they were all Milos vipers.

Stheno had red vipers for hair.

Kenji's voice came through our earpieces. *"Ollie just let a customer in."*

I rolled my eyes. Jeez Louise, Ollie. So much for keeping civilians out of the way.

"What's Medusa's other sister's name?" I asked Ian. "The only other one with snakes for hair?"

"Euryale." Ian squatted down next to me and saw what I was seeing. He swore. "Looks like we've got a family reunion in town."

"And the sisters had themselves one helluva catfight," I added. "Ruby must've had a front-row seat. No wonder she was so freaked out."

From upstairs, Ollie screamed.

Then, like Quinn and Carlos, his scream was silenced.

12

We all ran for the ladder.

Chaos would've ensued, but Sandra had seniority. Plus, she got there first. Ian clambered up at her heels. Claire and I followed.

When we reached the top, Sandra and Ian had guns out and glasses on, covering each other through the door and into the shop.

"Claire!" Ian shouted. "Keys!"

Claire tossed, Ian caught, and seconds later Claire's bike fired up in the alley. Ian roared down the street, presumably after who or what had made Ollie scream.

Ollie was standing behind the counter.

He wasn't stone.

I started breathing again. "Ollie, what was…?"

His eyes were fixed and staring. One hand was on the register, and a small stack of one-hundred-dollar bills lay untouched right in front of him.

That's when I *knew* something was wrong. He hadn't snatched up that cash.

Then I saw what was next to the money.

A dead rat. Not just dead, turned to stone.

The customer was a gorgon.

That explained why Ian had peeled out of here.

I ran around the counter and put my hands on either side of Ollie's face. His skin was still pliable and warm.

"Ollie." I lightly tapped him on both cheeks. When that didn't get anything out of him, I tapped harder. I admit I didn't mind doing that.

Then Ollie's mouth dropped open, he inhaled, and started screaming again.

Sandra winced. "I like him better petrified."

I grabbed his shoulders and shook him. "Ollie!"

Shaking him didn't stop the screaming, but seeing those Ben Franklins sure did. He squeaked in delight and snatched them up.

I didn't think gorgons could temporarily paralyze people. Just one more thing gorgon glasses might not work against. Great.

I turned his head to face me. "The. Customer. Do you know their name?"

No response. Though at least his eyes were trying to focus. On the money.

"Must be a delay with the brain coming back online," Claire said.

Sandra pointed at a dark reflective bowl set into the ceiling behind the counter. "Surveillance camera."

"Off...office," Ollie managed.

Sandra took the stairs three at a time to Ollie's office. I could only manage a double.

When I got there, I tried to call Ian. He didn't answer. Hopefully he was still in pursuit, and not lying paralyzed or worse in the middle of the street.

The last time I'd been in Ollie's office had been the night a grendel had smeared Dr. Adam Falke all over the place like strawberry jam, then taken a couple of body parts for souvenirs.

Sandra was already behind the desk booting up Ollie's computer. She indicated her earpiece. "I'm on with Kenji. He got a good shot of the bike from the camera across the street. He couldn't get the tag, and she was still wearing her helmet when she went in."

"She?"

Sandra flashed a grin. "Tight leather. Kenji noticed." Her eyes went back to the screen. "Okay, it's on. Work your magic, Ken."

I keyed my mic. "I'm with Sandra. Patch me in."

Kenji's voice came over my earpiece. *"Go ahead."*

"Ian's in pursuit on Claire's bike. Do you still have visual from his body cam?"

"That's a negative."

Dammit. "How about a location?"

"He just flew past Morton and hung a left on Barrow."

Toward the Hudson River. At least he was still upright.

"Getting in." Kenji's voice was punctuated with the

clicking of computer keys. *"Crappy excuse for a password... decent security...not a good time to have it... almost there... Okay, let's see who she is."*

Kenji had taken over Ollie's computer, had accessed the surveillance program, and was speeding through this morning's video. It was moving too fast for me, so I studied my shoes for a few seconds to keep from getting queasy.

"Got it."

I looked up. The video showed us coming in. Kenji ran it forward again—and I studied the ceiling while he got to where he was going—until our biker made her appearance. Kenji was right. She was wearing tight biker leathers, and she wore them well. She removed her helmet, revealing mirrored sunglasses.

Oh boy.

"When she takes off her glasses, look away," I said quickly.

She lowered the glasses for a fraction of a second, stoned the rat that'd just jumped on the counter, froze Ollie where he stood, and pushed them back up. She never looked at the camera, so we didn't get second-hand gorgon glare. So much for getting a field test of gorgon glasses. Stheno must have looked directly at the vault's surveillance camera when I got nailed.

Kenji froze the frame on the gorgon's face with her glasses down.

Oval face, olive skin, dark hair, dark eyes, shoulder-length bob with bangs.

Claire looked over my shoulder at the screen. "She's cute. Bangs totally work on her. I wish I could wear bangs."

Sandra keyed her mic. "You got enough for an ID?"

"Maybe. Running it now."

Moments later, Kenji swore.

Sandra leaned forward. "I'll take that as a yes."

Claire keyed her mic. "Have you tried calling Ian through the bike radio?"

"Duh. Yet another reason why I love you."

Nerve-wracking seconds passed, then Kenji's voice came over our earpieces. *"Ian, stand down. Repeat, stand down. She's a gorgon. Name is Zyta Kokkinos. Twelve hundred twenty-three years old. She's the commander of a military order called, get this, the Sisters of Medusa."*

We couldn't hear Ian's response, but we did hear the bike being throttled back. Wise man, my partner.

Being told you'd come close to catching a militant gorgon was like finding out a harmless snake was actually a cobra.

Once again, Kenji—and Claire—saved the day.

Hundreds of ships a day arrived in and departed from New York Harbor. Finding one Greek gorgon on a ninja bike on the Hudson River waterfront had needle-in-a-haystack odds. Though as far as a hideout went, it was brilliant.

"She called me last night asking if I still had that sixteenth-century Venetian hand mirror," Ollie was telling us. Waving those crisp, new bills under his nose had worked better than smelling salts. My little British buddy was now all kinds of alert.

"I told Miss Christatos I opened at one o'clock, and she said she would be here. I didn't see why I couldn't let her in."

His face lost its color again. "How was I supposed to know she was a gorgon?"

I thumbed the cash under his nose again. Ollie inhaled, closed his eyes, and smiled dreamily.

"Why did she paralyze you?" I asked.

He shuddered and his eyes popped open. "A rat jumped on the counter. A *rat*! Dear God, how embarrassing. She pulled down her glasses and it…it…"

"Yeah, yeah, Ollie. We saw. Keep going."

"I screamed. Then she glanced at *me*." He swallowed with an audible gulp. "I couldn't move." He stopped, thought, then frowned indignantly. "You slapped me. Why did you slap me?"

"It was a tap. And it was to keep you from turning to stone." I didn't know if that would've happened or if slapping would've helped, but it seemed like a good way to keep Ollie focused.

"What's so special about the mirror?" Ian asked him. He'd gotten back a few minutes ago and wasn't happy with not apprehending Zyta Kokkinos. If Ollie was less than forthcoming, Ian would be taking his unhappy out on Ollie.

"It had Medusa's face on the back." Ollie went a little pasty again.

"And?"

"And it's sixteenth-century Venetian. I've had it for years. This is the first time anyone has been interested." He held out his hand for the money.

I sighed and gave it to him.

"Miss Christatos paid the full asking price. In cash." The money disappeared into his jacket pocket with a speed that'd make a Three-card Monte dealer proud. "I unloaded old inventory for four times what I paid for it." He gave us a smug little smile. "So perhaps a little paralysis was worth it."

No need for an MRI. Ollie was fine.

Sandra raised her hand from the door to the backroom and waved us over.

"My guy found another red viper in the East River tunnel. Ruby sniffed out three of the gray and black ones in the Hudson River tunnel—and a lot more blood."

"Well, Stheno *is* the vicious one," Ian noted. "Sounds like they fought and went their separate ways. Zyta Kokkinos was headed toward the Hudson piers."

"All three toward the water. Can snake-bodied gorgons swim?" I asked anyone who would know.

"Their grandparents were sea Titans," Ian reminded me. "I think that'd be a yes."

"Manhattan's an island, so that doesn't help us any."

"I didn't say it would."

"It's a good thing Ollie has rats," Sandra said, "or we would've never known about Kokkinos."

Ian scowled. "We don't have her in custody."

"Not your fault," I told him.

"The hell it isn't."

"The way our luck is running, you'll get another up-close-and-personal chance. Maybe this time you'll have backup," I added meaningfully.

We had Medusa's actual sisters in town, along with an order that called themselves the Sisters of Medusa. And for the sprinkles on top, the boss's sister Tiamat was playing tour guide for at least one of them. We were up to our collective keester in Medusa's relatives, literal and otherwise. And the only gorgon on our side was vacationing somewhere in the Canadian wilderness.

13

Yasha's birthday party started shortly after sundown, but nearly a third of the guests wouldn't show up until after nine o'clock. Some were nocturnal by preference, some by necessity.

With his natural likability, Yasha had accumulated a *lot* of friends over the past century. Many of those friends had become SPI sources when the big Russian werewolf had come to work for us. With tonight being Yasha's one-hundredth birthday, any of his friends who could be here would be here. There was no way the venue could accommodate all of them at the same time, so the party was more of a drop-in affair. And with so many people coming through, there was no better time to put the feelers out about our gorgon problem.

The birthday boy was at the door greeting party guests with Kitty Poertner.

Kitty was another of SPI's consultants. In her day job, she owned and ran Kitty's Confections, a bakery on Bleecker Street in the Village. Her angel food cake was said to have made an actual angel weep. Her family came from a long line of portalkeepers who could open, close, detect, and destroy portals. Kitty was one of the best. She had once closed a portal linking Hell and Earth, while it had demons scrabbling up through it. My friend Kitty had nerves of steel.

She and Yasha had been a serious couple for over a year. She had even taken him home to meet her parents.

Naturally, Kitty had baked Yasha's massive chocolate birthday cake.

We were hosting the party at Yasha's favorite bar and restaurant, the Full Moon. It was only a short walk from SPI headquarters, which made it a popular agent hangout. But what really made it a SPI home-away-from-home were the owners, Bill and Nancy Garrison. Bill was the king of the barbeque pit, and Nancy had the brains for the business and the Southern charm and hospitality to keep the place full of happy customers.

They were also werewolves.

Best of all, they were from my home state of North Carolina.

I came here to get a literal taste of home.

The barbeque was slow cooked, the burgers were rare, the steaks could be ordered tartare, and the regulars went furry once a month. There was always a booth reserved for hungry SPI agents, and Yasha's Suburban was always welcome in the alley/delivery area out back.

No supernatural with a lick of sense would bring trouble over the Full Moon's threshold. In addition to Bill and Nancy, nearly the entire staff were werewolves. There weren't many supernaturals—magic-packing or not—who wanted to get up close and personal with a pack of werewolves who'd just had their den invaded.

That's exactly what the Full Moon was, a den. Family and friends were welcome, as were well-behaved patrons. Agents could speak freely here, and Bill and Nancy had become our surrogate parents, having stepped up for us more times than we could count. The restaurant and bar were decorated with dark wood, dim lights, and every werewolf cliché that existed. Yasha loved classic monster movies. Werewolf movie posters and props were on display, and everything on the food and drink menus had a werewolf or movie monster-inspired name. Nancy had hidden their werewolf natures in plain sight, and it had worked brilliantly and profitably.

The Full Moon was a fun place, with great food, and the best people.

The dartboards had been moved and an axe-throwing station had been added just for tonight. It was a birthday party, and what was a birthday party without games? Axes were merely the more lethal cousin of Pin the Tail on the Donkey. The Garrisons knew their walls were safe. We were professionals. We knew what we were doing. And no, I didn't include myself in that "we." I still couldn't throw for crap and wasn't about to embarrass myself in front of my friends.

Bill and Nancy had closed the Full Moon for Yasha's party. No balloons, no decorations, just an open bar and a barbeque buffet with all the fixin's, with the grill open for either burgers or steaks. All courtesy of Vivienne Sagadraco.

Before the Aegis had been stolen, she hadn't planned to

attend. She wanted us all to feel free to have fun. But she was here tonight. The Full Moon had two small rooms accessible from the back door where private conversations could take place. Kenji was working in one, Ian and Kylie in the other. Vivienne Sagadraco was ensconced in the restaurant's office, watching and listening to the exchanges in both. Four senior agents were working the floor out in the restaurant and would text any information of value directly to her.

A few people not on the guest list would be joining us. Everyone in yesterday's meeting had put out feelers, and Yasha had asked select friends to contact their contacts. Yasha was confident that some of the birthday presents he'd be getting tonight couldn't be wrapped.

Information.

Many times, it was not only who you knew, but also who *they* knew.

We had agents posted at both front and back entrances. The front was for guests who didn't mind being seen by anyone who might be watching. The back was for more circumspect entrances and exits.

Our people were calling in every favor we had.

I was in a corner booth, waiting to talk to a contact of my own when Rake slid into the seat next to me with a dazzling smile.

I kissed him. "You look pleased with yourself."

"Exceptionally pleased. I found the son of a bitch."

"Honey, you know many sons of bitches, but I take it you're referring to Marek Reigory?"

"I am."

"And he is…?"

"At the Carlyle."

"And where is that?"

Rake just looked at me.

"Sweetie, the only hotel I care about is yours."

"The Carlyle is on the Upper East Side."

"About as far away from the Regor Regency as he can get."

"Precisely. The Carlyle is legendarily discreet, nearly as discreet as the Regency. But what people fail to realize is that discretion rarely applies to hotel owners. Information I want is information I can get."

"Is he alone?"

"Surprisingly, yes." Rake snuggled in close. "But I found Gerald Blackburn in a posh rental on Riverside Drive. Marek and Gerald are two of Tia's favorites."

"Then she's in town."

"Almost certainly."

I pulled out my phone. "We need to tell Ms. Sagadraco."

Rake tapped his jacket pocket where I knew he kept his own phone. "Already have." His eyes went from one side of the restaurant to the other, taking in every face. I knew from experience that he'd memorized them all. I could quiz him a week from now and he'd be able to tell me every name.

"And where is dear Vivienne?" Rake asked.

"Bill and Nancy's office. The center of the web for tonight."

"Have you spoken with your secret source yet?"

"I wouldn't exactly call Ord secret, but the source he's got a line on is."

"And who is that?"

I leaned in and kissed the oh-so-sensitive tip of Rake's

ear and was rewarded with a shiver. "You've got your secrets, I've got mine."

As if on cue, Ord Larcwyde came down from upstairs and gestured me outside.

I gave Rake a wink. "Be right back."

Ord Larcwyde was a three-foot-tall gnome who'd always reminded me of Colonel Sanders, if the colonel was wearing a blue velour tracksuit and gold chains instead of a white suit and black string tie. Ord even liked fried chicken, though with his new office over the Full Moon, he'd gone hard-core into barbeque.

Ord had chosen his previous office space for the security of its old walk-in freezer. Now he was over a werewolf bar one block from SPI HQ.

My gnome friend had a financial goal and a life goal. Make enough money to retire well. Live long enough to enjoy both. He was an entrepreneur and a veritable information clearinghouse.

And out of all SPI's agents, I was the only one he would talk to.

Ord had transplanted from Atlanta about twenty-five years ago. Business was too good in New York ever to consider going back home, but talking to me helped ease his homesickness for all things Southern. Over the years, his fondness for my accent had turned into friendship.

When I'd first met him, Ord had his office in the back room of an organic greengrocer one block south of the Meatpacking District on Horatio Street in the West Village. He'd recently moved to an apartment over the newly expanded Full Moon. He was from Georgia, the Garrisons were from

North Carolina, so they essentially spoke the same language. Plus, they all got something out of it. Ord got the increased security of working above a werewolf bar, and the Garrisons got a new and continuous stream of customers. The scents of barbeque, burgers, and steaks that drifted up from the Full Moon tantalized the noses of Ord's clientele. They couldn't help themselves. They had to stop for takeout. It got to the point where they'd call in an order and meet with Ord while it was being cooked. Ord got more information. The Garrisons got even more business. Everyone was a winner.

If possible, the gnome looked even more pleased with himself tonight than Rake had.

"You did it." I didn't ask it as a question. It was obvious that Ord had indeed done it.

Ord spread his hands. "But of course."

"You're the best."

"I know."

Ord had arranged for a meeting between me and the rarest and most sought-after source of information in the city.

The gargoyles.

14

The Full Moon now had outdoor dining. Bill and Nancy had bought the tiny patch of dirt adjacent to the restaurant and had turned it into a fenced beer garden with three picnic tables and umbrellas. SPI used it quite often for casual corporate meetings and to meet with sources who got nervous being in the middle of four walls.

Like gargoyles.

Tonight, there were lanterns on the tables and white fairy lights around the edges of each umbrella. There were a few people out here, all SPI agents. I knew them; they knew me.

I cleared my throat. “I’m meeting a new source in a few minutes. They’re a little shy. Can we have some privacy for about half an hour?”

They stood and started back inside. A few nodded as they passed, others wished me luck.

"Thanks, guys. I really appreciate it."

A couple of years ago, I would've asked Ian to make the request. I had nowhere near the level of SPI cred as Ian, but in the five years that I'd been an agent, I'd earned some respect of my own. You'd think the cherry on top would've been that Cernunnos was my father. My fellow agents thought it was cool, but it hadn't earned me any more respect than I already had. I was glad it hadn't. Respect needed to be earned. It didn't matter who you were related to. Respect came by what you did. Since my first mission I'd done things—things that'd saved lives. And I'd risked my own while doing it. My fellow agents knew I had their backs; and while I couldn't fight at anywhere near Ian's level, they knew I'd fight with everything I had. I wouldn't back down. They knew I wouldn't leave any of them behind, and they'd do the same for me.

Ord had been working for years cultivating a relationship with the city's gargoyles, and it'd recently started bearing fruit.

Through his pixies.

Pixies were tiny, winged, and nosier than your worst neighbor. New York and Los Angeles were thick with the things. About the size and speed of hummingbirds, they were the eyes and ears of the city's supernatural paparazzi, and of individuals like Ord who dealt in information. Like hummingbirds, pixies lived on a liquid diet. Pay them with enough Mountain Dew, Red Bull, or any other high-sugar, high-caffeine drink, and they were yours for life.

Humans frequently mistook Ord's flock for real hummingbirds, thanks to a glamour he'd bought for them from a gnome mage in the Bronx.

At Ord's request, his pixies had begun taking street-level

news to the gargoyles. Recently, the gargoyles had begun reciprocating. As a result, if there was anything Ord didn't know, he could find out. The gargoyles were the last link in his information network.

New York had hundreds of gargoyle-festooned buildings. They were prime perches for watching everything that transpired above and below them. But while the gargoyles knew all, they didn't tell all, at least not to outsiders. Anyone who wasn't a gargoyle was an outsider.

To mundane mortals, gargoyles were an Old World import, both practical and ornamental. There they'd functioned as waterspouts to take rain away from the walls and foundations of buildings, most notably cathedrals. In medieval times, people believed gargoyles detached themselves from their perches at night and patrolled the city, protecting the good from the evil, returning to their places by sunrise.

Gargoyles in New York were no different.

SPI patrolled the city day and night. Occasionally, we'd get a call, and when the agents got there, our work had been done for us. Most of the time, we apprehended, cuffed, and took the miscreant into custody. Apprehension by gargoyles tended to be a more permanent solution to criminal activity. Often when a gargoyle had gotten there first, all that was left for our teams to do was cleanup. In the gargoyles' defense, stone hands weren't exactly made for gentle apprehension.

The city's gargoyles knew all, so they had heard of Ord Larcwyde.

And SPI.

The gargoyles had simply chosen to ignore us. Why, we could only guess because they'd never told us. What we did know was that the dragons they'd heard about from their European cousins were arrogant and didn't consider gargoyles worthy of notice. And humans had a bad habit of demolishing their buildings. Those buildings—with their brick and mortar—were literally a gargoyle's lifeblood. Separate a gargoyle from its building for longer than twenty-four hours, and it died. More than half of SPI's agents were human, and the head of SPI was a dragon. Do the math. The city's gargoyles wanted nothing to do with any of us.

I sat on one of the picnic table's benches to wait. "Who did you get to agree to see me?"

"Eh, not exactly a gargoyle, but close."

"What? You said—"

"I know what I said, but this is actually better."

I ignored "actually better" because knowing Ord, it probably wasn't. My gnome friend had an annoying tendency to put lipstick on pigs. Yeah, it was wearing lipstick, but it was still a pig. Though baby pigs were cute.

I sighed. Any help was better than no help. Take the lipstick, Mac.

"Okay, what have you got for me?"

"Bartholomew Herald, one of the two green-glowy-eyed bronze owls from Herald Square."

"I know you think you just told me a lot, but I don't know who that is."

"You're kidding me."

I didn't have much patience right now to begin with, and I was losing what little I had. "Ord, we've got Tiamat in town, and she's brought Medusa's big sister, and they're not here to go shopping. So you'll have to excuse me if I'm less than—"

"That's why the gargoyles cancelled at the last minute. As far as they're concerned, this is a family fight. They don't want any part of it."

"We're not asking them to get involved. We just want to know if they've seen or heard anything."

"Information is gargoyle currency. That'd involve them up to their stony necks."

"I can understand that, at least I can try. Instead of a gargoyle, I get a bronze bird. I'll have to be good with that. I take it the owl will at least be an intermediary between me and the gargoyles? They'll get the message?"

"I've been assured that is the case. Everything you say will be taken to their council."

"Good. What background do you have on Bartholomew?"

"Bartholomew Herald. His sister's name is Beatrix. All New York gargoyles take their surnames from the building, street, or park where they live. Bart and Bea are on top of the James Gordon Bennett or Bell Ringer's Monument in Herald Square. The monument's where the *New York Herald* newspaper offices used to be. It was a two-story building with something like twenty-six owls on the roofline."

"That's a lot of owls."

"Word had it Bennett was a lot of nuts. In addition to a thing for owls, Bennett was, shall we say, an alcohol enthusiast. He peed in the fireplace in front of everyone at his own engagement party. His fiancée's brother challenged him to a duel and both men survived due to being appallingly bad shots. He was fond of driving his carriage at full speed through the countryside, naked and yelling. Oh, and he had rumored links to the Illuminati. All a little much, even for me.

There were other incidents, but I'm trying to be brief. Oh, one more, I can't leave this one out. He wanted to be buried in a two-hundred-foot-tall, owl-shaped mausoleum. That didn't happen because the mausoleum's designer, Stanford White, was shot and killed by the millionaire husband of his former teenage mistress."

"I get it. Poster child for eccentric or even nutso-cuckoo. Both of them."

"And then some."

"Are we going to get to Bart?"

"Bart and Bea were on the roof of the *Herald* offices from 1894 until it was torn down in 1920. In addition to all the owls up there, there were a clock, a bell, an eleven-foot statue of Minerva, and two, seven-foot-tall bell ringers." Ord got out his phone and found a photo of the monument and showed it to me. "They built the monument and included Bart, Bea, Minerva, and the bellringers. Bart and Bea are there at the top on either side of the clock. Their eyes light up from dusk to dawn. In 2007, their green lenses and bulbs were switched out for green LEDs. With the exception of the time between 1920 and 1940, Bert and Bea's eyes have been glowing green and blinking disconcertingly since 1895."

"Statues are fully sentient after about twenty years. Normally statues and gargoyles don't associate with each other," Ord continued, "but the owls are less clique-ish, at least with each other. Winged gargoyles have access to more information. Those without wings are rather limited in their movements. Most of them won't talk to anyone. Those who can leave their perches have to be back by dawn. The ones with wings know the entire city and are the most social and willing to share their knowledge. Owls are generally the easiest to deal with. They love to share what they know, that is if you don't mind a little arrogance to go with your info."

"I'll put up with anything if he can help us locate Tiamat and Stheno."

"And they don't actually speak. It's more of a telepathy thing. Since you can hear dragons, you might be able to hear them. If you can't, I'll translate for you."

"Could be awkward, but again, I'll deal with it. Anything else I need to know?"

"Not that I can think of right now."

We sat and we waited. Ord had perched on the picnic table and was swinging his legs.

I had no clue how owls regarded punctuality, though you'd think they'd be all for it. I'd glanced at my watch for the fifth time when I spotted two glowing green eyes leveling out over the traffic on Thompson Street. A bronze owl. His wings flapped with metallic pings as he came in for a landing on the beer garden's iron fence.

Ord handled the introductions.

"Bartholomew, this is my good and trusted friend, Makenna Fraser. Makenna, this is Bartholomew Herald."

"It's an honor and pleasure to meet you," I said.

"The time I can spend here is limited. I have other places to be before dawn." The owl turned his bright green eyes toward Ord. *"Can the human hear me?"*

"Yes, the human can," I told him.

"Good. That will expedite things."

I didn't expect a time limit. Though I didn't expect a bronze owl, either.

"No small talk," I said. "I like it."

"Statues and gargoyles have always been reluctant to involve ourselves in the affairs of mortals or immortals, seeing that we are neither," Bart said. *"They see this as Vivienne Sagadraco's fight. It is her sister."*

"She would agree," I told him. "But Tiamat has made it about all of us. Tia may be starting with New York, but she won't be stopping here. She wants the world, and if you're not her slave or worshipper, you're food."

"We can't be any of those." The owl shrugged in a creak of metal. *"Though humans are useful for keeping the rust and pigeon dung off me."*

"I've had the misfortune of meeting Tiamat," I told him. "I've got news, the only statues will be of her. Have you heard or seen either her or the gorgon she's brought with her—Medusa's sister?"

"Nothing. Either one."

"Would you be willing to notify Ord or myself if you do come across any information?"

Bart thought for a moment. He wasn't moving or talking in my head, so I thought he was thinking. *"It would not be to our detriment to do so,"* he finally said.

"Probably as close to a 'yes' as you're gonna get," Ord whispered.

"We're already metal and stone, so we have no flesh and blood to paralyze," Bart said. *"We do have the advantage of seeing what many cannot. We can see through curtains and blinds. Nothing is hidden from us."*

Jeez. A peeping Bart.

"We see all as it truly is. Even those with magic cannot

hide or disguise themselves from us. On New Year's Eve five years ago, I was above Times Square. I saw your Vivienne Sagadraco, her sister, and the female grendel."

"You *do* see all."

Bart pulled himself straighter, preening. *"We also have exceptional night vision."*

"Impressive. I can see where that could come in handy. Ord has told me that statues and gargoyles know all. Then you would know what Vivienne Sagadraco has done for the citizens of New York, *all* of them. She has never hesitated to put her life on the line to protect and preserve us all."

Bart blinked. Ord was right. It was disconcerting as hell.

"Gargoyles govern and protect their own," I continued. "So does every other supernatural group. I understand your need for autonomy. We would be having this conversation even if Tiamat and Stheno weren't here. Ms. Sagadraco wants the gargoyles and statues to know that she wants to help you. You can't protect yourselves against developers, and by being attached to buildings, gargoyles are more vulnerable to modernization. Buildings are torn down to make room for what some believe is improvement. Sometimes gargoyles are broken during demolition; sometimes they're taken and sold. She knows that their buildings are gargoyles' lifeblood. Without them, they die. Vivienne Sagadraco has gone to great lengths to get herself appointed or elected to as many preservation groups in this city as she can to save the city's history and buildings. New York's rich history is what has made it in her opinion the best city in the world. She believes history should be revered and preserved whenever and wherever possible. Tell the gargoyles she wants to help protect them. If you see Tiamat or Stheno, she would gladly and gratefully accept that information. But it will not affect what she has committed and vowed to do."

Bart blinked again. *"Is that the message you want me to deliver?"*

I didn't think I'd forgotten anything. "It is."

Wings flapped, and Ord and I glanced up to see what looked like a pixie on steroids launching itself out of the beer garden's lone tree. It flew past a streetlight, and I got a better look at it. It was pale. Not albino pale, but limestone pale.

A gargoyle.

"You just delivered the message yourself," Bart said. *"That was Wentworth. She may be one of the smallest gargoyles but is among the most influential. She'll take your words back to those who need to hear them."* He ruffled his feathers in series of metallic clinks. *"I think we are done here."*

The sound of glasses breaking came from inside, followed by applause and laughter. When I looked back to the fence, Bartholomew Herald was gone.

Ord clapped me on the back. "Good meeting—and you're welcome." He scooted to the edge of the picnic table, jumped down, and went back inside.

I looked around the little beer garden, including up. No statues or gargoyles. I was alone.

I went back to Yasha's party.

15

When I went back inside, Rake had been joined in the booth by Vladimir Cervenka. Vlad was a vampire. And no, people didn't point out the irony of his name—at least smart people didn't. Partly because Vlad was a vampire, but mostly because Vlad was what folks back home called a big boy.

Between fighting together against the Fomorians, defending delegates trapped in the Regor Regency pocket dimension, as well as more recent missions, Rake and Vlad discovered they had quite a bit in common. Plus, they both had fangs that scared the bejeebers out of pretty much everyone, and both prized their honor and wouldn't violate it under any circumstances. However, any activity that didn't violate their honor, integrity, or reputation was fair game. In addition, both operated in the shadows and did it very well. Vlad knew the city's underbelly like the back of his hand. A hand with cigar-stained fingers.

Many vampires disavowed everything mortal after they'd been turned, but not Vlad. He was an undead blood drinker, but he was still a cigar smoker. Though, as he had told me when we'd first met, he was considerate of those less dead than himself. He would put out his ever-present cigar when mortals were around.

Vlad had white-blond hair, pale blue eyes, and a tan, which was surprising for a vampire. I'd found out in the years since we met that he'd spent a lot of time outside before he'd been turned. Vlad had been a Viking, the Kievan Rus variety. Now he sold his services to the heads of the major American and European vampire families. Vlad thought of himself as a security consultant, but his vampire employers considered him a mercenary. Vlad didn't like the title, but he was fond of the money.

Vlad had helped save Ian from Janus and the Fomorians by talking his erstwhile employer Ambrus Bathory into cooperating with us, and by going to Bannerman Island and fighting alongside us against the Fomorians. Alain Moreau had begun hiring Vlad and his team when SPI needed specialized vampiric help. Having allies who were deeper undercover than any of our agents was an invaluable asset.

That was why he was here tonight. Well, that and being one of Yasha's best friends.

I slid into the booth next to Rake.

"How did it go?" he asked.

"Highly productive. I think." I didn't need to say that I'd tell him later. That was understood. Vlad understood it, too. He also wouldn't be in the least bit offended. Any information he didn't need to know, he didn't want to know. Vlad was a direct sort of guy and didn't like his life cluttered with needless complications.

The vampire had a stein in front of him, and I caught a whiff of what definitely wasn't beer. In funding tonight's bash, Ms. Sagadraco would've provided for *all* the guests regardless of dietary requirements.

Vlad noticed me noticing. "The vintage is excellent, but I would really like one of those." He indicated the nearest table where four guests were seriously enjoying burgers and beer.

"I have had beer, wine, ale, and mead many times before," the vampire continued wistfully. "But I would really like to experience a hamburger."

"You've never lived anywhere before New York that…" I stopped, wishing I could suck those words back in.

Vlad grinned, exposing one tobacco-stained fang, the one that usually impaled a cigar. "No, I have not *lived* anywhere that had hamburgers."

"Sorry about that."

"It is not your fault that I am dead. I chose to become a vampire. The other alternative was unacceptable to me. I made the choice. My heart does not beat, but every other part of me is in perfect working order." He grinned wider. "I am stronger, my senses are sharper. When you think about it that way, I am more alive than anyone here. So, such questions are not offensive to me, nor do they make me sad that I am undead. I am happy as a vampire."

"Vlad's been telling me about a lady friend," Rake said. "Who is uniquely positioned to help with our current predicament. She's a Fury."

Vlad scrolled through his phone. “Her name is Akashar. She is an international security consultant, like me. Here is a photo.” He showed it to me but kept his hand over the lower half of the screen. Judging from the sultry smirk on her face, that smile was all she was wearing. A hot woman with fangs and bat wings.

I wasn’t sure what I was supposed to say to that. “Way to take one for the team?” was what came out.

Vlad shrugged. “I do what I have to do.” His voice dropped to a deep rumble. “But mostly I do what I want to do. I like bad girls.”

I’ll bet he did.

Rake saved me from the awkwardness. “She arrived in town three days ago. She’s a contract employee. Tiamat’s employee.”

Holy crap.

Vlad chuckled at my bug-eyed, open-mouthed reaction. “Have you ever been told you should not play poker?”

“Many times.”

“Good.”

“You just caught me off guard.”

“That is not good. You should work on that.”

I cringed inwardly. “I know. I’ve been told that, too.”

“This is Akashar’s first job for Tiamat,” Vlad continued. “She knows what Tiamat is and what she is rumored to have done.”

“And she took the job anyway?”

Vlad shrugged. “What she is being asked to do is not illegal, and it did not violate her honor. Plus, she is being generously compensated. Our business is rarely black and white. Most of it is gray.”

"Working for Tia is dark gray."

"Akashar is aware of that." The vampire paused. "How do I say this? It is…difficult to refuse work from such individuals as Tiamat and Viktor Kain. They take refusals very personally. Akashar would find it tiresome to watch her back to the degree it would be necessary should she have refused Tiamat's offer of employment."

"How long have you known her?" I asked.

"Seventy years."

I leaned forward. "Does she know where Tia is?"

"That she does not know. She is not guarding Tiamat. She is guarding a black box."

"Containing, as she described it, a crystal with flames inside," Rake added.

My heart fell into my stomach. "A magetech generator."

"I can't see it being anything else." He took a sip of his scotch. "But wait, there's more. Vlad?"

"Akashar often works with her two cousins. Tiamat hired them as well. Each is guarding a black box in separate locations."

I plopped back against the booth back. "*Three* magetech generators. Have you told Ms. Sagadraco?"

"I thought I'd wait for you to get back so you could also regale her with your 'gargoyle' encounter," Rake told me, using air quotes.

"How did you know—?"

"I went to the back door and took a peek."

"You spied on me?"

Rake spread his hands. "Darling, I *am* a spy. But in this case, my motives were purely protective."

"In that case, you're forgiven."

"I thought you'd see it that way."

I frowned. Weren't Furies goddesses of vengeance? If Tiamat had hired—

"You do see it that way, don't you?" Rake asked.

"Of course. I just had a disturbing thought. Three Furies are in town. They're known for chasing down criminals, punishing the wicked and guilty and all that. Vlad, has Tia asked Akashar and her cousins to do anything else besides guard those boxes?"

"Nothing yet, but she promised to tell me when she hears from Tiamat again."

I nodded absently, but my mind was racing. At Rake. He could talk to me in my mind while carrying on a conversation out loud with everyone else. Me? Not so much, though I was getting better. *"Stheno thinks Vivienne stole the Aegis and wants vengeance,"* I told him. *"Tia lied to Stheno to get her cooperation."*

"And you know this how?"

"Vivienne's theory."

"Sounds plausible."

"And now Tiamat hires three Furies. Coincidence? Not."

I was sure Vlad noticed something was going on, at least with me. Rake was a telepathy expert. However, the vampire rolled with it and kept talking. "Akashar is a bad girl, but a good woman. She did not want to work for Tiamat but took the job to keep her from hiring anyone else. I told her I was coming here tonight, and she asked me to find out what SPI knows."

"Do you trust her?" Rake asked.

"I do."

"And we trust you," I told him. Alain Moreau had done a thorough background check on Vlad. The vampire mercenary was a SPI agent in everything but name. Heck, we even had him on retainer.

The boss needed to know about this. Now. *"Ma'am, have you heard what Vlad—"*

"I have. You have my permission to tell him what we know. Akashar should know Stheno is probably responsible for her being hired. If Tiamat discovers she has been talking to us, even indirectly, Akashar would be in danger from my sister and Stheno."

"They're guarding generators now. Are they coming after you next?" I asked her.

"Unlikely. My sister is appeasing Stheno by hiring Furies. Stheno is from the time of the Greek gods and goddesses. If she wants vengeance, it is logical that she would seek out Furies. My sister wants the satisfaction of killing me herself. She believes she controls Stheno. She is mistaken. Dangerously so."

"So she hasn't taken out a contract on you with hit Furies?"

I could hear the smile in her thoughts. *"No contract. No hit Furies."*

Sisters of Medusa, literal and figurative. Mercenary Furies. And three magetech generators in a pear tree. I didn't believe it possible, but our situation had just gotten a whole lot worse.

16

By the next morning, it was becoming apparent just how much worse.

The day dawned with a hydra disrupting traffic in New York Harbor. Fortunately, the weather was foggy, which kept sightings and any accompanying photography from being proof positive. Three hours later, a minotaur appeared near the Wall Street charging bull statue and started terrorizing stockbrokers. No fog to fool the eye on that one. The minotaur would disappear and reappear a few buildings down the street. We dispatched a team, but by the time they arrived, the minotaur was gone. Whether it was for good or not, we had no way of knowing.

Kylie O'Hara, our director of Media and Public Relations, and her staff had to hit the ground running on this one. It was a speed they were used to. Unless any big stories had broken during the night, the morning news shows were hungry for anything juicy. Monster sightings in Manhattan were juicier than Godzilla stomping a whole grove of Florida oranges.

The mission had turned into a hunt for the magetech generators responsible.

Vlad had said he'd reach out to Akashar. He had, but she'd been unable to contact her two cousins until after two of Tiamat's mage couriers had arrived to take the generators (each concealed in a briefcase). The couriers had literally vanished with the briefcases in front of the Fury guards.

We didn't get the briefcases/generators, but Akashar's cousins gave her detailed descriptions of the two couriers. We immediately knew who they were because these two cabal megamages were on our Top 10 Most Wanted list.

Griselda Ingeborg and Gerald Blackburn.

Tiamat using these two as couriers was like sending Catwoman to shoplift a can of Fancy Feast.

This monster appearance scenario was what'd happened while we'd been locked inside the Regor Regency during the Centennial Supernatural Summit. Creatures from the attendees' various mythologies kept popping up. The only good thing about it had been that the manifestations had been contained inside the hotel.

Tiamat had significantly expanded the playing field.

The first model of the magetech generator had filled a midsize car trunk. The next generation was the size of a small carry-on suitcase. That had been a year and a half ago. We'd had the magetech generator's creator, Phaeon Silvanus, in custody since that time. The elven scientist was being treated like a visiting scholar. He was in a nice guest apartment in headquarters, but he was being watched—while also being given opportunities to redeem himself. Phaeon's older brother, Isidor, had made no effort to free him, and I think that was starting to sink in. Big brother only valued him so much. He'd reap the rewards of little brother's genius so long as it was convenient. Retrieving him from maximum-security SPI custody was about as inconvenient as it got. Isidor wasn't about to stick his neck out that far.

As a result, Phaeon was starting to be forthcoming about the magetech generator. He'd told us that the decrease in size was due to the change in power source. The first generation had been powered by a manmade crystal. The second generation was powered by a much smaller, naturally occurring crystal from Rake's home world. Apparently evil came in all shapes and sizes. Smaller size didn't mean less power. Quite the opposite. The new and improved magetech generator had been responsible for teleporting Rake's house from his home world to a vacant lot in Lower Manhattan.

That was the kind of power we were dealing with.

It was coming up on lunchtime when Yasha received another call from Vlad. A courier had arrived to take the generator Akashar was guarding.

A courier named Marek Reigory.

We had a tail in place for this one. Not SPI agents. Marek would've spotted them. I'd called in a favor with Ord.

One of his pixies had been waiting in a tree outside the apartment Tia had rented for Akashar and the generator. Marek had come out of the building carrying a messenger bag. He'd gotten into a town car and been dropped off at Central Park

West at 82nd Street, where he headed into the park on foot, glamoured as a blond, casually dressed human. The pixie lost Marek at that point. One of the park's hawks thought the pixie would make a tasty breakfast, and he'd had to hightail it out of there. Marek could look like anyone by now. He'd probably changed his glamour as soon as he was in the park, and at least twice more just for fun.

In other words, needle meet haystack.

I could see through any glamour. And Rake would know Marek, regardless of any disguise.

Rake and Marek were involuntary blood brothers.

Years before Rake and I had met, he and Marek had fought and tried to kill each other. They were evenly matched, magically and physically. Knives were used, blood was shed, the fight deteriorated into grappling, and Rake's blood got into Marek's system, and vice versa. Mage blood was potent stuff. It didn't take much to establish a link. The link protected each against some of the other's magic. So, any chance of one killing the other was limited to hands-on means.

Rake had no problem with that.

He and Marek had tussled again more recently in Las Vegas. Marek had escaped. Rake was determined there wasn't going to be a repeat performance today.

He promised Ms. Sagadraco that he'd behave himself. Neither one of them believed that, but the boss figured increasing the chances of apprehending Marek Reigory and that magetech generator was worth the risk. And of course, Gethen and his team would be sticking close to Rake. When it came to taking on the cabal, the more the merrier.

On the SPI side, Ian and I would be joined by Elana Tavitz.

I'd been working off and on with Elana since my first night at SPI. If there was a dark alley that needed investigating, Elana was the go-getter who wanted to go in first. She was *that* person, the one who didn't necessarily start the bar fight, but come hell or high water, she was gonna be the one to finish it.

Between Rake and Elana, we were guaranteed to have an eventful day.

Once we got to Central Park, Rake took the lead on tracking Marek Reigory. His nemesis could glamour himself as pretty much anything, but mage blood called to mage blood. Marek would be all too aware of that, but there was only so much he could do. Rake wouldn't be able to track him down to the square foot, but he'd have a good idea as to the general area.

That was how we ended up at Central Park's Great Lawn.

The Great Lawn at lunchtime on a sunny spring day was as public as it got. There were picnic lunches everywhere we looked, people sunbathing, dogs catching Frisbees. As a result, more than a few courses of action were off the table.

"What are we looking for?" I asked.

Ian put on his gorgon glasses, and the rest of us followed suit. "I have a feeling we'll know it when we see it."

As he had been many times in the past, my partner was right on target.

A group of runners came out of the trees. They were running faster than they wanted because they were being chased.

By five satyrs.

When people imagined satyrs, they thought of beautiful men from the waist up, and well-endowed from the waist down.

What came sprinting out of the trees wasn't a manifestation of anyone's mythological fantasies. These were goat men. No one's erotic imagination could possibly think that was hot, though I'd been surprised before.

Satyrs didn't have a sexual preference. If it was human and it ran, they'd chase it. If they caught it? Well, satyrs gonna do what satyrs gonna do.

That they'd be doing it in front of hundreds of phone-wielding witnesses put an unwanted twist on an already bad situation. Though at SPI, you dealt with it first and worried about witnesses later.

All of the pursuees were college-age, athletic, and wearing NYU T-shirts. I was guessing the young men and women were probably NYU's cross-country team. According to the SPI handbook, satyrs were sprinters. They had neither the build nor the motivation for long distances. If they couldn't bring down their quarry in the first hundred yards, they lost interest. And while the NYU team were young and nubile college students, there were plenty of options in Central Park right now. Hundreds, in fact.

And judging from the satyrs' pause and change in direction, they had just figured this out.

New Yorkers didn't scare easily, if at all. And nothing was going to make them leave the park on a gorgeous day, certainly not what they thought they were seeing.

With good costuming and makeup, humans could look like satyrs. So, the sight of what appeared to be humans dressed as goat men chasing college students through Central Park struck many of the people watching as funny. It was spring and satyrs were chasing college students. Must be some kind of frat initiation or college prank.

Then it hit those closest to the action that this might be something else entirely. Or should I say the smell hit them.

As I knew from goats on farms back home, there ain't no stink like billy goat stink. Flies were attracted to goats for a reason. And the aroma got kicked up a couple of notches when said goats were horny, as satyrs always were.

The bottom half of a satyr was all horny billy goat.

The laughter from those closest turned to stunned silence as they got a good look at the business end of a satyr.

Silence turned to running. Running was bad. Well, unless they wanted to be chased.

SPI's directive for dealing with a public supernatural event was to end it as quickly and quietly as possible. How that was best accomplished was left to each agent's discretion. SPI trained their people, then trusted them to make the best call in a given situation using the resources they had.

As former NYPD, Ian could simply tackle a satyr and cuff him. It wouldn't be the first time a former cop had done their former job. Rake's go-to move was to conjure an invisible wall directly in a fleeing perp's path. Most of the time they knocked themselves out, resulting in less work for everyone.

Our goal was obvious. Get the satyrs off the Great Lawn and back to wherever the heck they'd come from. But first we had to catch them, and they weren't making it easy.

Within seconds, the situation had gone from serious problem to total chaos.

People were running every which way. The satyrs had picked new targets and dashed off in pursuit.

Ian went after the closest satyr. Rake and Gethen took off

after two more. I didn't know which way Gethen's team had gone because I couldn't see them.

The remaining two satyrs had veered off toward a play area full of children.

Elana and I gave each other a look that said "Oh, hell no" and took off in pursuit.

Parents were snatching their kids off the playground equipment and running if they could or standing their ground if their children were too big to carry.

The satyrs clearly had not gotten the memo about not taking on a human mama or daddy protecting their young. Plus, these were New Yorkers, so the general attitude was "bring it and find out, perv."

All my money was on the humans to win, place, and show.

Heck, one of the dads even reminded me of Dave Bautista. A mini-me of her dad—and I do mean mini—was hefting a whiffle bat nearly as big as she was and looked downright eager to use it. That apple hadn't fallen far from the paternal tree.

I was running toward the playground, Elana right behind me.

We were attractive women. The two perps were horny satyrs. This should work.

In theory.

I gave an ear-piercing whistle to get their attention.

"Hey! Wanna piece of this?" I yelled.

They turned, they saw, and they obviously liked. Don't ask me how I knew.

Elana and I gave the satyrs time to change direction before sprinting toward the trees. To dodge a small playground with those bouncy fiberglass animals on huge springs, Elana veered off toward the bathrooms, the satyr hot on her heels. I didn't need to look back to know mine was gaining on me. His stink had already arrived.

When training me in hand-to-hand combat, Ian had taught me how to determine an opponent's next move. This one was easy. Flying tackle. I'd learned to fight without air in my lungs, because one of Ian's tackles always knocked the breath out of me. Training was worthless if your teacher pulled punches.

The terrain was now sparse grass and entirely too many trees. This was gonna hurt. Time to end this game on my terms.

I stopped running and spun to face the satyr—who was *much* closer than I anticipated.

And turning to stone.

In my peripheral vision, a ninja bike roared past, sending up chunks of dirt.

I had just enough time for *"Gorgon!"* to register in my brain before impact with a still-moving, satyr-sized rock.

I lost consciousness for the second time in as many days, and when I started coming around, everything was yellow, and I couldn't move my legs.

I panicked.

I inhaled to scream, and a hand clamped down over my mouth.

Rake.

"You're fine! Shhh!" He took his hand away, then used both hands to roll the satyr statue off my legs.

But everything was still yellow—oh yeah, gorgon glasses.

Was that why I hadn't been stoned, too?

After a couple of gasps to refill my lungs (and calm myself down), I started breathing normally.

The park outside the little grove was still in chaos, so I couldn't have been out for long.

Rake put a hand on the satyr, which was now lying on its side. I felt a surge of magic, and it disintegrated into pebble-sized rocks.

"Wait, he fell on top of me." I started patting down my legs. There was some pain, but nowhere near what it should've been. "How was I not crushed?"

Rake was helping me to my feet. "He fell face down, and landed on his…shall we say, kickstand."

What? Oh. "It didn't break?"

"It did not." Even Rake was impressed.

Dang.

Then Gethen was there. "Ian and Elana found the generator. In a food truck."

When we got to the truck, which had THE FOOD DUDE emblazoned on the side, Yasha had just pulled up next to it in the Suburban. Elana was waiting to load the magetech generator inside. When she saw the three of us, she jerked her head toward the back.

Gethen opened the door.

Inside, Ian was hauling a handcuffed man to his feet.

Rake looked in and swore.

Ian's catch definitely wasn't Marek Reigory.

He looked like a street person.

Brown hair and beard, both unkempt. Clothes were dirty and worn. An average build with an average face. The eyes were also brown…but they were anything but average. They weren't dulled by drugs or drink. They were intense. Intense and intelligent.

They were also familiar. I'd seen this guy before.

Then it hit me. It'd been nearly five years. A photo on an employee badge from the Department of Defense. Another photo, this one in the paper, on the society pages, announcing his divorce.

From Tiamat.

Her ex- and presumed late husband, Dr. Jonathan Tarbert.

"This isn't what it looks like," he said.

17

New York had a problem of the Greek mythology persuasion.

A gorgon had stolen the Aegis. A hydra had obstructed shipping traffic in New York Harbor. A minotaur had popped up next to the Wall Street bull and terrorized stockbrokers. Satyrs had chased college students through Central Park. A gorgon on a ninja bike had stoned the satyr chasing me—or had she been aiming at me and missed?

And for the chocolate chips on top, Tiamat's ex-husband Dr. Jonathan Tarbert had come back from the dead.

To quote the Coast Guard kid in *Overboard*, "It's a hell of a day at sea, sir."

We didn't have Marek Reigory in custody, but we did have the inventor of Tia's cloaking device, aka the hockey puck of hiding.

I called that a good day.

Rake didn't agree with me. His day wouldn't be complete until he had Marek Reigory's neck between his hands. He hadn't sensed Marek near the food truck. Reigory was a survivor. He had to have known Rake was on his tail. He'd probably activated the generator and run like hell. Rake had taken Gethen and his security detail and gone hunting. I had no doubt they'd bag their quarry before sundown.

As a bonus, we'd retrieved the magetech generator that'd turned five satyrs loose in Central Park.

When Ian had opened the door to that food truck, he'd found what appeared to be a street person stuffing the magetech generator in a garbage bag. It was pretty smart as far as concealment went. Not many people would look twice at a street person carrying a trash bag.

Ian didn't think twice about cuffing him.

He patted him down and found a gun, which Tarbert had wisely not tried to use against him. Unlike Tarbert, the gun was clean and well-kept.

After she and her satyr pursuer had dashed past me, Elana had run behind the bathroom and stopped. No one was around to see, so she was gonna kick some satyr ass. He rounded the corner, there was a flash of light and whiff of ozone, and the satyr vanished, much to Elana's disappointment. The same had happened to the other three while Gethen's guys were chasing them. By that time, Rake had already turned mine to gravel.

The magetech generator giveth, and the magetech generator taketh away.

Ian quickly loaded Jonathan Tarbert into the Suburban, and Elana and I piled in.

"Where are you taking me?" Tarbert asked.

"That depends on what you tell us in the next few minutes, Dr. Tarbert," Ian said.

Tarbert glanced nervously out the window. "Can we at least get moving?"

"Worried about your ex-wife torching you?" I asked.

Yasha looked in the rearview at our guest. "You should have given her something in the divorce. Pre-nup was smart, yet stupid."

"She kept the jewelry."

Yasha nodded in approval. "Wise. Dragons don't like it when you take their sparklies."

"Are you SPI?" Tarbert asked.

"We are," Ian said without hesitation.

Well, that did it. By confirming who we were, Ian all but came out and said that we wouldn't be releasing Jonathan Tarbert back into the wild anytime soon. While the boss had contacts in the intelligence agencies, Tarbert wasn't one of them. One, he was supposed to be in an urn in the Tarbert family mausoleum in Green-Wood Cemetery. But mainly, it was because he was her sister's ex-husband. Yes, they were divorced, and he was presumed dead, but he could still be working for her, directly or unknowingly. When dragons claimed something—or someone—they stayed claimed.

We believed Tia had married Jonathan Tarbert to gain access to his cloaking device technology. She'd gotten it. But perhaps that wasn't all she wanted from him. We had no idea what secrets were running around in our prisoner's head.

"I'm not working for or with my ex-wife. I am trying to stop her."

"From doing what?" Ian asked.

Tarbert sat back and clammed up. "I need to speak directly to Vivienne Sagadraco. Please take me to her."

Ian blindfolded Jonathan Tarbert, and we took him home with us to headquarters. Not because he'd asked to go there; because we knew Vivienne Sagadraco would want to have a chat with him, too.

It was a quiet ride. Tarbert actually leaned back in his seat and relaxed.

When your perps ranged from human to supernatural, from living to dead and quite a few levels in between, you got a firm grasp of what behaviors to expect from the newly apprehended.

Relieved had never been one of them.

Though if I was him, I'd be relieved knowing I wasn't where my ex could get ahold of me.

Ian was texting.

When I raised a quizzical eyebrow, he mouthed, "The boss."

Yasha didn't necessarily lengthen the trip to headquarters, but he threw in a couple of extra turns here and there to confuse Tarbert in case he was one of those people who'd memorized every pothole and speedbump in New York.

There were a gazillion parking garages in the city, and the most-used entrance to headquarters was in one of them. Yasha pulled into a private, SPI-owned garage on West Third Street a block from Washington Square Park and began spiraling down to the lowest level. Once there, he pulled into a parking space near the back. He pushed a button on the dash, and almost immediately, the Suburban began to sink. The trip ended in one of the city's abandoned subway tunnels, which had been converted to a street leading to the SPI garage and loading dock.

With Ian holding one of Tarbert's arms and Elana the other, the still-blindfolded and cuffed Dr. Jonathan Tarbert entered SPI headquarters to meet his ex-sister-in-law for the first time.

The good doctor would ultimately be taken to one of two places at HQ—a cell or one of our small guest apartments.

It all depended on how the next hour or so went.

Tiamat, as the former Babylonian goddess of chaos, was more than living up to her name. Headquarters looked like a hornets' nest that'd been given a good kicking. The red lights above all the hallways meant SPI was now operating all hands on deck and around the clock. We knew Tia and the cabal were creating distractions to spread us too thin to cover all of them. Problem was, we *had* to cover all of them. We couldn't just leave satyrs rampaging through Central Park. Or a minotaur doing the bull-in-a-china-shop thing on Wall Street.

And Tia knew it.

Ian seated our prisoner in the interrogation room and removed his blindfold. "Stay."

Tarbert stayed.

SPI didn't question suspects like you see on TV and the movies. We didn't put them in a room with a table and two chairs facing each other. There wasn't two-way glass along one wall. Most supernaturals could see—and hear—right through it anyway. Yes, we had barebones interrogation facilities. But for someone like Jonathan Tarbert, we went with the comfortable, casual chat approach. A small sofa, two chairs, and a coffee table, with cameras and mics built in. Tarbert had an intelligence background, so he knew that while he might be physically comfortable, there would be nothing casual about the chat.

The observation room was next door, but separating it from our suspects was a seriously soundproof wall.

Vivienne Sagadraco was going to question Dr. Tarbert herself.

I called Kenji and put him on speaker.

"You got time to catch us up?" I asked.

"Just the short version," he said. *"Kylie's team is monitoring social media for any more mentions of myth creature manifestations. She got one of her producer buddies in LA to admit to a costume and makeup test for a* Clash of the Titans *sequel. The production company has said they'll pay for all damages on Wall Street and in Central Park, but it'll really be the boss lady footing the bill. Dr. Milner's trying to come up with a plausible cryptocreature for the harbor incidents, maybe a new species of giant squid. The fog really helped us out with that one."*

Ian had just come in and caught the tail end of Kenji's report. "How about getting us some extra help in case there's more generators we don't know about?"

"The boss called in commando teams from the Atlanta, Chicago, and LA offices. She's headed in your direction now. Talk later." And he hung up.

I looked back to interrogation room monitor. Dr. Tarbert had been thorough with his disguise. He'd told us he'd been living on New York's streets for nearly two weeks, and judging from the smell, we had no reason to doubt him. Two weeks he'd been here, waiting. The Aegis had been stolen only two days ago, but he'd been primed and ready to literally bag that magetech generator.

Oh yeah, he had to know plenty.

18

Ms. Sagadraco looked at the monitor showing the seated and understandably nervous Dr. Tarbert. "Remove his restraints and have food brought. A selection of sandwiches. Heavy on the protein. Juices and bottles of water. And tea for me."

Ian went in to take care of the cuffs, and I got on the phone to the SPI cafeteria.

This might be an interrogation, and Vivienne Sagadraco was a dragon, but she wasn't barbaric. A predator's nose knew. Tarbert probably hadn't had many decent meals recently. Yet in that food truck, he'd skipped the edibles and gone for the magetech generator. It was that important to him.

We didn't do good cop/bad cop. Vivienne Sagadraco believed in taking a firm, yet humane approach to questioning, even though she wasn't human. If that method was productive, then there would be no need to go to the type of interrogation that was guaranteed to produce results.

We had people who were very good at what they did, namely getting information with no pain or injury to the suspect. Kind of like a Vulcan mind meld. As confirmation that we wouldn't need that department's services, Jenna Simon had just arrived in the observation room with us. Like Clarissa St. James back in my hometown, Jenna was a human lie detector.

Dr. Tarbert stood when Vivienne Sagadraco entered the room. It was instinctive, not contrived. Point in his favor.

"Please be seated, Dr. Tarbert."

He sat and added confused to his nervous. "Are you Vivienne Sagadraco?"

"I am."

"You and Tia are from the same…clutch?"

Ms. Sagadraco's lips twitched in amusement. "We are. You seem baffled by the age difference. My sister and I are the same age, but Tiamat looks much younger. Is that what you were thinking?"

Tarbert hesitated before nodding. Wise man.

"I've allowed myself to age past what most humans consider to be a woman's 'prime,' while Tiamat has gone to great lengths to preserve her youth." Her blue eyes sparkled. "There are many advantages to being perceived as a mature woman, Dr. Tarbert. My sister does not know what she is missing."

The door opened and a cart was wheeled in by a man I recognized as one of our head chefs. First, he placed a tea service before Ms. Sagadraco, then set a plate on the low table in front of Dr. Tarbert along with bottled beverages and a platter of assorted small sandwiches.

Even though Jonathan Tarbert was in dire need of a shower and clean clothes, Vivienne Sagadraco was treating him as if he was wearing a custom suit and they were having lunch at The Plaza.

"I assumed you didn't have any dietary restrictions," she said to the scientist.

"No, ma'am." Tarbert noticeably relaxed, realizing she considered him a guest and not a prisoner—or an entree.

Ms. Sagadraco selected two sandwiches from the platter for herself. "Then please, Dr. Tarbert, help yourself."

The sandwiches may have been small, but there was a pile of them. Easy to eat one, answer a question, eat another. Like high tea for sumo wrestlers. Tarbert must have wanted to wolf down the food, but maintained his decorum.

"Do you know why you were brought here?" Ms. Sagadraco asked.

"I was caught red-handed with a QTTD."

The boss paused, her teacup halfway to her lips. "I am unfamiliar with that term."

"Quantum Teleportation and Transference Device."

The teacup continued its journey. "So that is what my sister calls it."

"You have another name for it?"

"We refer to it as a 'magetech generator' due to its combination of magic and mortal technology. Had you succeeded in taking it, what were your intentions?"

"Make it one less that's available to my ex-wife, and if

possible, reverse-engineer it and determine how to counteract it." He opened a bottle of water. "Ms. Sagadraco, I assure you that Tia is as much an ex to me as it is possible for an ex-wife to be. She was…alluring when we first met. It took a few months before I realized she wanted me for my brain and not my body." He went a little pale. "Then I discovered that she was…and that I had been…"

Ms. Sagadraco smiled, showing her teeth. "Yes, I imagine that was quite a shock."

Tarbert was in the throes of a thousand-yard stare. "I'd been having sex with a giant lizard." He glanced quickly at the boss. "No offense."

"None taken. I'm not the one you had sex with."

"I didn't exactly handle the realization well."

"Few human males would. Tell me, was that the moment you decided you wanted a divorce?"

"I just wanted to get out of the bedroom alive."

"I'm surprised she allowed it. What Tiamat cannot possess she destroys. She must have still had use for you."

"She made that abundantly clear. I ran from the house, called my attorney, and began plans to fake my death. One thing I knew for sure about Tia, she wouldn't take rejection well."

"I'm impressed you had enough clarity of thought to take your phone."

Tarbert smiled, the first real one we'd seen from him. "I left my clothes, but I took my phone—and my car keys."

Ms. Sagadraco saluted him with her teacup. "Your priorities were in order." She selected another sandwich. "I do have questions regarding the contents of the crates we found beneath your family's mausoleum."

Ian and I had seen what was in those crates.

Human skulls with fangs. Vampires.

Massive wolflike skulls and pelts. Werewolves.

Baby dragons preserved in jars or in cross-sectioned eggs. Skulls of adults and stuffed younger and smaller specimens.

And other deadly-looking creatures I'd never seen or heard of before.

Each crate had documentation saying where they'd been killed or collected, and if photography had been available at that time, there was photographic proof of the successful hunt. They ranged from high-resolution, full-color digital prints, all the way back to grainy, turn-of-the-last-century sepia tones.

Photographic and scientific proof of the existence of supernaturals. Predatory and dangerous supernaturals.

All packed in crates, stamped "Property of U.S. Government."

Proof didn't get more official than that. It was SPI's worst nightmare.

Tarbert froze. "You have them?"

"Yes," Ms. Sagadraco replied.

"All of them?"

"All that were in the mausoleum the day your brother was killed."

"That was all of them. Thank God. If you have them, they're safe."

"No concern for your brother?"

His twin brother James had been killed while trying to sell off those crated body parts to the highest bidder, along with a flash drive containing his brother's cloaking-device research.

"My brother was an opportunist," Tarbert said. "The

only work he ever did was determining how best to avoid it. However, he did excel at one thing—getting his hands on other people's money after he'd squandered his own. He found the crates under the mausoleum before I could have them removed."

"And where did you get them?"

"From a warehouse owned by the CIA outside of Alexandria, Virginia. When I met Tia, she was working for them heading a task force charged with weaponizing supernatural beings. It didn't matter what government agency signed her paychecks, Tia has always worked for Tia. She wanted something from me and the CIA, so she lowered herself to human form for a few years. The project was deemed to have little chance of success, so its funding was cut off."

"So I had heard."

"Then you heard what they wanted you to hear. I was working for the Department of Defense. They had plans of their own when it came to supernaturals. They found out about Tia's task force and the contents of the warehouse. When securing congressional funding, it greatly increases your chances of success if you can produce tangible proof of your claims."

"You took the proof from both of them."

Tarbert nodded. "We humans have done enough damage to ourselves. Proof of the existence of supernaturals wouldn't have benefitted anyone. Well, with the exception of people like my ex-wife. I suspect the CIA and DOD knew I'd taken those crates. But even if they could prove it…" He spread his hands. "I'm dead."

"So, you burned every bridge you had and staged your own death."

"Nearly every bridge, and if I hadn't erased myself, Tia would've done it for me. I had a few people I knew I could trust, one of whom was a very good friend with a very remote cabin. Even better, he was known for lending it to academics who needed a quiet place to write up their research. The locals were used to strangers being there."

"You must have trusted this friend with your life."

"It was all I had left, and I was determined to keep it." His expression became haunted. "Had those task forces succeeded, the results would have been second only to the development of the atomic bomb. Einstein and Oppenheimer regretted the monster they helped create. Dragons are not monsters, but my ex-wife is. I know what she is, what she ultimately wants, and the lengths to which she's willing to go to get it. I owe it to myself and humanity to do all that is in my power to stop her."

"Do you know why she is in New York?"

"I've cultivated a contact close to Tia. We communicated via a series of intermediaries. My contact knew it was only a matter of time before Tia turned into some kind of Bond villain. My source recently told me she had crossed even his line. He overheard part of a conversation she had with Viktor Kain where she intended to, and I quote: 'end all life on this miserable little world.'"

"What did Viktor say?"

"Unknown, it was a phone conversation, but my source asked some discreet questions and found out she was talking to Viktor. Four days later, Tia went to Greece, then last week came to New York—in a rented cargo plane instead of her private jet. Tia likes her creature comforts. Something in that plane was so valuable that she wasn't about to let it out of her sight."

I let out a quiet whistle. "Like an eight-foot-tall gorgon?"

Ian tapped the tip of his nose twice.

"My source's questions must not have been discreet enough," Tarbert continued. "Two of our intermediaries had fatal accidents. I've learned during my time at the DOD that convenient fatalities are rarely accidental." His expression darkened. "One of those deaths was my friend with the cabin. I left as soon as I heard. I managed to reach my source. He said Tia was coming to New York and had informed him he would be coming with her. After that, he was watched constantly. He suspected his disloyalty had been discovered but had no way to avoid coming here."

"Did he arrive on the cargo plane with Tiamat?"

Tarbert shook his head. "He traveled with two of her other mages, Gerald Blackburn and Griselda Ingeborg."

"Other mages? Would your source by any chance be Marek Reigory?"

Oooh, Rake was gonna hate that he'd missed this.

Tarbert froze. "You are familiar with Marek?"

"Oh yes. Very much so." Ms. Sagadraco set down her teacup and steepled her fingers. "As well as Ms. Ingeborg and Mr. Blackburn. Please continue."

"When I arrived in New York, I contacted Marek directly. He wanted out of Tia's organization, and he wanted me to use my contacts at the DOD to make it happen. In return, he would give us the address of every safehouse, the location of every cave, any place Tia could run to and feel safe. He wanted to meet at that food truck. When I arrived, the magetech generator as you call it, was there, but he wasn't. He either ran or was taken. I have no way of knowing which." He leaned back on the sofa. "I heard about what nearly happened in Las Vegas, from old DOD colleagues and Marek. He first reached out to me a month after that. I wanted to get my hands on one of those generators. As incentive—or bait—for me to meet him, Marek said he'd be bringing one to that food truck."

"An offer you couldn't refuse."

"Hardly. By the way, I was disappointed that Tia escaped you above Times Square that night."

"As was I, Dr. Tarbert. I had to make a choice. Kill my sister, or the grendel that was seconds away from appearing and slaughtering innocents. I chose to save lives. I knew I would get another chance at Tiamat, preferably before she succeeds in one of her schemes."

Jonathan Tarbert leaned forward. "I feel responsible for much of what Tia did that night and what she's done since then. The cloaking device technology was mine."

"A cloaking device. That is what our scientists call it as well. Most of them are fans of that science fiction show, *Star Trek*."

"I am as well. Then they would also understand my belief that the needs of the many outweigh the needs of the few, or the one. My cloaking device and the QTTD are catastrophic technologies in the wrong hands, and those hands don't get any more wrong than Tia's. I've devoted what's left of my life to doing all I can to stop her."

"What can you do, Dr. Tarbert?"

The scientist's lips curled in a secretive smile. "My cloaking device, Ms. Sagadraco. I have a device that can turn it off."

Ian and I looked to Jenna Simon.

“He’s telling the truth,” she said. “All of it.”

Vivienne Sagadraco heard her.

“Dr. Tarbert, may I offer you a cup of tea—and a job?”

19

Dr. Jonathan Tarbert went from suspect to SPI's newest employee in ten minutes flat.

The cloaking device was the size of a hockey puck, but the off switch would fit on a watch band. We'd need to be within twenty feet for it to be effective.

Everyone was going to get what they wanted. Except, hopefully, Stheno and Tiamat.

Ian and I were happy campers.

Then the boss rained all over Ian's happy by assigning him as Tarbert's babysitter. She'd done the same on my first day, and Ian didn't like it any better now than he did then.

"I don't think Dr. Tarbert will be comfortable around me," Ian was telling her. "I cuffed and stuffed him in the Suburban."

"A shower and a change of clothes are all the comforts Dr.

Tarbert has time for," Ms. Sagadraco said. "He understands this. I need him to be productive, not comfortable. Time is a luxury we can ill afford."

"Yes, ma'am."

She opened the door to the interrogation room and gestured for Tarbert to join us.

"Ian Byrne is our best agent, and one of my most trusted. He will take you to where you need to be and introduce you to those you'll be working with in the coming hours. Directors Stanton and Fitzwilliam of our research and development department are expecting you."

Ian and Dr. Tarbert started for the elevators. The boss glanced at me and mouthed, "Stay."

I stayed.

Apparently, trusting the new guy only went so far.

She waited until the elevator door closed before speaking. "Alain is back with Helena. The friend she was visiting, Sophia Galanis, came with them. Alain says Ms. Galanis's knowledge and assistance will be incalculable." Her eyes shone with what I could only describe as triumph. "According to Helena, Sophia served with Medusa as one of Athena's priestesses." The boss turned and headed for the elevator. "And she wants to meet you."

It turned out being struck speechless was an actual thing.

I'd been too stunned for words a couple of times before, but those paled in comparison with now.

Sophia Galanis and Medusa had been coworkers. And I'd thought Jonathan Tarbert would know plenty.

Medusa's coworker wanted to meet me.

Holy crap.

"Why?" I asked the boss as we took the elevator up to her office.

"Alain didn't say, but I suspect it has to do with the Master of the Wild Hunt being your father. The Masters don't often sire progeny. You're a rarity."

"Right back at her," I muttered.

"Pardon?"

"Cernunnos is my dad, but she's…" Again, words were failing me. "Wow." Though one thought popped in my head and stayed there. "Is she a gorgon?"

"She is."

"How? Sorry, that must sound insensitive, but better to ask you than her."

"Alain did not say."

"Then I'll let you ask that one. You have tact. I don't."

Out of the corner of my eye, I saw Ms. Sagadraco's lips curl in a smile. "Agent Fraser, I have never heard you offend anyone. What you see as tactless, I consider to be a charming lack of pretension."

"Hopefully a 7,200-year-old gorgon will agree." I felt a little frisson of fear. "I don't have my gorgon glasses."

"Remember when you accompanied me to Helena's apartment?"

"Yes."

"She was wearing sunglasses then. Alain says Helena and Sophia are wearing sunglasses now out of consideration for you. Older gorgons can control their glare, so the sunglasses aren't necessary. We are all quite safe. Helena is a dear friend whom you've met before. Sophia is Helena's dear friend, and if I understand correctly from Alain, her mentor. In addition, Alain has vouched for Sophia. If he did not trust her completely, he would not have brought her here."

I was about to meet the woman who had been, quite possibly, Medusa's bestie.

Again, wow.

SPI had plenty of historians on staff covering all eras and nations. But for our situation, the boss had wisely called in a specialist. This person had something none of our experts did.

Helena Thanos had been alive when Socrates taught. She was also a gorgon.

Helena had not been a suspect the last time New York had a gorgon problem, and she wasn't a suspect now. This time, we knew exactly who we were dealing with.

Medusa's big sister. Stheno. The gorgon known through the ages for her viciousness.

Helena was about the same age as Ms. Sagadraco, give or take a century or five.

Sophia Galanis was as old as Stheno.

When Ms. Sagadraco opened the door to her office, I got my first look at Medusa's coworker. I'd only had a few minutes to imagine what she might look like.

My imagination could not have been more wrong.

Sophia Galanis appeared to be in her late fifties. Her hair had probably been blonde at some point, but was now that highly coveted shade of silver that couldn't be bought in any bottle at any price. She wore it in a long braid draped over her right shoulder. The peasant blouse and flowing, ankle-length skirts, seemingly containing every color in existence, were just the beginning of what I did not expect. The silver rings on her fingers weren't large, but they were on eight out of ten fingers. Silver bangle bracelets covered both wrists and half her forearms, and multi-loop hoops hung from her earlobes. The simplest adornment was her necklace: a silver chain with what appeared to be an old and battered Greek coin. Sophia Galanis looked like she should be reading your future in a crystal ball or handing out flowers in front of Whole Foods.

I could just see her sandaled feet peeking out from beneath her skirts. No anklets or toe rings—just a bright pink lotus-blossom tattoo on the top of her right foot.

All sported with a confidence and ease that reminded me of Edwina, the ancient oracle who lived near my hometown.

I liked her.

Helena Thanos was just a smidge over five feet. It was only in recent human history that people have been growing taller. In ancient Greece, Helena was probably considered tall, or at least average. I knew how old she was, but she looked to be in her early forties, a very attractive early forties. She still wore her hair in a stylish dark bob. She always wore elegant, neutral colors in shades of ivory, gray, and beige, tastefully accented with gold jewelry, and today was no exception.

Both women were wearing large Jackie Onassis-style sunglasses.

Must be a gorgon thing.

Their eyes didn't identify them as gorgons, but their auras sure did.

The auras of humans and supernaturals had one thing

in common—they encompassed the entire body. I'd seen Helena's before. Sophia's was identical. Their auras were centered around their heads. They were green, with lashing tendrils that bore a disturbing resemblance to the snakes I'd seen on Stheno. All subsequent gorgons had normal hair, but their auras showed their origins. Medusa. Helena had told me that all gorgons were descended from Medusa through her Athena-cursed and infected blood.

Alain Moreau appeared at my elbow. It happened often enough that I didn't jump anymore. My vampire manager made no sound whatsoever when he moved. The man didn't even displace air.

"Madam Sagadraco, I took the liberty of ordering tea and a light luncheon."

"Perfect, Alain. Thank you."

More tea and sandwiches.

Ms. Sagadraco wouldn't have dreamed of telling him she'd just consumed the exact same thing downstairs. However, she was a three-story-tall dragon. Filling that tank would take a gazillion tiny sandwiches and a tanker of tea.

Both women rose, and Helena came over to Ms. Sagadraco and they did the double-cheek-kissing thing. I wasn't at that level of familiarity with Helena, but last time, we had shaken hands. That was what we did now.

As a Southern woman, I knew that in an uncomfortable situation, polite and sincere small talk was called for. "I'm sorry you had to cut your vacation short, Miss Helena, but we really appreciate your help."

"No problem at all, Makenna. I simply brought my vacation home with me. Sophie's never been to New York.

Makenna, Vivienne, this is my dear friend and mentor, Sophia Galanis."

Sophia and Ms. Sagadraco shook hands, and after an only ever-so-slight hesitation, I went to do the same—and looked her in the eye while doing it. Or at least at the center of her sunglasses lenses where her eyes would be. When you were introduced to someone and shook their hand, you looked them in the eye. Anything else would be from the land beyond rude, even if they were a gorgon.

"Ms. Sagadraco has told me a few things about you, Ms. Galanis," I said. "It's an honor to meet you."

Sophia smiled and took my hand in a firm and cool grip. "And it's a true pleasure to meet the mortal daughter of the Eternal Hunter."

I inclined my head in acknowledgment, not knowing what else to do or say.

Everyone took their seats, and Mr. Moreau served tea.

"I prepared Madam Sagadraco's favorite Greek blend in honor of our guests," he said. "It's a pomegranate green tea blended with a mix of Greek herbs and flowers." He flashed a quick smile. "And one of Madam's favorites, dragon fruit."

Helena inhaled the aroma. "You'll like this, Sophie. It's become one of my and Alain's favorites at breakfast."

Breakfast?

Alain Moreau had been born in the 1700s and had Old World manners to go with each and every year. But judging from the glance that'd just passed between him and Helena, my vampire manager could and had set aside those impeccable manners and was equally good at being a bad boy.

No, this wasn't awkward for me at all.

"May I remove my glasses?" Sophia asked.

And adrenaline kicked awkward right in the teeth.

Hoo-boy.

Okay, I had to admit the sunglasses were problematic. Conversation was so much easier when you could see someone's eyes.

So was trust.

"Agent Fraser is the sole mortal present," Ms. Sagadraco said. "The decision is hers."

She's just like Edwina, Mac. Your gazillion great-grandmother. If the boss says it's safe, it's safe. Do it.

It still took me a few seconds to get the words going. "That would be fine with me. Actually, I'd prefer it. There's no time for me to be squeamish, and there's no reason." I looked directly at Sophia Galanis. "You're Miss Helena's friend. Please, be comfortable." I turned to Helena. "Both of you."

Since I was already looking in her direction, I saw Helena's eyes first. As I'd guessed when I'd first met her, her eyes were large and dark—and perfectly harmless. At least to me. I don't think I winced as I looked over at Sophia, at least I tried my best not to. Teeth clenching, I had no control over. Her sunglasses dangled from the fingers of her right hand, leaving me looking into a pair of eyes as blue as the Aegean Sea. The gorgon smiled very slightly and gave a single, approving nod.

Mr. Moreau took his seat. "I told Helena and Sophia about the incident at Barrington Galleries."

Sophia spoke. "It appears Stheno and Euryale are both here."

"That is what we believe," Ms. Sagadraco said. "You know both of them, correct?"

"I do. At least I did."

"To confirm," Ms. Sagadraco said, "Stheno has red Milos vipers for hair, and Euryale has a mix of gray and brown."

"Yes."

"They fought in a tunnel beneath Barrington Galleries. Both were injured, but it appeared that Euryale's wounds were more severe. At this point, everything we know is an assumption. My sister must have gained Stheno's trust, or at least cooperation, to take the Aegis from my vault. Another assumption is that Euryale attempted to stop her sister or take the Aegis away from her for her own purposes. We have intelligence saying Tiamat brought Stheno to New York from Greece. Did the Sisters of Medusa bring Euryale, or did my sister bring both?"

"That would be a question for the Sisterhood."

I half raised my hand.

"Yes, Agent Fraser?"

"Ms. Galanis—"

"Sophia, please."

"Sophia. I experienced a brief link with one of our battlemages whom Stheno killed. She wasn't defending herself. She ambushed them, showing her eyes first, then revealing the rest of her."

"Stheno has a device my sister has used in the past that renders her invisible," Ms. Sagadraco clarified. "Stheno wears it as a pendant. That is how we knew Tiamat is behind this."

"Stheno enjoyed what she did," I continued. "She wanted those two men to suffer."

Sophia set her cup and saucer on the table. "I can't say I'm surprised. Even before Medusa's death, Stheno had little regard for humans, and would not hesitate to kill them, much like humans would swat a fly."

"Speaking for us humans, we don't enjoy killing flies, at least most of us don't. Stheno *really* enjoyed killing our mages."

"Much like my sister would have," Ms. Sagadraco said. "I know my sister is evil, and since Stheno is partnering with Tiamat, has stolen the Aegis, and killed two of my battlemages, I'm inclined to think the same of her. I am less certain of how to categorize Euryale and the Sisters of Medusa."

"I can say with certainty that Euryale and the Sisterhood would be trying to stop Tiamat and Stheno," Sophia said. "Euryale is not like Stheno. She is more like Medusa."

"Does that put us on the same side?"

"I don't know if the Sisterhood would see it that way."

"Then how would they see it?"

"The Aegis has not been seen for over seven thousand years. The Sisterhood would hear rumors of a location, but when their agents arrived, it was gone—or had never been there to begin with. The Sisterhood was founded and exists for two reasons: to protect Stheno and Euryale, and to recover the Aegis. Until the Aegis was taken from your vault, the Sisterhood did not know that you had it."

"Regardless of their intentions," Ms. Sagadraco said, "they're involved in this, along with Tiamat. I need information. What do you know about them?"

"Everything," Sophia Galanis said. "I founded them."

20

I whistled before I could stop myself. "Sorry."

"Don't be," Sophia said. "It sounds more impressive than it was. Medusa was my friend. After what Athena did to her, I wanted to help. I wasn't in the temple the day she was raped. Poseidon had seen to it that none of us were. Only her sisters, Stheno and Euryale, heard Medusa's screams. Poseidon was gone by the time they got there." Sophia's voice was clipped with an anger that the millennia had not dulled. "Then Athena arrived. Medusa's sisters told her what Poseidon had done. They had no reason to lie, and Athena knew they weren't lying. Poseidon and Athena were rivals, and what better way to humiliate your rival than to rape one of her virgin priestesses in her own temple. But rather than protect her priestess, Athena blamed the rape on Medusa and turned her into a gorgon. And when Stheno and Euryale tried to defend their sister, Athena did the same to them. Yes, Poseidon was a god second in power only to Zeus, but Athena was the goddess of *war*. She wasn't a coward. Fear was beneath her—as apparently were her priestesses. We were just adornments for her temple, dolls to do her bidding, and no more. Medusa was the one who was raped, but Athena considered it an insult done to *her*. A humiliation, an embarrassment—*to her*. So, she got rid of Medusa, the embarrassment. That day, Medusa had no one to help her. Neither did her sisters. I swore my friend would never be without help again. The other priestesses joined me. We left Athena's temple, and never returned."

The only sound was the clock ticking on the mantle.

"Soon after, Medusa realized she was pregnant. She was ashamed, and one night while we slept, she went deeper into the caves where we had taken refuge. We searched but couldn't find her. Medusa had fled so deep she had gone into the realm of Hades. Athena could not pass into Hades's realm, so she sent Perseus. You all know the part of the story that followed. I founded the Sisters of Medusa to protect Medusa's sisters after her murder. To do for them what we were unable to do for her."

"Do you know their leader, Zyta Kokkinos?" I asked.

"I do not. I haven't had any contact with the Sisterhood in nearly three centuries. Admittedly that is a short length of time for me. Still, I don't recognize the name, so it must have been a recent change. Mortals easily lose contact with and drift away from each other over a few years. It's even easier with millennia. I've been in northern Canada most of that time. Every few centuries, I sleep. Though it's getting more difficult to find a place that won't be disturbed until I awaken."

Her beautiful eyes looked far away. "Stheno and Euryale were awake for their first few centuries, then like all of us, wearied of the monotony. They slept. Hibernated. The Sisters cared for them in their oblivion. There were only ten of us, and we realized that to keep our vow, we needed to expand our numbers."

"Were you all gorgons?" I asked.

"Not at first. After Perseus killed Medusa, Athena kept hunting for the rest of us. After what she had done, we had refused to serve her any longer." Sophia huffed a laugh. "Athena never handled rejection well."

Jonathan Tarbert had said the same about Tiamat. Sounded like she and Athena had more than a little in common.

"Athena knew the caves we were in, but she couldn't find us," Sophia continued. "Then she realized she didn't have to. There was only one source of fresh water, near the surface. Athena took blood from Medusa's severed head and poisoned the water with gorgonism. We drank the water and became gorgons. Only Medusa and her sisters had been directly cursed by Athena, so only they had the snake attributes. Our former goddess called down the well to us, telling us what we would have to do to survive. Hunt humans and turn them to stone. If we didn't, we would slowly turn to stone ourselves from the outside in. After that, she never bothered us again. She didn't need to. She had damned us for eternity, and she knew it."

"That psycho *bitch*," I spat, not even trying to stop myself.

"I've said the same myself, and many times much worse. That's an advantage to living as long as I have. I've had the opportunity to learn many languages, some seemingly made for cursing."

"German?" I asked.

"That's one."

"You should learn Goblin. It's seriously satisfying."

"I'll have to look into it."

"How did you learn to…"

"Live with it?"

I nodded.

"A few of us were driven insane by the curse, but mostly due to the solitude of the caves. So we turned our prison into a beautiful home, a small city beneath the earth, the one place where we would not be hunted. Still, four of the original ten fled and spread gorgonism into the world. Some of those newly infected women found their way back to us. We educated them on what they were—and what they could be—a force for good. We helped them get past their first few centuries to, as you mortals say now, 'pay it forward,' taking in and helping other young gorgons. Training the next generations, so the original few could leave for a time, taking sabbaticals of a sort. We found that time had weakened the curse. We no longer needed to kill to live, and we could control our glare. It's the closest we'll ever come to being mortal again."

"Had Stheno ever left the caves before?" I asked.

"In the time I was there, she had not. Neither had Euryale, but from what Alain says, that's precisely what happened. Stheno couldn't have travelled here on her own. Someone had to have brought her. She knows nothing of modern technology, nor does she want to know. In her mind, those responsible for her sister's murder have never paid. Perseus's line has long died out. The old gods have shrunken into insignificance. Mortal humans rule this world. Stheno and Euryale have the blood of the Titans in their veins. They are gods. Humans are servants."

"That sounds very much like Tiamat," Ms. Sagadraco said.

"Then you do understand them—or at least understand how they think. After all this time, Stheno now has the Aegis in her possession, and as she would see it, the power to have the vengeance she has longed for."

Ms. Sagadraco sat straighter in her chair. "Vengeance against an innocent world. Those who wronged her have not existed for thousands of years. I understand her desire to retrieve what remains of her sister. In her place, I would have similar anger. But she has stolen an object under my protection and murdered two of my agents. She has made it my very personal business."

"I'm not at all advocating what she has done," Sophia said. "Merely explaining why she may have done it."

"Ever since the Aegis came into my possession, I have treated it not only with the care due a powerful artifact, but with the respect and honor due to that which it contains. The Aegis is not only a protective shield, it is a reliquary of Medusa's remains. Her head and her blood, taken by Perseus in the most cowardly of acts. Murdered in her sleep. Her head cut from her body and taken as a grisly trophy. The Aegis is too powerful to be out in the world. It's been in my vault to keep it away from those who would abuse its power, like my sister, and now Stheno. You were Medusa's friend. I cannot imagine she would have wanted to be used in this way."

"She would not. Medusa was a caring and generous young woman."

"Then it seems Tiamat has found a kindred spirit in Stheno. The Aegis is still in this city. I can feel its presence, but not its exact location. Tiamat is somehow shielding it from me. What Tiamat has planned will be in New York. Last time she was here, she did not succeed. I know my sister. She refuses to accept failure. It is my duty as the guardian of this city to stop her and any who side with her."

"The Sisterhood has as little contact with the outside world as possible," Sophia said. "However, they would know that New York is yours. They would also consider this a gorgon matter and would not see how it involves you."

"Even with the Aegis in the possession of my sist—"

My phone rang. Loudly. I grabbed it and hit the mute button. "I'm so sorry." I looked at the display. Rake. Last seen hot on the trail of Marek Reigory. I had news for my honey, Tia was probably on his trail, too.

"I need to take this," I told Ms. Sagadraco.

"Do so."

Once outside her office, I took the call. "Did you find Marek?"

"No, but Zyta Kokkinos found me."

My heart skipped a beat. "Are you—"

"I'm fine. And I said that wrong. Ms. Kokkinos contacted me in my role as a neutral host. She wants to meet Vivienne here at the Regor Regency."

"When?"

"As soon as possible. I tried to reach her, but with Alain out of the country—"

"He's back, he's in the boss's office where we're having a big meeting of our own. I'll have her call you right back for details, but I know she wants to talk to Zyta Kokkinos. Set it up." I paused, mentally shifting through the pile of information I'd just had dumped on me until I dug down to Marek. "About our boy Marek..."

Silence from Rake. "What about him?"

"It seems he's not happy with his employer and might be coming over to the light side, or at least the gray side."

"What?"

I told him what Jonathan Tarbert had told the boss.

"And you believe him?" Rake asked.

"Jenna Simon, our human lie detector, said Tarbert wasn't lying. Marek could've been, but Tarbert believed what Marek told him. Or Tia found out her ex was alive and used Marek to flush him out. Though if she was using Marek as bait, you'd think he'd have been waiting when Tarbert got there so he could grab him."

"So you would think." Rake paused, and I could almost hear his wheels turning. "Or Tia knew Marek had betrayed her." He chuckled darkly. "If she'd just waited a little longer, she could've taken Marek *and* her ex-husband." He made tsking noises. "Patience is a virtue, Tia."

21

In the supernatural world, Rake was known as the host with the most.

When a goblin invited someone under the protection of their roof, they were obligated to protect them as they would their own family. For them to violate that trust would be to severely damage or even destroy the honor of their family and that of the goblin people.

Goblins took hospitality seriously.

A few years ago, Rake hosted the Centennial Supernatural Summit at the Regor Regency. Members of the cabal, intent on sabotaging the event, sealed us all in the hotel with a menagerie of monsters. That no one died during the three-day conference was nothing short of a miracle. The elite of the supernatural world had expected to be safe at the Regency. If they couldn't be safe, they trusted Rake to protect them.

Rake had come through with flying colors.

He'd played a big part in popping the pocket dimension surrounding his hotel and disabling the magetech generator that'd been sending in the monsters.

Of course, he wouldn't have been able to have done either without SPI's help. It'd been a true team effort.

As a result, Rake's reputation as a host had not only emerged unscathed, it'd been elevated to legendary status.

It seemed that Zyta Kokkinos had heard of Rake's daring deeds of hotel management and place of honor as a supernatural corporate meeting host extraordinaire.

Vivienne Sagadraco had called Rake back to tell him she'd be bringing two guests to the meeting—Helena Thanos and Sophia Galanis. Rake relayed the message.

Now Kokkinos *really* wanted the meeting. Sophia may not have heard of Zyta, but Zyta sure had heard of Sophia. She was the Sisterhood's founding mother. It'd be like an American having never heard of George Washington.

On the drive to the hotel, Ms. Sagadraco had taken another call. She'd done a lot of listening, and when she had spoken, her words were few and grim. She'd been silent the rest of the way.

The moment Ian and I walked through the front doors of the Regor Regency, followed by two gorgons, a dragon, and a vampire lawyer, everyone in staff uniform immediately snapped to attention.

I had to hand it to Rake, he knew how to make people feel important.

Rake was waiting for us, artfully framed between a pair of dragon-festooned columns.

Helena and Ms. Sagadraco each got a double-cheek kiss, Rake shook Mr. Moreau's hand, and Sophia Galanis found herself on the receiving end of an exquisitely proficient hand kiss. My honey knew how to weaken female knees. I didn't know if Sophia's knees had wobbled, but her smile said she'd allowed herself to be charmed.

The Regor Regency was a fully restored, thirteen-story epitome of art nouveau elegance near the Financial District. The hotel had been open for almost a decade and was now the preferred destination for the well-heeled financier, both human and supernatural. The staff were either supernaturals themselves or humans who were in-the-know.

Part of the hotel's supernatural friendliness was due to its location. The hotel's foundations had been embedded in the bedrock right above several ley lines of power, which emitted a low and pleasant hum to people and beings who were sensitive to such things. As a result, the beds were more restful, the food more flavorful, and guest reviews were glowing.

Since the events of the Centennial Supernatural Summit, Rake now used those ley lines to power the hotel's wards, ensuring absolute security.

Rake nodded to the doormen, who swung shut the massive front doors. The sound of locks resounded in the now empty lobby. The Regency's staff had an uncanny ability to literally vanish into the woodwork when needed.

Rake dropped his glamour. The human hotelier in a dark bespoke suit was replaced with a rakishly handsome goblin in the full regalia of his art as a dark mage, his station as a duke of the goblin court, and his office as the colonial governor of all goblins on our world.

Yum.

"The meeting of these two parties will be held in my secure sanctum," Rake was saying, his voice oddly formal. "Zyta Kokkinos is waiting there under protective guard. As my guest, she has given me her word and bond to abide by my rules as host for the duration of this meeting and until she takes leave of my domain, this hotel." He turned to Ms. Sagadraco. "Vivienne Sagadraco, do you acknowledge my authority as host, and give your word and bond that your guests will abide by the rules of my domain?"

"I do and they will."

Rake turned in a swirl of robes. "Please follow me."

We did, at least to Rake's private elevator. Then Ian, Alain Moreau, and I stepped aside. Ms. Sagadraco and Rake had prearranged what came next.

Ms. Sagadraco wanted me to attend, since I had been a witness of sorts to Stheno murdering our mages. Ian and Alain Moreau would be attending as Ms. Sagadraco's personal guards. The four of us, plus Rake, Helena, and Sophia, would've made for an awkwardly crowded elevator. For the duration of the elevator ride to the penthouse, Rake would accept responsibility for the safety of Ms. Sagadraco, Helena, and Sophia. They would go up first. Gethen and his security team were waiting in the penthouse. Rake would then send the elevator down for the three of us.

Our ride up to the thirteenth floor was quiet. Well, except for the humming of the turbo-charged ley line energy surrounding the elevator shaft. Bulking up the security around the penthouse included the elevator that went to it. The hotel had been built in the 1920s by an elf mage who was into some seriously freaky stuff. He'd summoned creatures that shouldn't have been summoned, and who took grave offense at having been called. The elf mage was destroyed down to the atomic level. The hotel had largely been abandoned since then and kept from decaying by the magic saturating the structure.

It'd taken Rake years to clean up the magical contamination. In his first years of owning the building, Rake told me he'd referred to it as Hotel Chernobyl. When he'd finished, he made a home for himself here. It was where he worked his most powerful spells. Thanks to Rake's work and care, the hotel was essentially sentient, and it was grateful for what Rake had done. Since he'd cleaned the building and then put his own magical print on it, the building wanted to talk to him. A lot. After the Centennial Supernatural Summit, the hotel had become rather protective of Rake.

The Regency's penthouse was furnished in actual art nouveau antiques. The furniture was warm woods carved into impossible shapes of smooth, flowing lines. The windows were clear in the center but surrounded by stained glass shaped into what looked like a garden of blue irises. A pair of large sofas faced each other on either side of a vine-carved wooden fireplace. The sofas were low, the cushions plush, the fabrics soft and silken.

The sofas had been cleared from the center of the penthouse's sitting room, and even the rug had been taken away. Now revealed was a perfect circle of pure silver embedded in the floor below. Rake himself had etched runes into the silver's surface for even more protection.

Zyta Kokkinos was seated on a chair inside the circle.

As a guest, she'd asked for protection, and as a host, Rake

had provided it. By seating her in his conjuring circle, Rake was not only protecting her as his guest, he was also protecting us from his guest.

Three chairs had been placed a few feet outside the circle. Ms. Sagadraco, Helena, and Sophia were seated there. No one was speaking. They'd waited for us.

I'd seen Zyta Kokkinos on Ollie's security camera, but even the best resolution was a poor substitute for face-to-face.

The leather jacket and helmet she'd worn at Ollie's had given the illusion of size. The chair she was sitting in was from Rake's dining room set. I'd sat in those chairs. The back came up to her shoulders, the same as on me. Her build was slender, but was probably more along the lines of steel cable. Her hair was so black that light wouldn't be able to escape from it. That and her short bob haircut would look severe on most women, but on Zyta Kokkinos, it merely emphasized her large, dark eyes.

That weren't hidden behind sunglasses.

And Ian and I weren't wearing gorgon glasses.

"I can control my glare, Agents Byrne and Fraser. Yes, I know who you are. Magus Danescu told me everyone who would be here." She aimed her intense gaze at Ian. "Agent Byrne, you ride well. It was a challenge to elude you."

Ian gave her the barest nod in response.

Zyta Kokkinos wasn't afraid. Heck, she wasn't even nervous. I guess you didn't get to be the head of an ancient gorgon military order by having anything less than nerves of steel. From what happened at Ollie's, she did have a problem with rats, but I wasn't gonna hold that against her. Some of our toughest agents and commandos had big issues with spiders, snakes, or rats. I didn't particularly care for any of those, either.

Ian wasn't bothered in the least that Zyta Kokkinos was staring at him. He was staring right back. He hadn't become SPI's top agent by having anything less than nerves of steel, too. Kokkinos was the one who'd gotten away. If she tried to skedaddle now, he'd be on her in two strides and a tackle. She knew it, and from her dangerous smile, she wanted him to try.

"Agent Byrne," Vivienne Sagadraco said without turning to look at him. She knew what Ian was thinking, but she didn't order him to stand down, just to stay put. For now.

Rake was standing outside the circle where he could see all four women. "Before I agreed to host this meeting, I questioned Ms. Kokkinos. I can attest that she answered truthfully to the following: she does not know the present location of Stheno, the Aegis, or Tiamat." Rake glanced at me. "She was in Central Park because I was there. Her intent was to make contact to set up this meeting. She was in the right place at the right time to be of assistance with the satyr."

"Thank you," I told her. "I think."

Zyta Kokkinos shrugged. "I underestimated the creature's distance and velocity, but I could see that you were not injured."

"Just my pride."

"That will heal."

"It always has."

She addressed Ms. Sagadraco. "I am here as a representative of Euryale. I will speak plainly. Tiamat brought Stheno here to take the Aegis from your hoard. Euryale helped us track her sister here. She confronted Stheno after she had taken the

Aegis. They had a difference of opinion. Stheno escaped, and Euryale has not sensed her since." Her expression hardened. "Tiamat is your sister. New York is your city. Tell me where to find her."

"Ms. Kokkinos, if I knew where to find my sister, we would not be having this conversation because it would not be necessary. I would have found Tiamat and dealt with her once and for all." Ms. Sagadraco paused. "I do not know what you have been told or believe. I obtained the Aegis in 1938 from a remote monastery northwest of Katmandu. I had it smuggled out of the country to keep it out of Himmler's hands. I brought it to my vault here for protection. Until two days ago, it was safe." Ms. Sagadraco paused. "On the way here, I received a report from SPI's Athens office. Knowing that both Stheno and Euryale were here, I asked the director in that office to make contact with the Sisterhood. Yesterday, he dispatched a team to your caves, attempted contact, and when there was none, they used drones equipped with conventional and thermal imaging cameras. They detected no signs of life but found dozens of ossified remains."

Sophia exhaled in a sharp hiss. "How many came here with you?"

The gorgon commander met her eyes unflinchingly. "Twelve. Thirteen counting myself. There were eight survivors in Greece, and four others were with me in Prague. Thirteen survivors out of ninety-six. Stheno killed them all."

22

Sophia spat a single word. I didn't know the language, but there was no mistaking the meaning.

"You have my heartfelt condolences," Ms. Sagadraco told the gorgon commander.

"We have protected Stheno and Euryale for thousands of years," Zyta said. "We never expected Stheno would turn on us, but in hindsight, the signs were there."

"Rage such as hers does not lessen," Sophia said, her eyes haunted. "It only grows."

Ms. Sagadraco nodded. "From what Sophia has told me, Tiamat would've found a receptive listener in Stheno."

"More than receptive. Eager. Her need for vengeance has increased past the point at which sanity can survive."

"She is insane then?"

"Completely. That is why Euryale insisted on coming with us. She hoped to be able to reach her sister. We owed her that chance. Stheno is beyond help and has slaughtered those who have devoted their lives to her care." Zyta's gaze grew distant. "I was not in the caves that morning. The survivors reported that Stheno killed in a frenzy. Euryale told me that a voice had been speaking to them for years in their sleep. She had thought it was dreams, but apparently the voice was real. As she killed, Stheno raved that we were holding her captive, that we were her jailers, not her caretakers, and the only way to escape was to kill us all. Stheno glared Euryale in her sleep. Thankfully, they are of equal strength and Euryale was able to reverse the paralysis before it could kill her."

Sophia spoke. "When I left for Canada, Stheno had just gone into a sleep phase. She has always remained asleep for at least five hundred years. What happened?"

"Her sleep became fitful," Zyta said. "She awoke halfway through. We helped her get back to sleep, but she awoke again after sixty-two years, then twenty-nine, then fourteen. Euryale told us she heard whispers in her slumber, first a male voice, and more recently female. The voices coaxed Stheno awake, promising her the opportunity to possess the Aegis if she escaped the caves."

Rake and I exchanged a glance. It sounded like Janus had gotten an earlier start than we thought. Janus had been thousands of years old himself. Decades or even centuries spent whispering in Stheno's dreams would've been nothing for him. It seemed Tiamat had picked up where Janus had left off. How many more beings' dreams had Janus haunted?

"Tiamat is the expert on feeding resentment and rage,"

Ms. Sagadraco said. "This has all the hallmarks of my sister's work. Manipulate and exploit the powerful to do her bidding. Tiamat can do what Stheno cannot. She can travel the world in a human form, whereas Stheno is a prisoner in the form with which Athena cursed her. Hope is what enables all living creatures to survive the direst of events. Stheno had no hope for a life of her own. Tiamat tempted her with the freedom she craved to have the vengeance she wanted. I am truly sorry for the part my sister played in this."

"The women of the Sisterhood were my responsibility." Zyta Kokkinos didn't say that she had failed them, but we all heard it.

Sophia's voice was kind. "You weren't there, and if you had been, as commander, Stheno would have hunted you down. Your survival gives the Sisterhood a second chance."

"We do the best we can with the responsibilities we are given," Ms. Sagadraco told her. "There will always be times when we fall short. I have fallen short with Tiamat, most recently five years ago. I had to choose whether to save many lives or to take hers. My choice saved lives then, but it has cost lives now. For that, you and the Sisterhood have my abject apologies. My sister has the Aegis. She and Stheno are still in New York, but I do not know where. Euryale knows her sister best, followed by you and Sophia. I have over two hundred agents and commandos who know every square inch of this city. I have brought in three additional commando teams from our Chicago, Atlanta, and Los Angeles offices. Our chances will markedly increase if we combine forces. You know Stheno. I know my sister, and SPI knows New York."

Vivienne Sagadraco's eyes unblinkingly regarded Zyta

Kokkinos. Waiting with a patience only a multi-millennia-old dragon possessed.

SPI doesn't mind playing and sharing with others, especially if we're after the same big bad.

"The Sisterhood entombed Medusa's body after her murder," Zyta said. "Our mission has always been to recover the Aegis and separate Medusa's head from it, and failing that, to entomb the Aegis with her. Can you swear to me that you will return the Aegis to us?"

"Once we retrieve it, I will do all in my power to find a way to free Medusa's head from the shield. I know talented individuals on innumerable worlds, realms, and dimensions. We will not stop until it is accomplished. This I swear to you."

Zyta searched Vivienne Sagadraco's face for any sign of a lie. "I believe and accept your promise, but another has the final say."

"I trust the honor of the dragon Vivienne Sagadraco." A raspy, heavily accented voice came from the dark, big-screen TV mounted over the fireplace.

Ms. Sagadraco glanced sharply at Rake.

"Forgive me, Vivienne, but Euryale wished to listen before being known. She could not attend in person."

The boss exhaled, her irritation fading. "Understood, Magus Danescu. Not preferred, but understood."

"May I be seen?" Euryale asked.

I realized the reason for the rasp. Humans slept for hours. Euryale slept for centuries. I couldn't begin to comprehend what that was like. Her words were hesitant and accented because English was far from her first language.

"Is it safe for my agents?" Ms. Sagadraco quietly asked Sophia—and Zyta.

"It is," Sophia said.

Zyta nodded.

Vivienne Sagadraco addressed the dark screen. "We would welcome seeing and meeting you."

Rake pointed the remote at the screen and clicked a button.

I'll admit my first glance at Euryale was out of the corner of my eye. *Look away then back. Away and back.* Rinse and repeat. No headache. No eye grit. I blew out a tiny breath, steeling myself. It was safe. Probably. I glanced at Ian. He appeared to have done the same.

I had seen Stheno via Quinn Walsh's memories. His memories had become mine. All Vivienne Sagadraco had seen was the sketch and tomb painting. Her gaze was calm and totally accepting. That did it. There was absolutely nothing in the world—or any other—that could rattle the boss.

I looked at Euryale, Medusa's sister.

Euryale was nearly identical to her older sister. She had gray and brown Milos vipers for hair instead of red. She had the same green eyes, but they did not glow and there was no hate in them. Even the vipers looked like they'd be nice and non-bitey.

Then I noticed two bald patches on her head where snakes were missing, and fresh cuts on her face and shoulders.

"Do you require medical assistance?" Ms. Sagadraco asked the ancient gorgon. "We have physicians able to care for many types of beings."

Euryale shook her head, the vipers gently waving with the motion. "My wounds will heal before the next sunrise." Her lips quirked in a sad smile. "Athena wanted us to suffer our curse in good health. Those like yourself have successfully adapted to modern times and are thriving. We have not and cannot. Part of Athena's curse prevents us from disguising ourselves as anything but what we are. Stheno was told you had stolen the Aegis to take Medusa's power for your own."

"That was a lie told by Tiamat."

"I know that now. Stheno probably realized it as well, but chose to believe what feeds her anger. I did not wish to harm my sister, but she did not have the same reservations toward me. I attempted to reason with her, but she is now far beyond reason. Like you with Tiamat, I intend for our next confrontation to be our last. I do not wish it so, but see no other solution." Euryale's gaze searched Vivienne Sagadraco's face. "You have recently suffered loss as I have. Was my sister at fault?"

"She was. Two of my battlemages, friends of mine for many centuries, attempted to stop Stheno from taking the Aegis. She paralyzed them to increase their suffering, then turned them to stone. You have lost more in number, but one loss is too many."

"It was intentional and explains much. Taking the power of those gifted in magic, their lifeforce, provides more strength than killing mere mortals. Stheno knew I would come for her, with what remains of the Sisterhood, to stop her. She strengthens herself. That was how she was able to defeat me and escape from the caves beneath this city."

Vivienne Sagadraco's expression darkened, and her dragon aura loomed behind her, flowing up the wall like a shadow. She couldn't help that she did it. I couldn't tell if it was a trick of the light, or if there was the daintiest wisp of smoke rising from her patrician nostrils.

"I was born a little more than three years after Stheno," Euryale told us. "We were always together, daughters of gods, granddaughters of Titans. We had no friends, only each other. Medusa was born different, a mortal. Stheno and I were understandably protective. We encouraged her to seek out Athena, to live in her temple, thinking she would be safe there. We trusted Athena to keep Medusa safe. Athena betrayed and cursed us all."

Possibly reacting to Euryale's anger, the vipers on her head hissed and struck at the air around them.

"Stheno and I once witnessed Athena using the Aegis with Medusa's head against an army," Euryale continued. "She caught the light of the rising sun in the shield's metal and cast it into the eyes of thousands of mortal men. Their screams of terror pierced the heavens. Within seconds, they went silent, turned to stone. That was the only time Stheno saw the Aegis used. I believe she seeks to recreate this against the mortals of your city. I saw the image of that event in Stheno's mind before she left our sleep chamber." Euryale paused. "And while I was trapped by Stheno in my sleep, I heard Tiamat tell her that together they would send the Aegis and Medusa to the heavens, to cleanse this world of its mortal stain."

23

Within the hour, the main conference room at SPI had become a hive mind with its queen at the center.

Department directors and agents came and went as they received information. They reported to Vivienne Sagadraco, and with a nod from her, Jenny Greene (formerly of Human and Supernatural Resources, now Ms. Sagadraco's private secretary) would condense and input the knowledge nuggets into her laptop, instantly broadcasting it to monitors throughout headquarters. What the boss learned, everyone learned.

It was teamwork at its finest.

It'd been my experience that previous meetings held in this room had occurred right before the world as we knew it went to hell in the nearest handbasket.

That was what we were here to prevent.

Knowledge was the ultimate weapon. Always had been, always would be. You could have the biggest army and the best weapons, but without accurate knowledge of your enemy, they'd only do you so much good.

We knew two things for certain. One, Tiamat, Stheno, and the Aegis were still in Manhattan. Two, they planned to unleash the Aegis to kill as many people in the city as possible. If Euryale's sharing of her sister's vision was accurate, the plan was to use the Aegis to reflect the rising sun. We didn't know how she was going to do that, but she did. We also didn't know the location—either of the Aegis or of the intended target.

Anywhere else, this would be a cataclysm of historic proportions.

At SPI, it was just lunchtime.

The main conference room was occupied by our commando teams, with Roy Benoit and Sandra Niles in charge. Vivienne Sagadraco and Jenny were ensconced in the smaller, adjacent meeting room. Wall panels had been pulled back to expand the boss's space to accommodate the flow of agents and directors and the updates they brought. We knew we were way behind, and not catching up was not an option.

I was off to the side, out of the way, taking a few minutes to eat. In my opinion, food was nearly as important as facts. When we had the facts we needed, we'd deploy. When that time came, I'd be fueled for whatever I needed to do. One of the many things I'd learned at SPI was how to eat before, during, and after almost anything. I'd learned that from our commandos, who had the cafeteria chefs busy keeping the food coming.

Our two teams here were focused on Tiamat and Stheno,

because the teams from Atlanta, Los Angeles, and Chicago had arrived and been paired with our local drivers and guides. They'd been deployed to deal with yet more of Tiamat's magetech generator-manifested distractions. Those boys and girls knew how to work big-city supernatural shenanigans. One urban jungle was pretty much the same as any other. Our citizens were in the best hands.

We had more than enough on our own hands.

Kenji had been hard at work, and our commandos were waiting to get their first look at Stheno. He'd scanned in Suzy's sketch and the most realistic of Amelia's art photos, combined with the measurements of Stheno's scale to get the dimensions right. Now Sophia Galanis and Zyta Kokkinos sat with him helping to fine-tune the finished product.

A life-size, photo-realistic, 3-D hologram of Stheno.

This had to be hell for Zyta Kokkinos, but she had no choice. Stheno had decimated the Sisterhood and was working with Tiamat to do the same to the city and potentially the world. Zyta had protected and cared for Stheno for hundreds of years. Now she would be helping our commandos find the best way to kill her. Zyta knew Stheno's weak points and was about to tell our people how to find and exploit them.

Kenji knew who and what Sophia and Zyta were, as did our commandos. Vivienne Sagadraco had assured our teams that the two women were trusted allies. Ms. Sagadraco asked for compassion for the two women while discussing the best way to kill the creature who had killed two of our own. The boss said she had full faith in their professionalism.

I had to hand it to our people. Cool, calm, and collected. At least on the outside. Their feelings they kept to themselves.

"Is there anything else?" Kenji quietly asked the two gorgons.

Sophia blew out her breath. "No."

"It's perfect." Zyta pushed back her chair, stood, and left the room.

I knew why. We all did. I waited a few seconds, and even though it probably wasn't the best idea, I followed her.

Zyta Kokkinos was in the corridor leaning against the wall, her eyes on the one across from her.

"I came out to ask if you're okay, but that'd be a stupid question. No one in your place would be okay."

Silence.

Again, not the best idea, but I kept going. "I can't imagine what it would be like to protect someone, care for them for hundreds of years, and then suddenly you have to help a group of strangers find the best way to kill her."

Silence.

"I'm here if you need anything. We all are." I turned to go back in.

"Thank you, Agent Fraser."

I paused again. "The chefs sent up some gyro wraps. Or is that something only Americans eat and think it's Greek?"

The twitch of her lips might have been a smile. "We eat them. But other than a bottle of ouzo and a dark corner, I'd really like a cheeseburger."

"We can do that. Well, at least the cheeseburger. Afterward, I'm sure we can find a couple bottles of ouzo; and if you're up for some company, I'll join you in that dark corner. We've had a couple of rough days here, too. Nothing like yours, but still bad. I'm not that much of a drinker, but I can toss back a shot or two."

"Sophia tells me you are the daughter of the Eternal Hunter."

"I am. I only recently found out about it myself."

"Cernunnos is your father. The Sisterhood considers Euryale and Stheno to be our mothers. In a way, they are. We even address them as Sacred Mother. We are all gorgons, all descended from Athena's curse. One of our mothers turned on us, betrayed our bond, and slaughtered her own children. Now she has stolen the Aegis, the tomb of her sister's soul, and will desecrate it and Medusa's memory, using it to kill millions more. Thirteen of the Sisterhood remain. We now must kill our mother. We have no choice. It is hard to lose a parent. It is even harder when that loss must come at your own hand." Her eyes glistened with unshed tears, but only for a moment. "Cherish your father, Agent Fraser. And may you never need to be the hand that kills him."

I didn't know what to say, but I knew what to do. My instinct was to hug, but I went with a handshake and meeting her eyes. "Thank you for sharing what you know and letting us help. Let's get this done quickly, and hopefully put the pain behind us."

Zyta Kokkinos clasped my hand—and my father's cuff grew warm. Not in warning, but in welcome. It was the cuff's way of letting me know I could trust the gorgon commander.

I so needed to know that.

In glancing down at the cuff, my eye caught another shiny, this one in silver sticking out of Zyta's jacket pocket. I recognized it, or at least the handle that was visible.

The mirror she'd bought from Ollie.

She saw me see it.

"You went to a lot of trouble to get that mirror," I said. "Care to tell me why?"

Zyta pulled it out of her pocket. I didn't know what a Renaissance-era mirror would look like, but it did look old. A little tarnished here and there, a couple of dents in the silver. And yes, it did have a rendering of Medusa's head on the back side.

"Perseus looked at Medusa's reflection in a mirror to kill her," Zyta told me. "Even though she was asleep, he was too cowardly to look directly at her when he cut off her head."

"Is this *that* mirror?"

"No, but it inspired the invention of those such as this. There aren't many left, and I tracked this one down to Mr. Barrington-Smythe."

"You can safely look at Stheno in its reflection?"

Zyta gazed down at the mirror and gave it a cold smile. "Yes, but it can also kill her."

I'll admit I wanted to take a couple steps back. I didn't. "How?"

"The technique for making these has long since been lost, but it gives a full-strength reflection of a gorgon's glare. In the 1700s, this mirror killed one of the ten original priestesses who served with Medusa and Sophia. She'd become a gorgon a few weeks after Stheno was cursed by Athena, so it should work on Stheno, or at least affect her enough to let us get close enough to kill her. My plan is to goad Stheno into glaring me, and then put this in front of my face. If successful, Stheno will be the victim of her own glare."

If not, Zyta Kokkinos would have sacrificed her life in the attempt.

Respect.

Time to lighten the mood, Mac. "By the way, Ollie seriously overcharged you for that, but if it can kill Stheno, it's priceless."

Zyta smiled and it reached her eyes. "I know he did. To the Sisterhood, it *is* priceless."

"Yeah, he can be a real jerk, but he's useful sometimes. Thanks for not stoning him."

Zyta laughed once. "He's a vile little man, but he had what I needed. I don't kill without good reason. I am a professional." The gorgon twirled the mirror by its handle like a dagger. "In the next few hours, I hope to put it to the ultimate test. Though Stheno is immortal." She shrugged. "I won't know if that makes any difference until I try."

Elana strolled by on her way to the conference room, eating an apple. "Nothing's immortal." She took a big bite. "Just means no one's managed to kill it yet."

Zyta saluted Elana with the mirror.

The girls had bonded.

Sandra stepped out of the conference room. "Commander Kokkinos. We're ready when you are."

Zyta nodded to me and followed Sandra.

"Thanks, Dad," I whispered, and went back inside.

24

Kenji saw us, clicked a few keys, and the SPI logo was replaced by a nightmare. And since it'd been created by Kenji, it was a rotating nightmare. The hologram formed from the tip of Stheno's snake tail to the top of her snake head. From the waist up, she looked more or less like a human female. There were no strategically placed snake scales to form a push-up bra.

"This is the only safe way to look directly at her," Sandra said. "So, look now and look well so you won't be tempted when you encounter the real thing."

That directive was mostly aimed at any of our commandos who couldn't resist gawking at a woman's bare boobs when the opportunity presented itself. Though in this case, her boobs would be the safest place to lock your eyes. They weren't the body part that would turn you to stone.

I knew from personal experience that there were ways to force you to look. In my case, it'd been a headlock from a harpy with her clawed fingers forcing my tightly closed eyelids open.

We knew from mythology (which in this case was history) that decapitation was the one certain way to kill Stheno. Medusa had been asleep when Perseus had cut off her head. There was no way we were going to catch her sister napping.

"For God's sake, Kenji, stop the spinning," Roy told him. "We'll walk around it."

Ian caught my eye and gestured me into the side conference room. Good. Stheno looming in the middle of headquarters was the last thing I wanted to see.

The whiteboard was filling up with potential targets. Big ones, both in size and global importance. Anything that happened in New York had worldwide ramifications. The city was a financial center. International businesses were based here, as were two of the world's largest and busiest airports. Then there were the geopolitical ramifications with the UN.

That was the problem. There were too many possibilities, too many targets. Though one event stood out as most likely to set Tia's supervillain nature to salivating.

The president of the United States would be addressing the United Nations General Assembly tomorrow morning at nine o'clock. The US president plus the leaders or high-ranking representatives of all 193 member nations were in town for the four days of the General Assembly.

Tomorrow was the last day.

The speech was less than twenty-four hours from now.

Bingo.

Five years ago, Tiamat hadn't gotten to hold her supervillain TV commercial/coming out party on New Year's Eve in Times Square. She was determined to stage one tomorrow.

"I've checked in with Sirene," Ian said. "Her merfolk have seen Stheno twice, understandably giving her a wide berth both times. Before dawn on the morning the Aegis was taken, two merfolk saw Stheno off the North Cove Marina headed north. Five hours later, she was spotted passing the Ellis Island Security Zone buoy number seven, headed roughly south. They said she was keeping to the deepest parts of the shipping channel." Ian pointed out both on a map of Lower Manhattan and its waterways that took up half a wall.

SPI has friends in watery places. The merfolk of New York's waterways knew who Ian really was, or at least who he was directly descended from. He was their Aquaman (the Jason Momoa version, not the one with the pompadour), and they loved to help any time they could.

"That gives us Ellis Island, Liberty Island, Governors Island, or any of hundreds of ships as a lair," Alain Moreau noted.

"Jenny, do you have any insight?" Ms. Sagadraco asked.

The water spirit/secretary shook her green-haired head. "I'm sorry, ma'am. All my family is north of Hoboken."

Right now, Jenny's hair was damp from a recent trip to the pool maintained on the lowest level for our water-dwelling employees to take a breaktime swim. Like the rest of us, Jenny knew she was going to be here for a while, so she'd gotten her dip in.

"The Aegis is still within a ten-mile radius of headquarters," Ms. Sagadraco said. "Apparently it amuses my sister to taunt me with this information. She is preventing me from determining its exact location."

Ian leaned back in his chair. "That's entirely too much real estate."

"I can say with certainty that Tiamat would want to use the Aegis in a highly symbolic place. My sister would not go to this much trouble unless she intended wide-ranging harm."

"Go big or go home," I muttered.

"Quite so, Agent Fraser. My sister has no intention of going home until she has accomplished what she came to do."

Sophia spoke. "Then there's the difference between Stheno's memory of the Aegis's use, and what would be possible here. The battle she witnessed was fought on a plain. It was relatively flat with no obstructions. Athena was on a hillside, aiming the Aegis down at the soldiers. Manhattan is a veritable sea of skyscrapers."

"The Aegis is highly reflective," Ms. Sagadraco noted. "And as Makenna experienced when she linked with Quinn, the Aegis can produce blindingly bright light. If Tiamat wanted to maximize suffering and death, she would position the Aegis to reflect light to as many points as possible. Light on one glass-covered high-rise would reflect like a prism to the next, rather like using mirrors to reflect candlelight in a room before electricity. Versailles has public rooms with walls covered in mirrors. The light was nearly as bright as what can be produced in modern times."

It sounded like Vivienne Sagadraco had seen it in person. I knew how old she was, but it was still unspeakably cool to hear specifics casually mentioned.

"Over the past twenty-four hours, I've given much

thought to how the Aegis could be used to effect maximum destruction," she continued. "We know Stheno can use the Aegis. Perhaps Tiamat brought her here not only to steal the Aegis, but to wield it as well. Perhaps Stheno will teach Tiamat how to wield it. Either way, you can be sure my sister has a detailed plan with every contingency addressed. As to the light source, Tiamat could have the Aegis provide it, or as in Stheno's memory, she could use the sun. I believe she will do both. The Aegis can produce light, but the brighter the light, the more points of reflection. Agent Hayashi assigned one of his team to create a model of how the sun's rays strike various locations and buildings from east to west, specifically during sunrise of this week of the year." She clicked a few keys on the laptop in front of her and the monitor on the far wall came to life. It was a timelapse of the sunrise, slightly sped up from the actual event.

There was a light knock on the conference room's doorframe. It was Claire. The man behind her was a surprise: Harald Siggurson, SPI's bladed weapons expert and metallurgist. Both looked incredibly pleased with themselves.

"Ma'am, we've finished the analysis of the residue found on Stheno's scales," Claire said.

I sat straighter. "Looks like good news."

"Possibly," Harald said, smiling slightly.

Claire gave the boss a printout. "We found traces of granite, steel, and copper on Stheno's scales. The lab keeps samples of stone and metals from the city's notable buildings and landmarks. All three are common throughout New York, especially the steel and granite. The scales from under Ollie's gallery had only traces of residue, but the one from outside the vault was the winner. Only two buildings and one landmark have the gray-blue granite that was mined in Blue Hill, Maine. And only one of those three also has the steel and copper." She smiled. "Fort Wood."

"Yes!" Ian popped the table with his fist. Everyone else was similarly enthused. Even Alain Moreau was smiling.

I was still clueless. "Share the joy, people. I'm not from around here."

Claire stepped aside, grinning. "I'll let Harald enlighten you."

"I know the sole source of that copper." The big Norwegian looked like his birthday had come early this year. "In 1986, the one-hundredth anniversary of this landmark, a research team investigated its origins. Its copper was tested against a sample from a mine in Visnes, Norway. It was a match. The Statue of Liberty, Agent Fraser. Or more specifically, where it stands—Fort Wood."

Claire's eyes were wet with unshed tears, the happy kind. "We can tell Mortimer Winters it was the scale Carlos Escarra and Quinn Walsh got for us. Carlos and Quinn just might have saved us all."

On the monitor, the rising sun struck Lady Liberty's golden torch. setting Lower Manhattan aflame with light.

25

"Uh, I'm still confused," I told everyone. "The Statue of Liberty ticks off the box for Tiamat's love of public dramatics, but how would Stheno get copper and granite on her sca—"

Claire held up a hand, stopping me. "The Statue of Liberty's pedestal was built in the center of Fort Wood, in the shape of an eleven-pointed star. Eight of its outer walls are in use today as part of the public areas. The other three remain as they were when the statue was erected. They were used for materials storage and sealed off once the construction was complete."

"The copper dust on her scale was pristine," Harald added. "No deterioration or exposure to pollution or salt water. That copper had to come from one of the storage areas."

"And Stheno has shown that she has no trouble getting

through solid rock. She proved that by penetrating my bank vault," Ms. Sagadraco said.

"Stheno and Euryale can secrete an acid from beneath their scales," Sophia told us. "Yet another part of the curse Athena placed upon them. They can't be touched by any living creature, denying them even that comfort in their torment. Now it seems the statue that welcomes visitors to this city has unwelcome guests."

In the five years I'd lived in New York, I'd never been to the Statue of Liberty.

That was about to change.

When I'd told Bartholomew the owl that the boss had devoted herself to the preservation and restoration of New York's buildings and landmarks, it'd been the truth. Now she told us that one of the landmarks she'd made substantial donations toward was the Statue of Liberty. There was restoration work being done right now to Fort Wood's outer walls. The repairs had started a year and a half ago and were nearly finished.

Vivienne Sagadraco made a few calls, and within the hour we were in her private helicopter flying to Liberty Island to meet a representative of the US Park Service and get a firsthand look at how her money was being spent.

As Tiamat's sister and the keeper of the Aegis, she would sense if they were on the island. She was hopeful that proximity would negate or at least lessen Tiamat's wards to give us confirmation. However, the reverse was also true. If Tiamat was on the island, she'd know the instant we landed. Heck, she was probably sensing us right now. Yeah, that was a happy thought.

There was only room for six passengers on the short flight, but we squeezed in seven to include Ruby in her disguise as a Belgian Malinois service dog. Ruby had gotten a good whiff of Stheno under Ollie's shop, so if the gorgon was on Liberty Island, Ruby's nose would know, wards or no wards. Martin entrusted Ruby to me, so she would be posing as my service dog.

One of the accepted reasons to bring a service dog into a national park was PTSD. That totally worked for me. If being on the same island with a sadistic dragon and psychotic gorgon who planned to use an ancient weapon to kill millions of New Yorkers and the leaders of the free world didn't give me the mother of all anxiety attacks, I didn't know what would. I wouldn't have to fake anything. Though my main reason for going was my ability to see portals, wards, and glamours. And for once, I wanted my handy-dandy Christmas present from Dad to zap the bejeebers out of me, confirming there was at least one bad gal in residence.

Ian went with us, taking Lugh's Spear, which likewise had the uncanny ability to sense evil. Sandra was there to scope out what could become a battlefield overnight. If that happened, I had a feeling the bill for the wall repairs would go way up after tonight. It wouldn't be the first time Vivienne Sagadraco had to cash in some gold bars to pay for SPI-inflicted damage.

Mortimer Winters was with us in case discreet, but heavy-hitting magic was needed. He'd originally conjured the ward around the bank vault and its twelve niches. He had also warded each artifact to keep them from reaching out beyond the confines of those niches. The nearly overwhelming come-hither Ian and I had sensed in that vault had been substantially muffled by Mortimer's magic.

Dang.

And last was Zyta Kokkinos. As the commander of what remained of the Sisterhood, she was likewise getting a look at the battlefield. And other than Euryale and Sophia, Zyta had been closest to Stheno. She knew her charge better than anyone else.

The last time we'd gone on a similar scouting mission had been to Bannerman Island, north of the city. Ian hadn't joined us that time because he was already there, having been kidnapped by Janus. We knew he had to be on the island, but Janus had him tucked away in a pocket dimension prison cell. We'd had no luck finding the pocket dimension, but we'd saved Ian from being sacrificed that night.

Rake had gotten us a private tour of Bannerman Island and the ruins of its castle. He'd called the foundation working to restore it and offered to make a sizeable donation. Nothing smooths the way like fistfuls of cash. Vivienne Sagadraco had already done that here, so our way came pre-smoothed. As her "friends and family," we got to follow along in her wake, roaming around, taking pictures, and just generally being touristy.

That meant we could also get up close and personal with Fort Wood's walls. The base was fenced off to everyone else, but since the boss was paying for most of the work, the gate was thrown open wide for us with the stipulation that we wear the provided hardhats. Considering what we suspected was looming on the other side of those walls, they got no argument from us.

We were wearing discreet body cameras. Everything we saw, Kenji and the team back at headquarters would see. If they wanted a closer look at anything, they'd tell us through our ear comms, and we'd go check it out.

Ian and I followed Mortimer Winters, Ms. Sagadraco, and her Park Service guide at a distance.

Still, I kept my voice down. "Maybe Tia knowing that we know she's here will get her to pull the plug on this thing."

Ian snorted.

"Yeah, I shouldn't hold my breath on that, should I?"

"I wouldn't."

I stopped and looked at the fort's granite walls. Ian did the same.

"See a portal?" he asked.

I shook my head. "Trying to decide which way to go first. Dang, these are tall walls."

"It *is* a fort. By the way, they're twenty-six feet."

"If I was making a portal to a pocket dimension, where would I put it?" I glanced up, *way* up, to get my bearings on the statue. The part of the fort wall under the torch was outside of the construction zone. That was as good a place as any. I jerked my head in that direction. "Let's start over there."

I tried to do a relaxed stroll and open myself up to subtle signs of magic. Ian stayed back a few feet so as not to block any signals that might be there. The Statue of Liberty was about as public as it got for an evil lair, but it made sense, not only for the symbolism of Tia using the Aegis from Lady Liberty's torch to kill the masses, both huddled and non-huddled. With the UN General Assembly going on, security in the city was on high alert, but Liberty Island had been deemed beneath that heightened alert. There weren't any security measures that stood out as odd to me. Since 9/11, all

New York landmarks had increased their security, but the Park Service folks in uniform looked relaxed, some even bored. The tourists looked like tourists as I went around another of the fort wall's star points. No one stood out to me as being on heightened alert or plotting heightened evil. Ian and I were doing our best to blend in and keep it casu—

Whoa.

I stopped in my tracks. So did Ruby. I glanced down at her. She was staring unmoving at the same thing I was seeing. Ruby could see portals, too. Good to know.

"Uh, Ian? Can you come take a look at—"

My partner was immediately beside me. "What is it?"

I pointed. "There."

"I see a V in a wall."

"I see a V and a glowing portal door. Well, not so much the door as the doorframe. Bright gold, like freakin' Vegas neon."

"That's unusual for a portal?"

"Uh, yeah. No one who's even in the least bit portal sensitive could miss this."

"Meaning…?"

"I don't know. All it needs are flashing arrows pointing to it. It's entirely too obvious. Obvious makes me nervous."

"Like 'Enter evil lair here, said the gorgon to the fly?'"

"Uh-huh. Like that."

"Want to get a closer look?"

"I don't want to, but we should."

We got closer, Ruby's hackles rose higher, and her growls grew lower. Ruby didn't trust any of this, either.

I stopped about ten feet from the portal. I could see

everything just fine from here. My instincts told me not to get any closer, and when it came to glowing portals to a probable ancient gorgon's lair, any warnings my instincts gave me, I was like, "Yes, ma'am." Oddly, the cuff was keeping any opinions to itself. Maybe it knew I had enough sense to steer clear without its input.

I didn't take my eyes off that golden doorframe. "Okay partner, you don't see anything, but do you feel anything?"

"I can sense something is there, but my instincts can't pinpoint it as being safe or get out."

"How about Lugh?"

"Same, though he's leaning more toward it's okay."

"Yeah, me too, and I still don't trust it. Let's continue around to be sure there's not another one. I don't think there will be, but let's be thorough."

26

We were and there wasn't.

The glowing golden portal was the only one. I'd considered the possibility that there might be another supremely subtle portal that led to the pocket dimension and that the flashy Vegas one was a trap. That theory didn't pan out. There was only one. We definitely needed Kitty's expertise to confirm my findings.

Time to report to the boss.

She and Mortimer were still busy with the Park Service rep, so Ian and I waited nearby.

We were facing Lower Manhattan. It was late afternoon, and the sun was still plenty bright in a clear, blue sky. "The weather folks say it'll be clear and sunny for the rest of the week. Coincidence, or is one of Tia's minions a weather wizard?"

"There is no such thing," Mortimer Winters said from behind us.

I jumped and Ruby growled.

"My apologies, Agent Fraser. Ruby."

I patted Ruby's shoulder. "No problem. We're just nervous."

"Understandable. Vivienne wanted me to tell you that her sister is not here. There is a presence inside the walls we both sense but cannot identify. The presence is also sensing us."

I glanced over at the boss. Sandra and Zyta had joined her.

"Vivienne is describing the presence to Commander Kokkinos," he added. "Hopefully she will confirm it is Stheno."

It wasn't terrifying in the least that an ancient gorgon could be slithering around behind those granite walls when just yards away, stonemasons were going about their work and tourists were snapping pictures of anything they found interesting. The sun was shining, birds were singing—and any moment, Stheno could dissolve those walls, slither out, and kill us all.

Nah, not terrifying at all. Not even mildly creepy.

I rubbed Ruby's ears. Good PTSD puppy.

I told Mortimer about the portal.

"Interesting. I wouldn't think Tiamat would want us to find her pocket dimension. Perhaps its creator needed to make it obvious so Tiamat could find it."

I hadn't considered that possibility. I'd tell Kitty what I found. She'd be coming with us tonight to open the portal and get us in to the pocket dimension. If there was another portal I'd missed, I was confident she could find and open it.

The rest of us were casually dressed, but Mortimer Winters was still in the dark, three-piece suit that was his work uniform. Though in deference to the sun, he was sporting a snazzy fedora and sunglasses.

I mentally scrambled back to the previous, and non-terrifying, topic. "So pocket dimensions are possible, but no one can move clouds around?"

"Correct. You implied it yourself. Pockets are small, especially when compared to the vastness of the sky and all that would be involved in affecting weather in even the slightest way. The weather pattern here began far above and even farther away, days, even weeks ago. It is dependent upon temperature and pressure, water or lack thereof, wind or calm, all interacting with each other and the lands or oceans over which they were formed or passed. Weather encompasses the world, with a complexity that is difficult to comprehend let alone be manipulated by us lowly mortals, even those of us able to use magic. As to pocket dimensions, I would be surprised if Tiamat doesn't have Stheno and the Aegis tucked away in one. The interior expanse of a pocket dimension is not limited by its exterior measurements. Tiamat could have the pocket be as small as one of the fort's star points, but inside be as large and lavish as she would like. I understand from Vivienne that this pocket dimension would be the work of Isidor Silvanus. He's her expert. If he was unavailable, we may be dealing with Gerald Blackburn's work, though he's not as talented as Isidor."

"Gerald's in town," I said. "Along with Griselda and Marek. We haven't heard anything about Isidor being here. And I'd be a happy girl if it stayed that way."

Jet engines roared overhead as a plane descended to land at LaGuardia. We all briefly glanced up.

Mortimer scowled. "That makes this even more dangerous. The Aegis's beam will be reflected all over the city. The Statue of Liberty is in LaGuardia's flight path."

A sick realization rolled though me. Pilots pointed out the Statue of Liberty to passengers. If it was your first time in New York, you looked.

"Thousands more deaths," Mortimer was saying. "Pilots turned to stone. Planes coming down, crashing into buildings, neighborhoods." He slowly turned, taking in the areas around Liberty Island. "9/11 would pale in comparison."

Across the harbor, one building stood out from all the others, both in height and reflective surface. The entire building was a multifaceted mirror.

One World Trade Center.

Oh no.

"Ian, look," I breathed.

"I see it."

"I'd like to say, 'she wouldn't,' but I know she would."

"That must be her main reflection point," Mortimer told us. "It's in a direct line from the torch. Light reflected from there would reach for miles."

The original Twin Towers had been destroyed by terrorists and thousands had died. Tomorrow, the cabal terrorists planned to leave the building untouched, but still use it to kill. This time millions would perish. Unless we stopped it.

"I'm not quite sure I understand how Tia plans to pull this off," I said. "She probably wants to use the Aegis from the torch balcony for maximum effect. It's closed, but Tia wouldn't care about that. I guess she could use one of Tarbert's disks. If she's invisible, she can go anywhere she wants, and switch off the disk when she's ready to rock and roll." I leaned my head way back to look up at the torch. "Anyone down here will see her up there, but after she activates the Aegis, it'll be too late to do anything about it." I remembered the Aegis's blinding flash at Quinn and Carlos. They'd instantly lost most of their minds—and then their lives. Any tourists here tomorrow morning would have the same thing happen to them.

We were standing at ground zero.

"Mortimer, I need you to look at something," Ms. Sagadraco said over our comms.

"On my way," the mage replied. "If you'll excuse me."

"Of course."

The boss hadn't asked us to come over, so Ian and I stayed put. There was plenty of time to tell her about the portal. I looked up at Lady Liberty's raised arm. I could see the railing and the top of the 24-karat gold-plated torch. There were sixteen spotlights around the torch to illuminate it at night. Even Vivienne Sagadraco's billions hadn't been able to get us up there. Ever since an explosion in New York Harbor in 1916, the torch had been closed to visitors. Park Service staff had to climb a narrow, forty-foot ladder to maintain the spotlights.

Part of what I wanted to look for were signs that Tiamat or her mage minions had added any hardware to the torch base or railing, then warded it to keep it from being seen. They'd need to mount the Aegis up there, though maybe Tiamat planned to hold the Aegis herself. Only Zeus and Athena had ever wielded the Aegis. Oh yeah, Tia wanted to do it herself.

I shielded my eyes with my hand, trying to see it better.

"You can look at it on my phone."

I squinted at my partner. "Pardon?"

"EarthCam. There are cameras on the torch railing with live shots around the clock of the torch, the crown, and the harbor. Kenji's people are monitoring them for any signs of tampering."

"The cameras or the torch?"

"Both. Kenji has software that can detect if surveillance footage has been put on a loop. His people went back over the past week, and for the past three mornings, all between four and five a.m., the torch feed was 'unavailable' for seventeen minutes." Ian was intent on his screen and frowning. "Well, you could look at it on my phone if it was working. No signal and the battery's down to ten percent. I just charged it."

"That doesn't sound suspicious at all."

"Not in the least."

My cuff shocked me. "Ow, crap!"

Ian rolled his shoulders. "Lugh's making himself felt, too."

My partner was wearing a light jacket, but I could just see the spear's glow coming from under his collar.

Then I felt the cause, or at least the trigger.

Mortimer Winters was standing at the fort's outer wall, a hand resting on one of the granite blocks. To anyone who wasn't a magic sensitive, it didn't look in the least bit odd, merely a well-dressed older gentleman admiring the quality of the stone. To those of us who were sensitive, it was as if Godzilla had hauled off and punched it. A surge of ancient power shot from Mortimer through the wall and into anything or anyone inside.

Zyta Kokkinos was standing just inside the fence. She went rigid.

Ruby howled and nearly pulled me off my feet trying to get to where Mortimer was standing.

And the Aegis rang like a giant silver bell.

At least I think it rang. A squeal of feedback from my comms might have just punctured my eardrum. I jerked it out. Ian did the same and spat a few choice words.

No one else heard him because they were hearing, feeling, and seeing everything else.

All around us, cameras and phones became too hot to hold and were being dropped and tossed. Two skid steers carrying pallets of granite blocks jerked in fits and starts, then stopped, smoke billowing from their overheated engines. Spotlights around Lady Liberty's base and around the torch railing popped, exploded, and showered tourists with sparks and glass. And something must have blown up in the museum and shops inside the base that sent people running outside, tourists and park staff alike.

Dang, Mortimer. When he rang a doorbell, he didn't mess around. That was exactly what he'd done. I guess we needed to be sure who was home and if the Aegis was there.

Mission accomplished.

Vivienne Sagadraco stood beside her senior mage with a look of grim satisfaction. She had her confirmation. The Aegis and Stheno were here. The boss was done playing around and she wanted her sister to know it.

Good for her.

She and Mortimer shook hands with the Park Service representative and the construction company foreman.

"Meet at the helicopter," she told me telepathically.

I relayed the message to Ian.

"We'll return tonight," she continued, *"and we won't leave without the Aegis. In the meantime, we have much to do."*

27

"My apologies," Ms. Sagadraco said once we were airborne. "I dislike overt actions, especially in public, but I was left with no choice. I apologize for any damage or injuries."

"That was my fault, ma'am," Mortimer said. "The wards on that pocket dimension were unexpectedly strong. You wanted confirmation of who and what was inside, so I pushed."

And blew out every electronic on Liberty Island, and those of hundreds of tourists. That was some push. Fortunately, the helicopter was unaffected. All SPI vehicles were equipped with a device to keep them from being tampered with, either mechanically or magically.

"I don't think anyone was seriously hurt," Ian said. "My ears are fine. Everybody else?"

They all nodded, and I joined in even though my right ear was still ringing. I'd deal with it. I knew I wasn't alone. Half the tourists being herded to the dock as we were taking off had been shaking their heads or rubbing their ears. Our Park Service tour guide said they were closing the island for the rest of the day to assess the damage, which worked in our favor.

"Did you sense Tiamat?" I asked.

Ms. Sagadraco shook her head. "I did not."

The pilot passed a headset back to the boss.

"I felt Stheno scream," Zyta said. "Whatever you did hurt her. Not critically, but she felt it."

"I'm sorry, Commander Kokkin—"

"Don't. I needed it, and she deserved it, and more. Tonight, I'll finish her off." Zyta glanced at Sandra. "With SPI help. It'll take all of us. That was my first contact with her since before I left for Prague. Even after what she did to my sisters, I had doubts about killing her. Those doubts are gone. She wanted to hurt us and enjoyed every life she took. There's no trace of the Stheno I knew. You surprised her. We won't catch her unawares again."

Vivienne Sagadraco held up her hand for quiet. She had put on the headset. "Go ahead, Alain." She listened and frowned, then put one hand over the mic. "The body cams didn't work on the island," she told us. "When we landed, all communication with headquarters was cut off." She removed her hand. "Alain, how did—" She listened intently and went absolutely still. "When? You sent Helena and Sophia? Good." More listening. "Yes, please patch him through." As she listened to whoever the new guy was, her lips narrowed into a thin line. It was the only part of her that moved. She didn't even seem to be breathing. "You did the right thing," she told him. She glanced out the helicopter's front window. "We can be there within five minutes. Is the roof landing pad available? Good. We'll be there soon."

I expected her to tell Mortimer, Ian, or Sandra what had happened.

When she looked at me, I stopped breathing.

Oh no.

"Makenna, that was Gethen. Stheno attacked Rake through the TV monitor. He's alive. Sophia and Helena are with him now keeping him stable."

Oh God, no.

I knew an older gorgon could turn a younger one to stone. They could also reverse the glare of a younger one. Helena had once saved Yasha that way.

Stheno was the oldest living gorgon. Sophia was younger. It wouldn't work.

"Stheno is older than Sophia. She can't reverse—" I heard myself say.

"By less than a year," Zyta hurried to assure me.

All I could see were Quinn and Carlos's faces forever marbleized in terror before Mortimer had broken their bodies to free their trapped souls. Euryale said Stheno had killed them to strengthen herself. She might have attacked Rake for the same reason.

Because of what we'd just done on the island.

No, no.

"How long ago?" I managed.

"Gethen said less than fifteen minutes ago. By taking out

our communications on the island, Tiamat or Stheno kept anyone contacting us."

I hadn't felt the attack. I'd always known when Rake was in trouble. Tia had taken out both out both types of communication, manmade and magical.

Ian put his arm around me and pulled me close. I lost all track of time as the helicopter descended into the shadowed canyon between the high-rises surrounding the Regor Regency and settled on the roof.

One of Rake's bodyguards waited grim-faced by the door that led into the hotel. I'd been this way many times before when Rake and I returned from a weekend upstate. On the other side of the door was a room with an elevator that went down into the hotel, and a security door that opened into the penthouse's foyer.

Getting from the helicopter to the foyer was a blur.

Once inside, I broke away from Ian and ran into the living room.

Time was standing still, and so did I.

Rake was on his back on the floor inside his conjuring circle. The rug covering the silver floor with its etched protective spells had been torn aside. The mage robe Rake had worn yesterday covered his body like a blanket. The wall-mounted TV where Euryale had appeared looked like it'd been hit by a fireball, presumably thrown by the goblin stalking before the fireplace, enraged he couldn't do the same to Stheno—or do any more to help Rake.

Sophia Galanis knelt on the floor just outside the circle, her pale blue eyes calm and steadily gazing into Rake's still warm and dark ones. He saw me and winked.

I ran to the circle and fell to my knees beside Sophia, vision blurred with tears.

Rake's lips twitched, trying to smile. "Now you know how…I felt when I heard…Stheno glared you." He closed his eyes and swallowed painfully. Just that small effort had cost him.

"Stop talking!"

He talked. Or at least tried. Then he took a shuddering breath and opened his eyes. *"How about this?"* said his voice inside my head.

I started to reach for him, and the protective shield crackled and snapped in warning.

The silver circle with its protective spells, even more protections woven into the silk and velvet of his robes. Sophia's eyes locked with his.

All keeping him alive, keeping him from turning to stone.

Helena appeared at my side. "His goblin physiology may be helping. Sophia can keep it from going further, for now."

Sophia kept her eyes on Rake's. "With his help, I may be able to reverse some of what was done, but I can't heal him without the Aegis."

"It heals?"

Sophia nodded once. "Medusa's gaze can kill, or it can heal. It depends on the person wielding it."

"Can you do it?"

"Medusa was my friend. She loved me and I her. I believe she would do this for me."

I touched my lips to my hand then held it up just outside the invisible barrier. *"I love you,"* I told him silently. *"You're going to be fine."*

"Of course, I am." Rake smoothly inhaled and exhaled. *"It's definitely easier to talk this way. Gethen will tell you everything. Let me get back to work."*

"Lady Makenna." Gethen's hand appeared beside me, an offer to help me stand. I took it.

We followed Gethen into the dining room. He closed the door behind us, then turned to face us, hands clenched into fists by his sides. A red glow seeped from beneath his fingers. His eyes were blazing. "I received a call almost half an hour ago from you, Commander Kokkinos. Euryale wanted to speak with Rake."

Zyta stared at him in disbelief. "I made no such call. I was on Liberty Island with—"

"Lady Makenna, did she make any calls?"

I didn't know what she had or hadn't done. I'd been with Ian and Mortimer, not Zyta. Gethen was barely controlling himself, and most of what we knew about Zyta had come from Zyta herself. One word from me, and Gethen would kill her where she stood, risk of her glare be damned.

"Gethen, I trust Zyta. I was with Ian and Mortimer, but if Zyta says she didn't make that call, she didn't."

"It sounded exactly like her."

Sandra spoke. "She was with me on Liberty Island. The entire time. She made no calls."

"My sister could easily mimic the voice of another," Ms. Sagadraco told Gethen. "She did it to plant doubt. She fears us or she would not risk striking so brazenly. Before we left for Liberty Island, I called Rake and Kitty to request their help in opening the pocket dimension if we found one on the island." She paused, then swore under her breath. "Ian, call Kitty and—"

"On it." Ian pulled his phone out, then remembered it was fried. "Gethen, can I—"

Gethen unlocked his phone and gave it to him, and Ian left the room.

"Have Kitty picked up and taken to headquarters," Ms. Sagadraco told him.

"And tell her not to take any Zoom calls," Gethen shouted after him. His shoulders slumped. "Forgive me, Commander Kokkinos."

"Zyta, please. And no forgiveness is necessary. Stheno and Tiamat have deeply hurt us all. We're exhausted and our nerves are at the breaking point, which is how they want us. But we won't break. We will do what must be done—starting with the two of them. And we will reclaim the Aegis and restore Governor Danescu to full health. This I swear."

When I'd seen Stheno, it'd been on a video and she'd been cloaked. Rake's exposure had been live. "Did he look directly at her?"

Gethen almost smiled. "Goblins are naturally paranoid. Rake even more so. He was off to the side when she appeared on the monitor. He'd already closed his eyes and was diving out of range when he saw it wasn't Euryale. His exposure was a fraction of a second. Then she screamed in what sounded like pain. I shattered the monitor, then I ripped the carpet off the circle, carried Rake to it, and covered him with his robe. He told me to get Sophia or Helena." He looked at Ms. Sagadraco. "I tried to call you, but it didn't go through. Then I called Alain. He sent Sophia and Helena through SPI's mirror. He then patched me through to the helicopter." Gethen paused. "Neither Rake nor I had time to hurt her. I don't know what did."

"That would be Mortimer," I said. "He punched the pocket dimension she was in. Hard."

Gethen stepped forward, hand extended. Mortimer accepted his hand and shook it. "Sir, you have my undying gratitude—and Rake's as well, at least you will when I tell him. He'll want to shake your hand, too, when he's back on his feet."

When, not if. From Gethen's lips to God's ears.

Two days ago, Vivienne Sagadraco had hugged Mortimer to comfort him.

I hugged him now in gratitude. When I let him go, the mage looked slightly embarrassed, but there was a little smile there, too.

Ian came back in. "Kitty's fine. I told her to close the bakery and lock the doors. No phone, laptop, or TV monitors. I called Alain. He's dispatching Yasha and a team to bring her to headquarters."

"Is there any possibility of obtaining the Queen of Dreams?" Ms. Sagadraco asked.

I'd forgotten about that. The goblin diamond was one of the Dragon Eggs. It could cure any disease or condition. That would solve—

"We thought of that," Gethen replied. "All mirrors and communications are down between here and the palace. Our end is fine, the problem is on their side. Dr. Jules, our hotel healer, is unable to help. Gorgons are unique to this world."

Dammit.

Helena was listening by the now open door. "I'm sorry to have to say this, but we need the Aegis within twelve hours. Rake will remain stable and may even improve, but after that, the effects of Stheno's glare will begin to override what Sophia is able to do."

I glanced down at my watch. 5:26. Rake had until just before dawn tomorrow.

We returned to the living room. Gethen stopped. "I want to go with you, but I need to remain here."

"Exactly," I told him. "You saved him once; you may need to do it again. If it hadn't been for you, he wouldn't have had a chance. He needs you here. If Tia finds out Rake is still alive, she might try something else."

Gethen glanced at Rake. "The hotel itself helped and is continuing to help," he said quietly. "Rake cleaned the magical stain from the hotel and brought it back to life. He saved it, and today it saved him."

Twelve hours to keep Rake and thousands, maybe millions, of New Yorkers from being turned to stone. I was determined that Stheno and Tiamat had even less time remaining in their evil lives.

I had to tilt my head back to look into Gethen's eyes. "Tiamat and Stheno started this. We're going to finish it."

Gethen's expression went utterly blank. Goblins didn't show any emotions that they didn't want you to see. For the next twelve hours, Gethen Nazar would be everything he had to be for Rake.

Gethen extended his hand and forearm to me. I knew what this was. A goblin warrior hand grip, given between brothers- and sisters-in-arms on the battlefield. Exchanged before the fighting started as encouragement—and in case there wasn't an after.

I clenched my jaw and accepted it.

Gethen clasped my forearm around my father's cuff, his big hand wrapping entirely around it. My hand could only grasp part of his forearm.

"You can, and you will," he said solemnly.

"I—or someone—will be back before dawn tomorrow. With the Aegis. I promise."

"It will be you." It was a pronouncement, said with utter certainty.

I replied with a tight nod. I couldn't get any words past the knot in my throat.

Gethen released my arm, and my gaze went to Rake and Sophia. I wanted to go to him, just for a few moments, but the last thing I wanted was to distract either of them from the work they were doing.

Helena appeared silently by my side. "We'll remain here with him until you return with the Aegis."

"Thank you." I took a deep breath and said with a lot more confidence than I felt, "I'll do the rest."

Vivienne Sagadraco stepped up and put her arm around my shoulder. "*We* will do the rest."

28

We got back to headquarters with a little more than an hour until full dark. None of us liked it, but we had to wait until then to return to Liberty Island. I didn't know the logistics yet, but when I needed to know someone would tell me. I had more than enough ricocheting in my head. Too much. Besides, that wasn't my job. My job was what it always was. See portals and monsters that everyone else couldn't, pepper the monsters with paintballs, then get out of the way so the commandos could fill them with lead, silver, or whatever would kill them.

I was determined to stay focused. I'd tried to act calm and confident in front of Rake and Gethen, and I was starting to feel that way, if only a little. What was the saying? Fake it until you make it. Rake was going to be fine. I'd told him he was, and he'd agreed with me. I simply wouldn't allow myself to consider any other outcome. Not now.

Ian and I were on our way down to the commando armory and staging area. We'd made a stop by our desks where we kept our weapons. Kenji fell into step with us and caught us up with what had happened while we were gone.

Kenji was an avid collector of comics, movie memorabilia, and dirt on supernatural-owned, multinational corporations.

He told us he'd located Viktor Kain—ancient dragon, tsar of the Russian mafia, incinerator of failed lackeys, and Vivienne Sagadraco's number two enemy, right behind her draconic sis who had perpetual dibs on the numero uno spot.

"Vik's at the Baikonur Cosmodrome," Kenji said. "Arrived two weeks ago."

I frowned. "That place sounds familiar."

"Russian spaceport in Kazakhstan," Ian said. "Flights to the International Space Station launch from there."

That was not good. I would've felt dread, but I was all dreaded out.

"A couple of years ago," Kenji continued, "Viktor bought a Russian media company. In two days, the company is launching a new satellite into orbit. The rocket is on the launchpad with the satellite, but a 'critical component' hasn't been installed yet. Bob and Rob theorize he's waiting on the Aegis. They'll attach it like a mirror, launch it into space, and stone the planet one time zone at a time."

Ian and I traded a sharp glance. Euryale had heard Tiamat tell Stheno that they would send the Aegis to the heavens and cleanse this world of its mortal stain.

I pushed the button for the elevator. Jonathan Tarbert had

called Tia a Bond villain. James Bond only had to deal with one villain at a time. We got two. Lucky us.

"Global extortion," Ian said. "Depending on how precise he can make the beam, Viktor could take out entire countries, or target cities, sections of cities, or even individual buildings. Pay and you get to live, at least for another trip around the sun. Life or death subject to the highest bidder."

"Or if your enemies pay more," Kenji pointed out, "you still get stoned."

And Tia planned to use New York as the test run.

The elevator arrived. Ian and I got on. So did Kenji.

"You're going with us?" I asked.

He grinned. "You guys are about to get Jonathan Tarbert's negator. I haven't seen it in action yet."

"Negator?" Ian pushed the button for Sublevel 3.

"It negates the effects of the cloaking device. Roy pushed for calling it a 'negator.'"

I leaned against the back wall, resting while I could. "Let me guess, because of 'gator.'"

"You got it. Kind of catchy."

"Between Janus and then Tiamat talking to Stheno in her sleep and Viktor buying a company that uses satellites, they *have* been planning this for years."

That reminded me of something Rake had said several years ago. Evil individuals' schedules are usually quite full. Villainy—when you truly commit to it—is time consuming.

We couldn't do anything about Viktor, at least not now, but he could forget about Tiamat delivering that critical component.

The elevator stopped and the doors opened. Time to lock and load.

When it comes to hunting monsters for a living, you could be all grim about it, or you could consider it the ultimate adventure. Our commandos went with the classic "It's not a job, it's an adventure."

Think positive, be confident, and heck, even have some fun.

There was nothing wrong with enjoying and taking pride in your work.

Yes, you were killing, but you were killing things that needed killing. A successful mission could save hundreds, thousands, or even millions of people. That right there is some serious job satisfaction.

We were in SPI's commando armory and staging area. I hadn't seen our commandos this pumped up in years. Not since the possibility that a gazillion baby grendels had hatched and were on the loose under Times Square on New Year's Eve.

Things that caused normal people to freeze in their tracks or flee and keep fleeing made our commandos go all hooah. They weren't worried about being killed; they were busy figuring out the quickest and most efficient way to kill Stheno, and Tiamat if they got lucky. A proactive bunch, our commandos. Though the boss had dibs on Tia. We all knew their history, or at least the parts Ms. Sagadraco had shared with us. What we did know put the boss at the head of the line. If she wanted help, our folks would be glad to step up and provide it.

Zyta had gotten over any guilt for killing Stheno. Her enthusiasm was contagious. Actually, it gave our folks the green light to express what they'd been suppressing out of consideration for her.

We knew we were going to Liberty Island and into a pocket dimension inside Fort Wood. Our people had been told Mortimer had essentially kicked the door to get confirmation that the Aegis was there. Recovering the Aegis was the critical goal. Stheno and Tiamat were secondary. Stheno already knew we were there. Wherever Tia was, I couldn't see her not knowing by now as well. Having the element of surprise was good, but none of our commandos seemed in the least bit bothered that we no longer had it.

I spotted Kitty across the room talking with Yasha. If Yasha was here, he was going as Kitty's bodyguard. Pocket dimensions had at least one way in. I'd found one of them in the fort's outer wall. I could find portals, but I couldn't open them. That was Kitty's superpower. She could open them, and slam 'em shut when you had a horde of demons on your tail. To make sure Stheno didn't try to leave with the Aegis in the next few hours, the merfolk were in the water surrounding Liberty Island. They'd send Ian a telepathic message if Stheno tried to take another swim.

What was still a big question mark was how big the inside of the pocket dimension was. If Isidor Silvanus had had a hand in creating it, we could be looking at anything from the size of a tollbooth to…well, pretty much anything. Tiamat would want Stheno to be comfortable, and the gorgon was an eight-footer. Tiamat in her dragon form was three stories tall, so we knew the space would at least have high ceilings. We'd previously dealt with two Isidor-crafted pocket dimensions—the Hell's anteroom/cavern containing a small lake of molten brimstone, and the one that'd completely engulfed the Regor Regency. Since those had both been supersized, we assumed he'd made a similar-sized abode for Stheno and Tiamat—and the unknown number and species of guards certain to be between us and them.

Three teams would be going. Our two commando teams and Zyta's team of six gorgon commandos.

I'd been on multiple missions with our two teams, though I knew some of them better than others. I trusted these men and women with my life. Our commandos were a mixed bag of races and species who worked flawlessly together. We had humans, elves, goblins, vampires, werewolves, and a couple of supernatural species I hadn't been aware existed until I started working here.

I'd become particularly close to Liz and Calvin. Rake and I had even double-dated with them a couple of times. They were another of SPI's workplace romances, even though neither were what you'd call romantic. Calvin had done three tours in Iraq as an army infantryman and field medic. He was a foot taller than me and had a bull neck, bald head, and biceps the size of my thighs. Liz was a former Marine who could've shown up Ellen Ripley in *Alien*. She and Calvin were a monster-hunting dynamic duo.

Sandra let out a whistle that instantly stopped all conversation and weapon prep.

Everyone quickly found a seat. The briefing room was adjacent to the armory and had chairs lined up in rows with a screen and whiteboard at the front. Ian and I took seats at the back. Kitty and Yasha joined us. Our people left the front row vacant for Zyta and her six gorgons. Yes, we trusted Zyta, but her team had just arrived, and I guess our folks didn't want to tempt fate by having gorgons sitting behind them, even though you had to lock eyes with a gorgon for the glare to work. The gorgon commander took a seat with a bemused smile, her team following suit. Just to be extra cautious, half of our commandos were wearing their gorgon goggles. The others had theirs perched on their heads or hanging on their straps around their necks. We didn't know if they'd work against Stheno, and there was only one way to test them. If they worked, they worked. If they didn't, they didn't. We'd find out soon enough.

"We'll be taking a dinner cruise to Liberty Island," Sandra said. "When we get close, Cate and Parker will cloak the boat." She nodded to indicate a pair of battlemages seated on the front row. "If the electricity's back up by then, Director Winters will cause a temporary blackout on Liberty Island, including the spotlights on the statue. Mac and Kitty will confirm the portal entrance to the pocket dimension. Kitty will open it, we'll go in, then Director Winters will turn the lights back on. Two of his battlemages will remain with the boat and keep it docked, cloaked, and safe until our return."

"Once we find Stheno, Commander Kokkinos and her team will take the lead and use the mirror. She considers Stheno their responsibility and has requested to take the brunt of the first attack."

You could've heard an itty-bitty bullet casing drop. Zyta blamed herself for Stheno's escape and didn't want anyone other than her and her team to risk their lives if possible.

"Euryale will meet us on the island and go with us into the pocket dimension. According to Commander Kokkinos,

Euryale considers this her fight. She wants to finish what she started in that tunnel without risking anyone else. Euryale is the only gorgon capable of killing Stheno with a glare. Thanks to Commander Kokkinos's knowledge, we now know Stheno's weak points. There aren't many, but they can be exploited. We'll use quick, micro-targeted attacks. Strike and move. Make room for the next team member."

"Sharing is caring," said a voice from the center of the seated teams. A couple of snickers and snorts followed.

"We don't know what we will face in terms of terrain or opposition," Sandra continued. "In other words, it's just another day at the office. Eliminating Stheno is *a* goal, but that's secondary to recovering the Aegis. Snag it, bag it, and get it to Rake."

Sandra met my eyes with a solemn nod. "We couldn't save Carlos and Quinn, but we can and will save Rake. He's one of our own." Then her attention went to the back of the room, just behind me and Ian. "We have one last team member joining us."

Everyone turned to see who it was.

When I saw, I gasped, then grinned.

It was Vivienne Sagadraco. The dark business suit had been replaced with body armor. Not the matte-black armor our commandos wore. The boss was rocking seriously custom body armor with scales like her blue dragon form, neck to toe. A helmet resembling a stylized dragon head was tucked under one steel-scaled arm.

Her eyes were glittering. "Is there room for one more?"

29

"Oh hell, yes!" Roy Benoit blurted. "Uh, ma'am."

There were grins, approving nods, and fist bumps going around.

As Ms. Sagadraco made her way to the front of the room, Ian leaned toward my ear. "The boss lady's thrown down with us before. You're in for a treat."

"She's that good?" Not that I was surprised.

"Better than. She means to have her sister's head tucked under her other arm before this is over."

I was all for that. I also understood why she was going with us. Like Euryale, Vivienne Sagadraco considered her sister to be her responsibility.

A couple of minutes later, Alain Moreau arrived with Dr. Jonathan Tarbert and the Roberts—and the new negators.

They looked like a wristwatch with a button on the side. Press button, see cloaked monsters—though that applied only to monsters wearing Tarbert's other invention, the hockey puck of hiding. Spotting any beasties that used magic or other means to keep us from seeing them was still up to me.

To demonstrate, Mr. Moreau picked up one of the hockey pucks, activated it, and disappeared. I could still see him, as I'd been able to see the grendels and Tiamat years ago. Tarbert handed a negator to Roy, who put it on his wrist and pressed the button on the side. From the reactions of the commandos, they could now see him, too. They gathered around for further instructions and distribution.

I made my way over to Ms. Sagadraco. "How much do you trust him and those?"

"I trust the devices. The Roberts have thoroughly tested each one. I mostly trust Dr. Tarbert. He's been closely watched. As a former government contractor, Dr. Tarbert is accustomed to being monitored." She gave me a quick smile. "I also told him I'm putting the lives of my agents in his hands and would be most disappointed if any harm came to them because of his work. He understood perfectly."

I grinned and nodded in approval. "Ketchup packet, meet foot."

Ms. Sagadraco considered it. "Grisly, but effective."

"If Tarbert screws us over, everyone in this room will be lining up for the honor of hosing your foot off."

The negators were being given to team leaders, snipers, and those commandos who were exceptionally gifted when it came to killing monsters in one-on-one combat. Ian was considered one of those even though he technically wasn't a commando.

I knew one other who had more hunting experience than everyone in this room combined.

My father.

As the present incarnation of Cernunnos, my dad had inherited the hunting knowledge of all previous Masters of the Wild Hunt. And with the final death of the First Master of the Wild Hunt, my dad had inherited his skills as well. The First Master had hunted most of the great dragons to extinction. If anyone would have tips on how to take out Tiamat and Stheno, it would be my father.

I hadn't wanted to make a habit of running to him for help, but if I could get information that could save the lives of the men and women in this room, millions of New Yorkers, and billions of people around the world, I at least needed to ask.

Though if I asked, he would come.

I saw Rake lying in that circle, all but paralyzed. Sophia and his own weakened magic all that was keeping him alive. If Stheno was killing mages to top off her tank, Dad would be a feast.

I couldn't bear to lose my father and Rake.

"Mac."

I jumped.

It was Ian. He was right in front of me, and I hadn't seen or heard him until he'd said my name.

Way to be alert, Mac.

"I tried not to startle you," he said. "We're leaving in about ten minutes."

"Good." I went to where we'd been sitting and started gathering my gear.

Ian followed me. "Do you need to talk about it?" he asked quietly.

"Not really, but I do need another brain on this. Mine's not working too well right now." I told him what I'd been thinking—and the decision I didn't know how to make.

He studied my face as I spoke. "That's easy," he said when I'd finished.

"It is?"

"Yep. It's not your decision. It's your father's."

"That's not helpful."

"No, it's helpful. It's just not what you want to hear."

Ian was right. I didn't want to hear that, either. "If I call him for advice, he'll come. But if I don't call, and people die…" I felt myself tearing up. Stop it, Mac. "He might know how to get the Aegis back or kill Stheno with less risk. He's the expert hunter. He could tell us how to do it, but I don't want him coming here. I won't take that chance with his life. Mom just got him back. I just got a father, period. I can't do that to her."

"And if he and your mother lose you on Liberty Island?"

That I knew the answer to. "Then I won't be here for them to yell at."

"And how will he feel to lose the daughter he's only known for two months?"

I just looked at him. "I hate it when you use logic."

My partner gave me an aw-shucks grin and shrug. "It's one of my many gifts." The grin vanished. "Don't take this the wrong way, but you're too emotionally involved."

"How else am I supposed to be? The man I love is dying from the outside in. And unless I—"

"Unless *we*. We're all going in, not just you."

"But I'm the—"

Ian held up his wrist with its new negator. "Tarbert's new

gadget works, so you won't be the only seer on this mission." He looked at someone over my head and held up five fingers.

"You're asking them to wait while I talk to Dad, aren't you?"

"We've got time until full dark. This is five minutes worth taking."

We went into the now empty commando locker room. I sat on one of the benches and put my arm with the cuff across my chest and over my heart. I bowed my head over it.

I called out to him in my mind.

Nothing. Just the buzzing of florescent lights overhead.

I took a deep and hopefully calming breath and tried again.

Still nothing.

"Oh great," I muttered. "Now I have to worry about Dad, too."

"I recall you saying there might be times when you couldn't reach him. This is merely one of those."

"The timing could be better."

"Timing could always be better. It's the story of my entire career." He stood and gave me a wink. "Don't worry, we've got this. Let's go."

Vivienne Sagadraco had made it a point to own strategic businesses near SPI offices. Not only in New York, but worldwide.

After the events on North Brother Island, where our commandos had to rely on a pair of small party boats to get them there—only to have those boats get blown up—the boss had purchased a dinner cruise company.

Saga Cruises operated five yachts from a terminal near Chelsea Piers that could be booked for weddings, private parties, corporate events, bar and bat mitzvahs, charity galas, and of course dinner cruises. One yacht was always kept available for SPI use.

Tonight, we would be on the *Saga Princess*. The crews were clued in to SPI and the supernatural, so no one batted an eye at commandos disembarking from the two small tour buses with blacked-out windows. And the catering trucks that had arrived before us hadn't been carrying food.

Yasha still looked human, but Ruby was her adorable-to-us but imposing-to-others hellhound self. Yasha would go werewolf once we were on Liberty Island. Both would be invaluable in finding Stheno before she found us.

This wasn't the first time we'd fought on an island for the survival of many. North Brother Island had been to save all the supernaturals in the tristate area. Bannerman Island had been to save Ian and millions of others if the Fomorians had been freed from their curse. Liberty Island was for every living being on the planet. Not only were the stakes higher, but an island in the middle of New York Harbor was as public as it got.

We left the terminal later than usual for a dinner cruise. Once we were out on the Hudson River, the sun had already set with only a dark orange glow barely visible behind the Statue of Liberty. We needed full dark before we could ward the yacht and approach the island's dock.

There would be six nighttime guards on duty. Two would be in the security office monitoring the dozens of cameras inside and outside the statue as well as the entire island, covering anywhere tourists were supposed to be and not supposed to be. Part of Mortimer Winters's job would be to temporarily take down all security cameras along with the lights. Four of the battlemages assigned to our commandos would ward us for sight and sound. We'd have three minutes to get where we needed to be, and Kitty would have maybe another three to get us inside. No pressure on Kitty.

I'd only sensed one portal in Fort Wood's outer wall. I could tell it'd been there awhile, and was stable. I didn't trust it, any of it. It was too obvious to anyone who could see a portal. Like Ian said, it was like a big flashing arrow with "Enter evil gorgon lair here" in neon letters. I hoped it was still there—neon lights and all—or this was going to be a real short trip.

Our larger weapons were waiting for us on board. I checked and rechecked my guns—both paintball and bullet. My knives were always sharp, especially the one my dad had given me. He'd told me I'd never need to sharpen it. Even Harald Siggurson hadn't been able to determine the blade's metal. However, he'd confirmed nothing would ever nick or dull it. I was wearing body armor, but the left arm had been modified to accommodate my dad's cuff, leaving it exposed. The shine would never dull, but I still took a cloth and buffed it, more to occupy myself than anything.

"Still not there?" I whispered to Dad.

Silence.

I had to try.

I put on my helmet, which automatically activated the built-in comms. Others were checking in with Kenji and I did the same. He'd be our lifeline, as he'd been many times before.

We had helmet-mounted cameras, so he'd see everything we saw.

I was just about to sit down and close my eyes for a few minutes when I saw Ian with his ancestor's medallion clutched in his fist, his gaze unfocused and looking out over the water. Then he silently spat one of his favorite words, turned and headed straight for Zyta.

Oh crap. I followed him.

"There's a gorgon in the water," Ian was saying. "She came from a Greek ship, in the North Cove Marina, the *Manticore*."

"Relax, it's Euryale. We borrowed the *Manticore* from a friend of the Sisterhood. Euryale will remain in the water until we dock, then join us on shore."

Ian blew out his breath. Yep, I wasn't the only one wound tight.

He nodded. "I'll tell the merfolk she's on our side, but to continue to keep an eye out for Tiamat's hydra."

Zyta blinked. "Excuse me?"

Ian and I hit the high points of magetech generators and Tia's attempt at keeping our agents and commandos busy.

Zyta huffed a laugh. "If the hydra's stupid enough to attack Euryale, you won't need to worry about it anymore."

Ian went to the bow to have a chat with the merfolk.

The sun had set behind the Statue of Liberty's pedestal. The *Saga Princess* would circle Liberty Island once, arriving at the dock under a full ward after Mortimer had knocked out the lights and security cameras.

Zyta's eyes were on Lady Liberty in the fading light. "The torch of one lone woman," she mused. "A goddess, freeing the prisoners, the enslaved, the victims. This would appeal to Stheno. She sees herself as a victim; and even after what she's done, she *is* a victim." Zyta gave a bitter little smile. "Athena would be pleased with how this will end. Stheno driven mad with her need for revenge, even though those who wronged her are no longer here for her to kill. It was easy enough for her to transfer her anger to humanity. They were the reason she could never leave the caves. Humans had the entire world. while she was the prisoner of her curse."

Suddenly, the lights went out on Liberty Island. We all looked at Mortimer Winters.

"That wasn't me."

Oh hell.

A series of muffled booms came from behind us. I knew that sound—electrical substations. In quick succession, sections of Manhattan and New Jersey went dark.

A total blackout.

30

New Yorkers don’t react well to blackouts.

We didn’t react well to our communications not working.

“This is so not needed,” I muttered.

“Take it easy, people,” Roy called out. “It’s probably just temporary, at least the comms.”

“So’s life,” someone muttered from the patch of darkness to my left.

The yacht’s emergency lights came on. That was all we needed to see each other. We had flashlights, helmet lights, and NVGs, but for now we didn’t need them.

Sandra’s voice came over my helmet’s headset. “Who can hear me?”

We all started checking in. We could still talk to each other, but Kenji was a no-show. He’d hacked into the island’s security cameras to feed us info on anything he saw that we needed to know. Our guardian angel was flying blind, and so were we.

"Negator test, folks," Roy said. He took out a disk, flipped it on, and vanished. I could see him.

Sandra activated her negator. "Gotcha."

"Yep," Ian said.

Zyta and the four sharpshooters could see him.

"Good." Roy turned off the disk and put it back in one of his armor's pouches.

Each of the team leaders had one of Tarbert's disks. We'd be going with magic to shield us from sight, not mechanicals, but our commandos were all about having backups for their backups.

Bringing both of our nine-member teams, plus the seven gorgons, and the boss sounded like a lot, but we might need every one of them. We were prepared for attrition. By the time we reached Stheno and Tiamat, we would need enough survivors to get the Aegis and get out.

One of the crew hesitantly approached Ms. Sagadraco. He spoke with her for less than a minute. The boss frowned, and the man made himself scarce.

"The yacht is running without instrumentation," she announced. "The captain can still dock at Liberty Island, but it'll take a little longer than expected."

One thing was greatly simplified by the blackout—warding the yacht from sight and sound. With the blackout, tour boats were headed back before it got full dark. If our instruments were wonky, so were theirs. No captain wanted to dock expensive tour boats in complete dark with no instruments.

Cate and Parker quickly went to the bow to get the ward in place once all other craft were out of our path. They'd do the same for us once we were on shore. Without Kenji, we didn't know where the Park Service security guards would be patrolling. With no electricity, they'd probably still be making the rounds, but they'd use flashlights now that the island's spotlights were out. That was no problem for our wards. The light would shine right through us as if we weren't there, same for the yacht.

Once the ward was in place, the crew got ready for docking. Cate extended the ward to cover them when they jumped to the dock to secure the lines. There was no sign of any security guards. Mortimer and his mages would maintain the wards on the yacht, while Cate and Parker rejoined their teams.

We all knew our jobs. Kitty and I were with Sandra's team, as were Ian, Yasha, and the boss. Parker warded the team, and we moved out. Roy's and Zyta's teams would wait for Euryale's arrival, then join us.

We went straight from the dock uphill to the base of the fort. Ruby and I were close behind Parker, scanning the granite walls that were nearly five times my height. One advantage to having the island's ridiculously bright spotlights out was that any other portals would be easier to see. There were none. The obvious entrance was our only entrance.

I gestured for Kitty to join me. I got two for one. Yasha wasn't about to let her go anywhere without him. He was still human, but his eyes had gone wolf. The better to see you with.

All I'd told Kitty about the portal was that it was suspiciously obvious. I wanted to see her reaction. What was "holy crap" to me might be normal for her. We rounded the corner and Kitty stopped in her tracks. After realizing she wasn't next to him, Yasha did the same.

Ruby stared at the portal and growled. She didn't trust it this afternoon, and she didn't trust it now.

"I see what you mean," Kitty whispered.

"Looks like something Wile E. Coyote would've built for the Road Runner, doesn't it?"

Kitty nodded. "All it's missing is a pile of birdseed out front. Someone *really* didn't want us to miss this."

"That's what bothers me."

"There are no other candidates?"

"Not a one and believe me, I looked."

"This is concerning."

"Yeah."

"Can you open it?" Sandra asked from directly behind us.

Kitty jumped. I would've, but my armor was too heavy.

"If they wanted us to see it, they want us to get in," Kitty told her.

"Then let's get it open."

I dropped back for a moment to where Ian waited. "Any opinions from Lugh?"

"Not a flicker. The cuff?"

"Not even a tickle."

That should've reassured us, but it didn't.

"Roy here," he said in our earpieces. *"We're joining you."* He paused. *"With a special guest."*

Special was the ultimate understatement.

I'd seen Euryale on-screen. I'd seen her sister in Quinn's memory. I'd seen Kenji's 3D hologram.

None of those prepared me for an eight-foot-tall gorgon slithering up the hill toward us. Ruby emitted a single whine and pressed her body against my hip.

Euryale moved like a cobra, holding her torso off the ground while her serpent back half flexed and coiled, sinuously moving her body forward. Also like a cobra, she was hypnotic. In that instant, I was even more grateful she'd be coming with us. Everyone would be getting a good look. By recovering from the shock and awe now, it'd be easier for them not to stare at Stheno when the time came. With her Milos viper hair, Euryale had to be nine feet or more. When the gorgon crested the top of the hill, Cate dropped the ward that'd kept the rest of our people from seeing her.

Stunned silence met the sight.

Kitty's full attention was on the portal, and it needed to stay that way.

I hurried over to her, leading Ruby with me. "How's it going?"

"Easy. Too easy. Another minute and we're in." Out of the corner of her eye she saw Yasha staring open-mouthed at Euryale. "What are you look—"

I put a hand on her shoulder, keeping her from turning around. "Not a thing, sweetie. Let's focus on the task at hand."

Zyta was quietly introducing Euryale to Vivienne Sagadraco, Sandra, and Roy.

A few seconds later, the portal unzipped like a tent.

Now my mouth fell open.

It was a cave, and it was huge. Stalagmites and stalactites met to form columns on either side of a wide path stretching into the distance. Every couple of columns had a torch embedded in the stone. The torches were lit and flickered in welcome.

Zyta Kokkinos appeared at my side, her eyes wide. "This is the entrance to our gorgon city caves in Greece."

"Uh, Kitty. Please tell me we're not in Greece."

A soft scrape of scales on stone came from directly behind me. I stiffened involuntarily. Zyta noticed.

"Makenna, this is Euryale. Sacred Mother, this is Makenna Fraser, mortal daughter of the Eternal Hunter."

I turned and looked up and up. I instinctively bowed my head. "It is an honor."

"You risk much for us, and I am grateful." Euryale peered inside, and the vipers on her head leaned forward with her. "This is not our home."

Whew. It was only a pocket dimension.

"I can see beyond the torches on either side of the path," she continued. "There are no walls, only shadows. This is but a copy of our home." The gorgon inhaled deeply. "I smell copper, iron, steel, and the oil of machines." Her eyes narrowed. "And my sister."

Vivienne Sagadraco stepped through the portal into the cave. She went to the first pair of columns and stopped. She remained motionless for nearly a minute. When she turned around, her eyes glowed blue with a slit pupil. Her dragon eyes. "My sister is now here as well—as is the Aegis." Her eyes glittered in predatory anticipation. "They know we are here and are waiting for us."

"You heard the lady," Roy said. "Let's get inside and get to work."

Kitty kept the portal open until all our people were inside.

Vivienne Sagadraco came back to the door. Mortimer met her there.

"Vivienne, they do not need me at the yacht. If you will not allow me to come with you, I will stand guard here."

"I want you to remain here."

Mortimer briefly bowed his head in disappointment. Vivienne took her old friend by the hand across the portal's threshold. "Mortimer, whatever happens, do not allow my sister to escape. If I do not return—"

"You will."

"If I do not return, hunt Tiamat to the ends of this world and beyond."

"I will not fail you, Vivienne."

"I know you won't." She kissed him on the cheek and stepped back inside.

Kitty closed the portal.

31

"Kill the redhead," Sandra was telling the commandos. "Not the brunette."

A good reminder. The gorgon sisters were nearly identical. In the dark and heat of battle, mistakes could be made.

Roy and Zyta were busy putting tape on Euryale's upper arms and wrists. We'd used it before to mark our teams to each other. The tape was highly visible with NVGs.

"Sorry, ma'am." Roy was looking anywhere except the gorgon's eyes—and her boobs. For a 7,200-year-old, they were plenty perky. Athena sure hadn't cursed those.

Ruby was busy sniffing Euryale's coils. She already knew Stheno's scent from tracking her in the tunnels. Ruby stopped sniffing Euryale, trotted down the tunnel a few yards and sniffed some more. She turned her head back to Euryale.

Sniff. Back down the path. Sniff, sniff. Then she trotted back to me, wagging her tail.

Ruby had Stheno's scent and was ready to go. Good girl.

Kitty's job was done for the moment. This was the entrance. She'd taught me that it might be the exit, or it might not. When the time came to run like hell and get out, there might be a closer way out. Pocket dimensions were rarely created without multiple exits. Isidor Silvanus had given himself at least one back door to his Hellpit dimension.

While I might be able to see a more convenient exit, Kitty was the only one who could open it. She had just become the person to be protected at all costs. Yasha had gone werewolf and was wholly focused on Kitty's safety. There would be nothing leisurely about our exit, and Kitty was our only key to the door out.

You didn't walk through a portal unless you were qualified to handle what you found—or what found you. Problem was, other than Tiamat and Stheno, we had no clue what was in here with us. We also had no choice.

So we were safe. Until we weren't.

I remembered what Rake had once told me. "I would rather know everything my adversary had planned, but there are times when it simply isn't possible. I accept that, plan for every contingency I can, and prepare to be flexible if it becomes necessary."

SPI was created to protect and to serve, and at no time in its history would that be truer than during the next few hours. Vivienne had put all her pieces into play. All or nothing. Win or lose. Live or die. If she was carrying any weapons, they weren't apparent to me.

Gorgon goggles on, negators activated, the three teams fanned out. Two mages on each team deployed a magical version of a camo shield in front of their teams as they moved. It wouldn't stop or deflect weapons, but it'd confuse the heck out of an opponent's aim. Most of our people also carried telescoping spears. Ian had the market cornered on magical spearheads, but our teams' steel spear tips had been forged with enough iron and silver to provide instant discomfort to the widest range of supernaturals.

Euryale was leading with the Greek team behind her. If there were any traps, they wanted to trip them. Next was Sandra's team, with Roy and his people as rear guard.

Still nothing from my cuff. A glance at Ian told me Lugh likewise didn't have anything to say. No glow. Ian had Lugh's spearhead on a telescoping shaft like SPI Scandinavia's grendel spears. When you were fighting something that could open you from stem to stern with one fingernail, keeping your distance went a long way to keeping you in one piece.

Euryale slithered in front of us, the faintest rasp of her scales on the stone floor the only sound. Stheno would move the same way. The gorgon sisters were slightly shorter than the grendels, and probably just as quick, but deadly in a completely different way.

I totally approved of my partner's weapon choice, and suddenly wanted one of my own.

We moved as fast as we could and still maintain vigilance. I could see through glamours and portals. Half of the people on our commando teams could see wards, illusions, and magical traps of every known kind. With their collective skill, any surprises between us and the Aegis would be found before they found us.

We'd discussed tactics before leaving headquarters. We had a plan, and if events kicked that plan in the teeth, we'd go to Plan B, then C. We had more, but those three had a preferred added benefit—all of us got to live. Probably. With each successive plan, the survival rate declined. Though as always, we'd do what we had to.

Stheno would be fast. With any luck, not fast enough. One of our weapons would be seriously bright light. Retina-frying light worked wonders on ghouls, vampires, and any creature of the night who couldn't take light. Zyta had told us Stheno didn't like light. Blinding her, even temporarily, would keep her from seeing us and using her glare.

I checked the time. It was 6:52. It hadn't been much past that time when we'd come through the portal.

I got Ian's attention, tapped my watch, and raised my eyebrows.

"Watches aren't working in here either," he said quietly.

We had to get the Aegis to Rake by sunrise, and until we left the pocket dimension, we'd have no idea how long we'd been in here. Dammit.

We kept moving. So far nothing had charged out of the shadows to kill us. Ms. Sagadraco had said Tiamat and Stheno knew we were here. When you'd gotten used to being worshipped as a goddess, I could see where you'd consider those who served you so far beneath you as to be microscopic. But just because something was microscopic didn't mean it wasn't lethal.

Ian had his spear ready. I held my paintball rifle low but ready to snap into position. My attention went from our surroundings to Ruby and Euryale. The hellhound was moving like she was out for a walk. Her tail wasn't wagging, but it was relaxed. If Ruby said there was nothing to worry about, there wasn't. Yet.

When the attack came, I wouldn't wait to see if it was visible to our shooters or not. Microseconds counted. I'd immediately hit it with glow-in-the-dark paintballs. Sam, SPI's armorer, had fine-tuned my rifle to increase its range and accuracy. If the target wasn't warded and our people could see it to fill it full of lead, great. If it was invisible to them, they used my glowing paintballs like tracers. They never waited for them to land. Too much of what we hunted was too fast. They trained for it. I'd trained for it, too, until I could consistently nail a fast-moving target. The lives of my friends counted on it. I always went for headshots first. Eyes were the best. Paint would temporarily blind them; bullets would go straight through to the brain. A win-win. Chances were, glowing paint in Stheno's eyes wouldn't blind her, just slow her down for a second or two. In our line of work, that could be the difference between survival or a messy death.

"It's as if sections of our caves have been the pieced together," Zyta was whispering to Ms. Sagadraco. "These are only what Stheno is familiar with."

"My sister wants her to be comfortable and cooperative."

"This has to be Isidor's work," Ian murmured to me.

"Hopefully without the collapsing walls and ceiling," I muttered. I turned and gestured for Kitty and Yasha to join us. "Can this be collapsed?" I asked her. "Like a balloon animal?" Kitty knew what I meant. When Isidor Silvanus knew he'd lost, he "popped" the pocket dimension containing the Hellpit. If we'd been only slightly slower, we'd have been trapped.

Kitty shook her head. "This is too big. Plus, it's more solid than the Hellpit dimension. Have you noticed the repeats?"

Way to be dim, Mac. "No."

Kitty pointed to a grotto just ahead to the left of the path. "We've already passed that. The first time, it was on the right. It's impressive work, but hurried."

Ian spoke. "I'd say Isidor created what Tiamat wanted as fast as he could and left."

That sounded smart. "Run fast and run far."

Kitty nodded, still studying the vaults. "He must have believed this would be Tia's last stand. Much of this is unfinished. Solid, but unfinished. It's too big to be malleable."

"That's good, right?"

"It's very good."

"So the Hellpit pocket dimension was a balloon animal and this is a..."

"Fortress, quite frankly. Either he assumed no one would be able to get in, which is unlikely considering the obvious portal. Or he didn't care because he wouldn't be here, and it wouldn't be his problem."

We came to a split in the path. Both were torchlit. Both appeared identical.

Even Ruby and Euryale appeared confused as to which way to go.

Vivienne Sagadraco and Zyta went forward to speak to Euryale.

I followed and stopped as both paths came into clear view. Something was different, but I couldn't put my finger on it. I tried to relax and let my seer vision take over.

Ruby stuck her nose in the air, sniffed, and froze.

Then I saw it. It was a third path, superimposed over the one to the left. Not just a path, an entirely different cave. Ghostly stalactites and stalagmites descended from a barely visible ceiling and rose from a nearly translucent floor. The stone was yellowish and smelled like…sulfur.

I didn't dare take my eyes off it. "On the left path, does anyone see another path on top of it? The rock is yellow and smells like sulfur."

No responses. Ian appeared next to me. "No one else sees it."

"Ruby smells it, too. The ceiling is much lower here," I added.

"I don't smell anything, and the ceiling still looks high to the rest of us."

If this is Isidor's work, why would he…

I knew. I'd seen it before. "Ian, this is the pocket dimension that led to the Hellpit. All that's missing is the brimstone river, but if Isidor was in a hurry, he wouldn't have bothered."

"What are you saying?"

"I'm not sure." I started thinking out loud. "Rake once told me that Isidor spends most of his time on our world. He likes it here. He has businesses here. Tia killing millions of people in New York and all over the world would be bad for business. Isidor wouldn't defy Tia openly, but he made sure we'd find the portal, and knew I would see and recognize the Hellpit dimension. To Tia and Stheno, it's a recreation of the gorgons' caves. He had to know SPI would get involved. He knew I'd be here and see this. He made the entrance obvious because he wanted there to be no way I could possibly miss it. He must think I'm dumb as a stump."

I ventured a few feet down the ghost tunnel. "If these

lower ceilings continue, there won't be enough room for Tiamat to go dragon. On the downside, neither would you, Ma'am."

"My sister prefers to assume her primary form so she can burn and crush her enemies."

"She may have ordered cathedral ceilings, but these aren't. If she tried to go dragon, she'd whap the heck out of her head."

And Isidor Silvanus would laugh his ass off.

"Isidor, you clever boy," I breathed.

Ian knew where I was going with this, and more importantly, where Isidor Silvanus was going.

"Isidor works with Tiamat only when they have the same goal," he said. "They use each other, like she and Janus did. If we find and kill Tiamat, Isidor gets rid of her but takes none of the risk."

"Murderous and manipulative," Kitty added. "That's Isidor, all right."

I started to smile. "As is thinking I'm dumb as a stump. If this isn't a needlessly complicated trap, the son of a bitch is actually helping us. He's like, if Tia or Stheno kill us, oh well. But if we kill them, Isidor benefits bigtime." I turned to the boss. "Ma'am, does that make sense to you?"

Vivienne Sagadraco's eyes were glittering. "We go left—and follow the yellow brick road."

Three words I thought I'd never say, at least not together. "Thank you, Isidor," I murmured.

I couldn't wait to tell Rake about this.

32

We picked up the pace. There was another fork in the road and one outright intersection. Each time, we followed Isidor's Hellpit path with the hope that it'd take us to the Aegis. Where the Aegis was, Tiamat and Stheno would be.

The wizard had all but told me to follow the sulfur yellow brick road.

If he was lying, he'd better hope Tia got to him first.

Euryale still sensed Stheno. The boss sensed her sister and the Aegis. Ruby still smelled all the above. The farther we went, the stronger the scent and sense.

A scream echoed from up ahead. A man's scream, equal parts fear and rage, followed by presumably that same man cussing a blue streak.

In Goblin.

I knew that voice. So did Ian. "You have *got* to be kidding me."

We ran toward the screams. Well, more like a brisk jog. We weren't about to risk an ambush to save that goblin's miserable hide.

The path opened into a small cavern, and there, chained to a stalagmite like Andromeda as a snack for the Kraken, was Marek Reigory.

He was mostly naked, and something on the cave floor around him was…moving.

Correction, hundreds of somethings were moving.

Roy came up behind us. "Snakes. Interesting choice."

"Not just snakes," Zyta said. "Milos vipers."

I snorted. "Looks like we're not the only ones who hate this guy."

Apparently, Milos vipers weren't climbers, or at least not very good at it. Marek was chained high enough to keep the snakes from reaching him. Probably. But he was low enough for them to scare the living daylights out of him. Definitely.

I couldn't have approved more.

Liz stepped up. "Want me to torch 'em?" she asked Sandra.

Sandra grinned. "The snakes or Marek?"

"They're an endangered species," Zyta said. "The snakes, that is. I don't know about the goblin."

"Oh, he's endangered, all right," Ian growled.

"They will not bite me," Euryale told us. "Shall I fetch the goblin?"

"If you would, please," Ms. Sagadraco said. "I have questions for him."

Our commandos didn't even try to hide their disappointment. They'd come ready to throw down with a great gorgon, and they even had the boss's blessing to open up on a great dragon. They were pumped up, and all they had was a half-naked, terrified goblin and a pit of snakes. Yeah, they were poisonous, but they'd break their fangs on our armored boots. A couple of Kong-sized pythons would at least have been fun.

Euryale slithered into the snake pit, and they parted for her like the Red Sea. With that many snakes, it was doubtful Tia had rounded them up and brought them over from Greece. They were magical constructs. Looked like the real thing, bit and poisoned like the real thing, but they'd vanish along with the pocket dimension. We weren't going to be in here long enough to have to deal with them again. Better to save the fuel in Liz's torch tank for something that really needed killing.

Liz glanced at Marek, then came up next to me and leaned over close. "He's hot."

I couldn't disagree. "But he knows it."

"Aww, too bad."

"He also tried to kill me twice." I held up one finger. "Vaporize." I added another. "Throw me off a Vegas hotel roof."

"Son of a bitch!"

"Yeah. He also pushed one of my predecessors off the Empire State Building."

Liz's eyes widened. "That was Clark Mason."

"So I understand."

"Dammit, I liked him!"

Roy turned to the boss. "Ma'am, we can't leave him behind us, and we don't have anyone to spare to guard him. Kill him? That is, after your chat."

Then I remembered. Remembered and realized.

I spat my favorite minor cuss word. Once didn't slake my rage and frustration, so I spat it again, and again, until I was cussin' like castanets. "Kill Marek and you kill Rake."

"Huh?" Roy looked at me like I'd lost my mind.

Liz blinked. "What?"

I gave them the condensed version of Rake and Marek's messy knife fight/wrestling match that'd resulted in a little of each's blood finding its way into the other's system, making them some kind of twisted magic blood brothers. Whatever happened to Rake, happened to Marek. That meant no lethal solution to our annoying Marek problem.

Euryale plucked the chains out of the rock as if picking flowers, then scooped Marek up like he was a toddler. The goblin mage weakly swatted at her, pathetic little sparks coming from his fingertips. That was some sad defensive magic.

"That explains why he ain't moving too good," Roy noted. "So, if he gets bit, Rake gets bit."

I nodded. "From what Rake told me, yes."

"Meaning we have to take care of that sorry excuse for—"

"Yeah, we do."

"That ain't right."

I nodded again. "Agreed."

Our teams were even less happy, if that was possible. Liz didn't even get to torch the snakes. No one got to kill anything, Marek Reigory got rescued, and even worse, we had to take him with us.

"Sometimes being a hero sucks," Roy muttered.

Euryale started to set Marek on his feet. The question

was, would he be able to stand on them? The answer: kinda sorta, but not really.

"Euryale, would you hold on to him for a few minutes while I speak with him?" Ms. Sagadraco asked.

There was one question I wanted to ask first. "Who'd you piss off this time?"

"I imagine that would be my sister," Vivienne said with a smile. "We have Jonathan Tarbert and know about your alliance, and I imagine so does Tiamat," she told the goblin. "On top of that were your failures. First in New York with the teleportation of Rake's family home. Then in Las Vegas when you failed the entire cabal by ruining my sister's evil scheme that had been years in the planning. In addition, two days ago, you lost a magetech generator."

"Three strikes and you're snake chow," I muttered.

There was laughter in my head. Rake's laughter. Weak, but it was there. *"And he committed record amounts of treason back home."*

I gasped. "You can talk to me here!"

Ian knew I wasn't referring to Marek.

"Tia's using him as bait and a delay," Rake said. *"She's probably hoping you'd forgotten about our link and would kill him, and thereby me."*

"I can help you," Marek was telling Vivienne Sagadraco. "I know where Tia will be taking—"

Smoke started coming out of the boss's nostrils and her eyes were beginning to glow.

Marek talked faster. "If I die, Rake dies. I don't want to die. I can help you get the Aegis. I'm exiled on this world, but I like it. That crazy bitch wants to kill everyone."

Zyta snorted. “Which crazy bitch?”

“They’re both nuts,” he said. “I can tell you where they’re going.”

The boss wasn’t buying it. “To the torch.”

“But you don’t know how they’ll get there.”

“Via a portal or Stheno burns through the wall with her acid. There is no assistance you could provide to redeem yourself. You killed one of my seers.”

Marek gave a weak grin. “Just following orders doesn’t make up for that, does it?”

I couldn’t believe what I was hearing. “Following orders? You tried to vaporize me! Then you tried to throw me off the roof of a hotel.”

“Again, orders. Following. Jeez.”

“Ma’am, would you mind too terribly if I punch him repeatedly in the face?”

“If you’d like you can consider it an order, so you could merely be following it.”

My responding grin must have looked downright evil. Marek actually tried to get closer to Euryale.

Ms. Sagadraco smiled up at the ancient gorgon. “Thank you for your help. Please set him down.”

Ian pulled out a set of magic-sapping manacles.

“No!” Rake said in my head.

I frantically waved my hands. “Stop! We can’t use those.”

“Why not?” Ian asked.

“Rake’s using magic to stay alive. If we cuff Marek, Rake’s magic suffers, too.”

“Are you sure?”

“Yes, he just told me. *Any ideas?”* I asked Rake.

Silence.

I panicked. *"Rake?"*

"I'm thinking."

I glanced at Marek Reigory. He was smirking. He knew we couldn't hurt him.

"Marek knows we can't hurt him."

"Unconscious would be fine," Rake said. *"I can work around that."*

"I do get to punch him?" I said that part out loud.

"If you must. Fainting would be better."

"Just how am I supposed—"

"Marek is terrified of spiders." I felt Rake's smirk. *"I am not."*

"We don't have any of those. Would conjured spiders work?"

"Yes. Just make it big and hairy. Hissing and clicking mandibles would be a nice touch. Let him see it first, then put it between his shoulder blades where he can't reach it."

"But he'll know we can't let it bite him."

"That won't matter."

"He's that scared of the things?"

"Pathological."

"We'll get it done," I promised. *"Lydia's good with conjuring creepy-crawlies. You need to rest."*

He ignored me. *"Is Yasha there?"*

"Kitty's here so Yasha's here. Stop talking and res—"

"Has he gone werewolf?"

"Of course."

*"Once Marek's unconscious, put regular handcuffs on him, then have Yasha throw him over his shoulder. Someone

will need to carry him, and Yasha has strength to spare." Rake chuckled. *"When Marek wakes up dangling over a werewolf's ass..."* The chuckles turned downright evil. *"Have Yasha growl and he'll faint again, guaranteed. Marek once had a truly unfortunate incident with a werewolf."*

"Good to know. Now rest! We've got this. I'll see you soon, and we'll bring you a big, shiny present."

"I love you."

"I love you, too," I managed. I turned to one of our battlemage commandos. "Lydia, I need a favor."

She did the favor, and Marek did what Rake said he'd do.

I had to hand it to my honey. If he hated you, he'd know *all* your weaknesses.

33

Yasha was a happy multitasker. He could protect Kitty and terrorize Marek at the same time.

Rake's suggestion had worked like a charm. One shriek at Lydia's freakish arachnid handiwork, and Marek was down for the count.

We moved out, continuing to follow the Hellpit path. There were other forks in the road, other choices, but we ignored any I didn't see with a sulfur overlay. Ruby's nose confirmed we were on the right track.

We came to what wasn't so much a tunnel as a narrowing of cave. There was only one way forward. Isidor's sulfuric path faded into the darkness. His trail ended here. I hoped that wasn't a foreshadowing of our own fate.

Vivienne Sagadraco stepped forward, her draconic eyes

intent on the darkness inside. "Is that the direction we need to go?" she asked quietly.

"Isidor's path ends at that tunnel," I told her.

Euryale slithered toward the opening, her scales a dry rasp on the stone. The gorgon had to bend to at the waist to put her head inside. Her tail thrashed in response to what she sensed, as did the Milos vipers on her head.

"Sisssster."

Silence from the darkness beyond. Ruby growled, her hackles rising.

Neither were signs of impending good times.

Ms. Sagadraco silently went to stand beside the gorgon. She leaned forward, listening, letting the air flow over her heightened senses.

She turned to her two commanders and gave them a single nod.

Here we go.

Part of me was relieved. A quick glance around told me I wasn't the only one. Game faces were on, and weapons were readied. None of us trusted not being attacked. We liked it, we just didn't trust it.

The boss's armored form shimmered and transformed into what she'd been hatched as—a Great Western Dragon. Her true size was three stories tall. She went with being slightly smaller than Euryale, just the right height to fit into that tunnel.

Euryale gestured Zyta and her gorgons forward to join her. This was the part where they'd take the brunt of Stheno's initial and—if they were successful—only attack.

My cuff vibrated and Lugh's Spear flashed.

That was all the warning we got.

The attack didn't come from the tunnel.

It came from everywhere else.

Ghouls and harpies. Bigger, stronger, and faster ghouls and harpies.

Unexpected and definitely unwanted, but it made perfect sense. Tia and her cabal had used ghouls and harpies before. It paid to stick with the classics. Attacks by land and air. Fun for the whole family.

When the harpies appeared, the gorgons looked up. We all did, but *our* startled glances didn't turn those harpies to stone. That was bad, for the harpies and us. Flying harpies became falling statues. Our people were nimble and got out of the way. The gorgons considerately refocused their attention on the ground-bound ghouls.

Every monster killed immediately regenerated in a flicker of squiggly lines, even the harpies that had shattered on impact.

"Magetech generator!" Ian shouted. "They're constructs. Kill 'em enough and they won't get back up."

It didn't matter that they weren't real, the dead they could make you was.

We didn't have time or anyone to spare to locate the generator. Tia probably had Marek program the ghouls and harpies into the generator, *then* chained him to the rock as a snake snack.

That was the thing about constructs. You could recreate a regular ghoul, or you could make them stronger and faster. Any villain worth their evil master plan was an overachiever. If Marek was responsible for these ghouls and harpies, there was gonna be some face punching in his future. I took a quick glance back. The goblin mage was still swinging limply from Yasha's shoulder.

Ian had his teeth bared in a fierce smile.

I wasn't sure if he was having the time of his life, but my partner did seem to be taking a more than the usual enjoyment in his work.

A ghoul attack while Ian had been with the NYPD had led to him coming to work for SPI. Two years ago, ghouls had overpowered and kidnapped him and hauled his unconscious self to Bannerman Island for a midnight sacrifice. He hadn't encountered ghouls again since that night.

Payback was a bitch, but for the one delivering said payback, it was intensely satisfying.

It didn't seem to bother my partner in the least that the ghouls he killed were regenerating. All that meant was he got to enjoy killing them again and again.

Lugh's Spear was getting quite the workout. Seeing my partner slice and dice his way through every ghoul that made the poor choice to get within range made my heart happy. Unfortunately, I didn't have much time to enjoy it. I was busy blinding any monster I could hit with a paintball. I felt like I was in a shooting gallery.

Our battlemages were torching, vaporizing, and shredding ghouls and harpies. One especially creative mage liquified the ground at a trio of ghouls' feet, and as soon as their heads went below the surface, she resolidified the cave floor, sealing them inside.

Vivienne Sagadraco was efficiently dealing with ghouls whose innate ability for survival had often been compared to that of cockroaches. It turned out that roaches and ghouls were equally susceptible to stomping.

Euryale was a triple threat. She was glaring with her eyes, slashing with her claws, and swatting with her serpent tail. One harpy hit in midair slammed wetly against the cave wall, briefly sticking there before sliding limply down.

The harpies regenerated nearly as fast as we dropped them from the air. We were making good progress toward that tunnel. Once inside, one team would be enough to hold it against anything that came at them.

Our commandos had a guaranteed lethal response to anything an attacker could dish out. Constructs were created to do whatever the real version did best, and if they were destroyed, they'd reappear to do the same thing. Wash, rinse, repeat. They weren't creative thinkers because they hadn't been created to think. Already some of them had been killed enough times that they weren't getting back up.

Over the thunder of automatic gunfire, multiple roars came from the tunnel, and the cave floor shook with the footfalls. It felt like a monster stampede.

Over a dozen yellow eyes emerged from the shadows, followed by nine heads.

"Hydra!" Calvin shouted. This wasn't his or his team's first hydra rodeo. Though the one in that Chelsea apartment building laundry room had been this one's micromini-me.

Euryale, Zyta, and her gorgons hit it with a simultaneous glare. As the stone heads dropped off, two more appeared. The ladies kept up their attack.

Ruby darted between the hydra's legs and into the tunnel beyond.

It'd be a waste of breath to try to call her back. To Ruby, her work here was done.

The gorgons lured the hydra out of the cave just enough for a few of us to dart inside. Euryale broke off the attack and followed us. We paused long enough for her to get out in front. She had called dibs on her sister. We respected that.

The growling and barking from up ahead wasn't coming from a great gorgon. I recognized Ruby's bark, but not the others. The bark was too deep, and the growl shook the floor.

At the other end of the tunnel was Ruby.

Standing its ground in front of her was one dog.

With three heads.

Cerberus.

No squiggly lines were running through him. He wasn't a construct. He was real.

Crap.

Roy skidded to a stop and swore. "Anybody bring Milk-Bones?"

We had a hydra behind us and Cerberus in front of us.

As far as Ruby was concerned, Cerberus was her one and only target. It didn't bother her in the least that the top of her head came to the base of his chest. Her determination and ferocity were a match for the largest of Hell's guardians, but that girl was barking way out of her weight class.

Euryale whistled.

Cerberus looked up in surprise. Heck, so did we.

But we looked *to* Euryale. Cerberus looked *at* her—and Euryale was looking right back.

He went from monster hound to monster monument in two seconds flat.

Ruby gave Euryale a glare of her own, then trotted over to me, growling under her breath.

I rubbed one of Ruby's ears. "Such a good girl."

Ruby's tongue lolled out the side of her mouth as she grinned up at me.

Euryale slowly slithered out of the tunnel, Vivienne Sagadraco beside her.

The rest of our people joined us. The hydra didn't. Another win.

I could sense her. She was here, waiting for us. All of us. She had started to feed on Rake, but he'd escaped. She hungered. She waited.

Stheno.

34

There was no good way to sneak into a great gorgon's lair.

Especially when said gorgon knew we were there and how many we were, as well as our intentions and armaments. We'd given Stheno a thorough demonstration of what we could do with those weapons right outside her lair's front door. She was half serpent and all predator. We must have looked like mice to her, huddled by the door and walls. Mice were tiny and had even smaller feet, yet a snake knew when even one had entered their den.

Our boots touching the floor had rung the dinner bell.

Stheno, big sister of Medusa, granddaughter of Titans, was ready for us. All of us.

The room was huge and filled with a forest of carved

pillars, each at least twenty feet high, and wider than Yasha's werewolf shoulders. Isidor had skimped on the rest of the pocket dimension with only an illusion of size. This was no illusion. The room was dimly lit from unseen sources and offered plenty of places for Stheno and Tiamat to hide.

"It's a copy of our home caves' audience chamber," Zyta said quietly into our comms. "There's a dais directly ahead on the far end where Euryale and Stheno received visitors."

Right where all the pitch dark was.

Between here and there was who knew what.

"Room size?" Sandra asked.

"One hundred meters long and seventy meters wide," the gorgon replied.

"In American, that's a little bigger than a football field," Roy told any of our metric-challenged commandos.

An eight-foot gorgon was somewhere on a dark, pillar-filled football field.

I glanced up at Euryale. Her eyes locked on something across the room, not directly ahead, but a little to the right. She then slowly tracked what she saw or maybe just sensed. Looked like Stheno wasn't waiting on her dais to receive us as visitors. Euryale's tail snapped from side to side and her hair vipers hissed in anticipation.

I couldn't see Stheno, but I knew she was there, too.

The great gorgon was stalking us. That certainty had nothing to do with my seer ability. It was the primitive instincts of a human in the presence of an apex predator.

I wasn't alone in my assessment. Our commandos scanned the shadows as hands readied weapons.

My adrenaline had been known to override my good

sense. Not anymore. Stheno was waiting in the darkness to stare us into statuary.

I still had my paintball rifle ready. Never had "aim for the eyes" meant more. If I could blind Stheno, her stone-turning days were over. Thanks to Jonathan Tarbert, everyone with a negator would be able to see Stheno. This time I wasn't the only one who could see her, but if I could keep her from using her glare, our teams could do what they did best.

We quickly moved out, executing the plan we'd agreed on.

Euryale slithered forward into the darkness in search of her sister, the gorgons fanning out around her. Our two teams of nine commandos split into six squads of three, moving along the walls like wraiths, code named Alpha through Foxtrot. The inner circle of attack would be the gorgons, code name Greek.

Ian, Kitty, Yasha, the boss, and I were what Roy called a special team, in football terms. We were coded Zulu. We'd do what was needed where and when it was needed.

The only presence I felt was Stheno.

No Tiamat.

"Ma'am?" I said in my mind to Vivienne Sagadraco.

"I know. My sister is not here, nor is the Aegis." The boss relayed that over comms to the others. "Tiamat has left and taken the Aegis with her. Makenna, Kitty, there is a door or portal in this room. Find it now."

"In our audience chamber, there is a door behind the dais for the sisters' use," Zyta told us.

Bingo. Maybe. If Isidor had conjured an exact copy. And it did make sense to have Tia's exit as far from our entrance as possible.

That was now our team's goal.

"Delta, cover Zulu," Sandra ordered. "All other squads, corral the target."

Yasha unceremoniously dropped Marek by the door, freeing both of his arms for whatever would happen in the next few minutes.

I approved. Marek was still out cold and half paralyzed. It wasn't like he'd be going anywhere without us.

We all wore gorgon glasses. We had no way of knowing if they'd work with Stheno, and we weren't counting on it, but if they bought us a fraction of a second, they'd be worth it.

Stheno couldn't look everywhere at once. One squad might go down, but the others would finish the job.

There were ways to kill Stheno without looking at anything above her neck. Zyta had also warned us that the great gorgon had one heck of a come-hither, like siren level. It was up to each of us to counter it in whatever way worked. Count backward from a hundred. Sing your favorite song in your head loud and proud. Anything to keep your mind from doing what a goddess was demanding you do. It wouldn't be easy, but it could be done. Our stubbornness had to be stronger than her call.

We only had to resist long enough for one of us to get a spear up under her scales. No one had ever killed a great gorgon this way. Perseus had decapitated Medusa, but her big sister wasn't going to lie down and take a nap for us.

"Dragon, you have stolen our sister to guard your ill-gotten hoard," said a heavily accented, sibilant voice inside my head.

Stheno.

"Ian, do you—"

"We all hear it."

"Such evil and desecration cannot go unpunished," Stheno continued. *"All you love, own, and protect shall fall beneath my glare. You will never leave this place, nor will the mortals and monsters you command. My traitorous sister will not escape me again. I will have the vengeance that has been denied me for untold ages. My beloved Medusa was murdered by the mortal coward Perseus. The gods have elevated and protected mortals while we were cursed as monsters, hated and exiled. They have spread like locusts, tainting, consuming, and destroying all that was good, leaving desolation and depravity in their wake. Poseidon defiled Medusa,and Athena cast her out and cursed us. Poseidon and Athena are beyond my reach, but their precious mortals cannot escape my wrath. I will see to it that this world will be wiped clean, free to begin again. First will be the mortals of this city, and you, Vivienne Sagadraco, their protector."*

My Grandma Fraser had a saying: Her cornbread ain't done in the middle.

Never had it applied to anyone more than Stheno.

The great gorgon and Tiamat thought humans were good only for slaves and food, but even entrées got lucky sometimes. It'd be the ultimate insult for them to get killed by humans.

I had news for them: this buffet was about to unleash some serious fury.

"The dragon Tiamat lied to you," Euryale shouted to her sister. "She has taken Medusa and the Aegis and left you to die. You told her how to wield it, and now she has no use for you. She is not coming back. She tricked you into stealing our

Medusa, to use her to kill innocents. You know Medusa would not want this. She isn't a murderer. Help me save her!"

In that moment, I felt both great gorgons. The weight of the millennia they'd lived and slept. I sensed how Janus and then Tiamat had turned Stheno's dreams to nightmares, a constant and unending stream of horror. How mortals had overtaken those once thought of as gods. Overtaken, and then dismissed, forgotten. Some mortals ascended to godlike heights, others fought for status, power, and money. Scheming, battling, killing. All to rule over other mortals. Destroying everything and everyone who stood in their way with no one to stop them.

Until now. Stheno had sworn to stop them, to remove the mortal stain from this world, and neither Euryale nor even Medusa could restore the sanity Stheno had willingly abandoned.

We moved quickly through the darkness, with no sign or sound of Stheno. Now, in this room, Vivienne Sagadraco was the great gorgon's primary target. Was Stheno tracking her now, waiting until she had a sure kill?

I was beyond grateful Kitty was here. If Isidor had disguised that door in some way, it wouldn't be all on me to find it.

This was the first mission involving both teams since Christmas Eve night, when the commandos who were here now had seen me take on Janus. For that one night, I'd had the mantle of the Master of the Wild Hunt to call on, and I did. The strength of past masters had surged through me, my voice had commanded Janus to obey, and I'd been told there'd been a glow of raw power around me.

I'd returned the mantle to my father once Janus was dead. Tonight, I had no power to call on.

I was just me, Makenna Fraser.

No one had said anything since then, but I had a feeling a lot more was expected of me. I couldn't suddenly sprout godlike abilities, even if my dad had sprouted antlers from his head when he'd become the Master of the Wild Hunt.

I also couldn't control anyone else's expectations—or my own guilt and devastation if I failed to get the Aegis and Rake turned to stone while I was helpless to stop it. Or if anything happened to the men and women around me. Or my partner at my side.

But Lugh Lámhfhada had killed King Balor of the Fomorians with a spear through his eye.

The spear that Lugh's descendant, Ian, now carried.

My cuff gave me a gentle pulse. Calming, reassuring.

I slung my paintball rifle across my back, and smoothly drew my father's hunting knife out of its scabbard. As I did, the knife's pommel brushed against the cuff's edge. Both weapon and cuff pulsed once as if they'd been switched on.

My father had said he'd used the knife many times and used it well.

"It is now yours to wield," he'd told me in the cold hours of that night. "May it be for you as it was for me."

It'd been a proclamation, a blessing. Cernunnos, my father, believed in me.

I felt my lips twitch at the corners. Who was I to disagree with the god of the hunt?

Ian was on my right. Vivienne Sagadraco on my left.

I felt the ancient hunters in them both, primitive and alive.

The same had always been inside of me. A gift from my father, and from the Masters of the Wild Hunt before him.

I sensed Vivienne Sagadraco in an entirely new way. Not the human. The dragon. Not as an employer, but as a fellow hunter. For this night, she was the female version of my father, an ancient and powerful predator, one of the last of the great dragons, ready, able, and eager to match tooth and claw against her sister, if Tiamat had the guts to face her tonight.

I glanced at her. She was watching me, her smile slow and dangerous. She knew.

Ruby growled in approval.

My father wasn't here, not physically. But the skills he'd bestowed upon me when I'd been conceived that night in a Scottish stone circle were here for me to call on and wield.

In that way, he'd been helping me my entire life.

I pushed down my fear, worry, guilt, everything a hunter wasn't. Everything I now wasn't. I embraced what was left, listening to what my instincts were telling me.

Just hunt.

Stheno was prey. Our prey. Mine and Vivienne's and Ian's.

We hunted together.

Nothing moved in the shadows until it did.

Stheno was fast, cobra fast, beside us and then, with a lash of her serpent body, looming behind.

There was no time to think, only act.

Stheno was more deadly to me than Janus had been that night. The slightest glance would do it.

I spun, my eyes focused on her scales, slashing with my father's knife. Ian stabbed with his spear. Both went through the great gorgon's armored scales as if they didn't exist.

Stheno screamed and raked downward at us with her claws.

Ian dropped, rolled, and was back on his feet attacking again a second later.

I wasn't nearly as nimble. Instinct took over and I parried Stheno's claws with the edge of my knife, taking two fingers from the gorgon's hand.

The scream rose to an enraged shriek.

Then Euryale was there, between us and her sister, pushing us back, their tails lashing and entwining, hands grasping, claws slashing.

Ian grabbed my arm. "Come on!"

Kitty and Yasha were behind the dais. There was an open door, now lit by flashlights.

Behind us, the great gorgons battled.

"Euryale risks her life to give us time," Ms. Sagadraco said in my mind as she darted past me toward the door. *"Accept the gift."*

Time to stop Tiamat and save our world.

Waves of power emanated from Stheno. The power she'd taken from Carlos and Quinn—and to a lesser extent, from Rake. There was no way Euryale could match Stheno. She knew it, but fought with all she had. For the love of her little sister. For Medusa.

I knew I shouldn't, but I stopped running and glanced back.

Mere seconds had passed since Stheno had ambushed us. Zyta, her gorgons, and our commandos, were only now closing in on the combatants.

The sisters' arms were wrapped around each other in a

lethal embrace, their glowing eyes locked in a death stare. Stheno's eyes flashed even brighter, and Euryale went rigid in her arms.

No.

Whether because of Euryale's great age or the strength of Stheno's glare, Euryale's body turned white as the finest marble, then crumbled into dust.

I'd often wondered what it was like to live for centuries or millennia. My conclusion had always been the same. I was glad to be mortal. I wanted a long, healthy life, but that was it. I couldn't imagine living as long as Stheno or Euryale, cursed as a monster for all eternity.

Euryale hadn't sacrificed herself. She'd been offered a chance to end her life with meaning. On some level, dying in the embrace of one sister to save the other was as good a death as she could've hoped for. Euryale was finally free. Probably her only regret was that she hadn't been able to end Stheno's suffering as well.

A thunderous roar of rage and betrayal went up from the Sisters of Medusa as they descended on Stheno.

Stheno was no longer our prey. Tiamat was. If she lived to use the Aegis, millions would die.

I let Ian pull me through the door and into the passage beyond.

35

Vivienne Sagadraco had the best chance of stopping her sister. Our job was to ensure that she got that chance.

A bright light from ahead illuminated the passage's narrow walls and ceiling. Ian and I had seen an identical passage, connecting Ms. Sagadraco's bank vault to the natural tunnels beyond.

Stheno had created it using the acid from her body to eat through solid rock.

The light at its end was also familiar.

A portal. Standing open like the iron door we'd just passed through, its frame glowing green. Tiamat either couldn't close the portal—or had left it open deliberately.

Vivienne Sagadraco was running toward it, seconds away from passing through and into whatever was beyond, focused only on catching her sister before she could use the Aegis. The portal frame flashed and began to collapse as soon as Ms. Sagadraco crossed the threshold.

The portal was closing.

Ian sprinted past us, spear held low, the tip glowing like a tiny sun. He thrust Lugh's Spear between the two portal halves that were inches away from touching.

Instinct screamed at me to close my eyes.

White-hot light blazed through my squeezed-shut eyelids. Shutting my eyes was great for not getting my retinas fried, but crappy for running, so I went with a squint. I didn't know how the light affected Ruby, but she kept pace with me.

Ian's entire body glowed as he pitted his strength against the closing portal. "Kitty!"

Yasha had already scooped her up and put on a burst of werewolf speed toward Ian.

Violent explosions shook the passage behind us, and it was all we could do to stay on our feet.

"Mortals!"

Stheno. Alive.

The explosions were the great gorgon slamming the iron door behind her and her serpent tail hammering the walls, collapsing the tunnel in front it.

Tons of rock, piled against the iron door.

Our people—if any were left alive—were trapped on the other side.

We were trapped inside. With her.

Hunters killed, but they also knew how to survive.

Run.

I risked a glance back but kept my eyes down. Stheno

was digging her claws into the stone floor to propel herself forward with a speed of which I wouldn't have believed her capable.

Run faster.

Kitty thrust her hands into the closing portal, grabbing either side like elevator doors, and through sheer skill and force of will, pushed. The portal fought Kitty for control. It had to have been Isidor's work. Just because he'd wanted us to get in didn't mean he intended for us to leave.

Isidor Silvanus versus Kitty Poertner.

I was betting on Kitty.

We all were.

My baker bestie screamed with effort, forcing the light to part just enough for us to squeeze through.

"Go! Quick! I can't hold…"

Ian shoved me through, Ruby right behind me, but when he then tried to do the same with Yasha, my partner had significantly less luck. Yasha wasn't going without Kitty.

"Do what I say!" Kitty shrieked.

Yasha went, then Ian. Kitty wedged her body into the opening and pushed herself out with an oddly wet plop on the other side.

We'd forgotten a supremely icky detail about leaving an Isidor Silvanus pocket dimension.

Exit portal ecto-goop.

It was a small price to pay for escaping Stheno.

We were in the concrete lobby of the visitors' center. There were two levels, main floor and mezzanine, with a wide staircase leading to double doors. Above them was a sign.

TO PEDESTAL & CROWN

"I'm climbing the ladder to the torch," the boss said in my mind. *"Tiamat is already there."*

Kitty was cussing, and it wasn't because she was coated in ecto-goop.

The portal was closed—at least it had been. Stheno's clawed fist had punched through the portal's seam. That shouldn't have been possible, but if Tiamat had been going in and out...

Isidor. He'd keyed the portal to Tia and Stheno so they could come and go as they pleased.

Isidor had just skipped the line ahead of Marek for a thorough face-punching, and had won himself a bonus ass-kicking.

Stheno was forcing her massive body through the portal and taking out most of the concrete wall around it.

Ian pushed me in the direction of the stairs, which I took two at a time wondering whether a snake-bodied gorgon could climb stairs.

Turned out she could, and quite well.

"Stheno! Face me!" I knew that voice, but it couldn't be.

It was Zyta Kokkinos.

The gorgon commander staggered clear of the ruins of the wall and its now destroyed portal, her entire body pale gray.

With dust. She hadn't been glared, at least not yet.

Zyta sprinted toward Stheno, her spear slashing at the wounds Ian and I had inflicted on the great gorgon's lower body. Stheno bellowed in pain and rage—and turned to glare Zyta Kokkinos into oblivion.

The commander bared her teeth in a fierce smile. "That's it. Look right at me."

Stheno flowed down the stairs, her tail excitedly lashing the air.

I'd seen this before. The last scene in *Jurassic Park* with the T. Rex in the island's welcome center. That dinosaur's tail had totally destroyed that room. Stheno did the same now, even copying the T. Rex's eardrum-piercing battle bellow.

I didn't have time to be impressed or worry that my ears might be bleeding. Zyta was buying us time, but we weren't about to leave her here alone.

We kept our eyes down and our blades moving. Yasha waded in with his claws. Between the three of us, we inflicted a satisfying amount of damage. Damage that Quinn and Carlos never got a chance to do. They had taken a scale. We took her tail.

Zyta darted in and out with lightning quick attacks, all the while shouting a steady and taunting stream of what I assumed was ancient Greek. If the literal froth at the corners of the great gorgon's mouth was any indicator, the commander was hitting every raw nerve Stheno had.

It worked. Stheno's eyes flashed, her glare aimed at Zyta and Zyta alone.

The commander had been fighting with a spear in one hand, biding her time with the weapon in her left, held low by her thigh. When Stheno's eyes glowed, Zyta brought her left hand up in a flash of Italian silver, putting the mirror directly in front of her face, tilted up to the great gorgon's line of sight.

Stheno went rigid, her final glare hitting the mirror to reflect back with deadly effect. For an instant, for the first and last time in over seven thousand years, Stheno was once again as she'd been before Athena's curse.

Beautiful. Smooth, flawless alabaster skin frozen in a single moment in time.

Then she crumbled, pieces of her falling, crashing to the concrete floor, then collapsing into dust.

"The doors are locked!" Kitty shouted, pulling at the doors to the pedestal and crown. She looked closely at the seam between them. "They're *fused*."

Laughter echoed in my head, in everyone's.

Tiamat.

In my mind's eye, I saw Tiamat in her human form, wearing armor similar to her sister's, but red and black. She was on the torch balcony, holding the Aegis like the shield it was, Medusa's face turned toward Lower Manhattan.

We ran to the doors leading outside. They weren't fused.

It was still dark, the lights still out here and all around us, but there was a faint glow on eastern horizon.

"Dawn's in less than half an hour," Ian said.

Meaning Rake had less than half an hour before Sophia could no longer help him. I looked up, tilting my head as far back as it would go. The only thing that could help him was up there, on the torch balcony, in Tiamat's hands.

"You are forcing my hand, little mortals," Tia said in our minds. *"I must do this earlier than I wanted, but this is only a test. What is it they say about New York? It's the city that never sleeps. Medusa's face can blaze brighter than the sun. It will be as if it has already risen. Humans are such stupidly curious cattle. They will look at the light and they will die. I will make the Aegis blaze again and again, luring sleep-dazed humans to their windows, each flash killing thousands more. Little hunter, the light will penetrate your goblin lover's tower.*

He foolishly believes you can save him. He is with us now in spirit and will feel you fail. Goblin, glance at the light that will soon appear in your windows, and you and your human paramour can die together. I will use one of dear Jonathan's devices, render the Aegis and my dragon form invisible, and fly to where Viktor awaits. Then the game will truly begin." There was a pause. *"Ah, Vivienne, there you are. Come, sweet sister, and receive Medusa's kiss."*

36

This took sibling rivalry to new heights.

The boss was three hundred feet directly above our heads, possibly at the mercy of her murderous sister, and there was absolutely nothing we could do to help.

The sun wasn't up, and the power was still out. Our helmets had lights, but they weren't nearly powerful enough to illuminate the torch.

Ian flipped down the thermal imaging over his right eye. "Nothing. Yasha?"

"Dragons too cold to see," he managed through werewolf dental work.

"Mortimer!" Ian called into our comms.

No reply.

"Mortimer!" I screamed in my mind. I had telepathy with dragons, and the mage was human, but I had to—

Running feet pounded the concrete behind us, coming fast. We spun to meet the threat.

Mortimer Winters found himself on the business end of half a dozen barrels and blades. He raised his hands. "You called; I came."

I pried my heart out of my throat. "The boss's up there with Tia. Tia has the Aegis. We can't see to shoot. Can you…?" I frantically wiggled my fingers in what I hoped was an inoffensive imitation of doing magic.

Mortimer looked up at the torch, his eyes intense. I swear they were glowing. Then he spat a word I didn't think Old World gentlemen used under any circumstances.

"I can't get a fix on Vivienne," he said. "There's too much distortion from the Aegis."

A sick feeling rolled through me. There was nothing any of us could do.

An image appeared for an instant in my mind, then out. A few seconds later, in again, then out. Sound was also cutting in and out.

Vivienne Sagadraco was trying to communicate or show me what was happening.

The sick feeling now had nothing to do with dread, and everything to do with nausea. She was fighting hand-to-hand with Tia. She fell against the balcony railing, and my view was straight down with us looking up at her. Tia no longer had the Aegis. It was behind her, leaning against the railing.

Facing Vivienne.

Oh no.

As if the waves of vertigo weren't bad enough, I felt surges of seeking magic from Mortimer alternating with Ian's aura pulsing with anger and frustration.

Then I realized they were keeping me from hearing the boss.

"Aura and magic. Can't hear," I shouted as I tried to run, but mostly staggered, to put distance between me and them. I found a low cement wall and ducked behind it. That did the trick. I now had audio and video.

Medusa's face was aimed directly at Vivienne, but her eyes were closed.

As long as Tia wasn't holding the Aegis, Medusa's glare remained inert.

The sun was rising. I saw a glint of light on metal in the distance. No, it couldn't be. I blinked and looked again.

A pair of fighter jets were coming in low from Manhattan, their altitude on a collision course with the torch.

The jets' wings flapped, building speed.

Flapped?

Not jets. Eagles. Stainless-steel eagles shining in the dawn light. What'd looked like landing gear were claws.

I realized what they were and where they'd come from.

The eagle gargoyles from the Chrysler Building.

They descended toward the torch, and Tiamat dove for the Aegis. The instant her hands touched it, Medusa's eyes flew open.

No!

One of the eagles banked to the side, claws extended, and tore the shield from Tiamat's grip.

I started breathing again—until the eagle with the Aegis went into a dive.

Directly at me.

And dropped the Aegis at my feet, then with powerful

beats of its wings—that knocked me the rest of the way to the ground—flew back up toward the torch to join the fight.

Suddenly, the torch balcony tilted, dumping a body over the railing.

Tiamat.

Her human body shimmered as it fell, turning dragon, wings folded tight to her body in a dive.

She was coming after the Aegis.

I was being divebombed again, but this time there would be no stopping until I'd been either torn to shreds or crushed into the concrete.

Everything slowed down. At least it did in my mind. The survival mechanism humans were born with that helped us live through the unlivable.

Instinctively, I lunged for the Aegis, and did what soldiers had done for thousands of years: held it over me like the shield it was, and braced for impact.

The instant my hands touched it, I saw through Medusa's eyes.

Her heart had stopped beating the day Perseus beheaded her, but part of her consciousness remained. She had felt it when Athena forced her head into the Aegis, the metal softening and engulfing her head, holding her immobile, muting her screams.

Athena knew Medusa still lived, still suffered.

She *knew*. I couldn't breathe with the horror of what Medusa had endured, and tears streamed down my face. Athena knew and she used Medusa against the enemies of the gods and her favored mortals, used her to murder hundreds and thousands again and again.

Medusa was aware that Vivienne had enshrined her in the

vault to keep her safe—and others safe from her. For the first time since her imprisonment in the Aegis, Medusa had been at peace and slept.

When Stheno had entered the vault, Medusa was overjoyed to see her. Minutes later, Stheno had used her to kill the human mages. Medusa did not understand why. They had not been a threat. They'd only been trying to protect her.

Later, when Euryale had appeared in the tunnel, Medusa forgot what Stheno had done. Joy returned. She was reunited at last with her beloved sisters.

Then her sisters had argued. Over her. She knew not why. She tried to call out, reason with them, make them stop. When Athena had imprisoned her in the Aegis, all she could use were her eyes. She could hear, but she could not move or speak.

Stheno attacked Euryale. The sisters fought and bled while Medusa cried and silently screamed.

Medusa screamed now, in rage at the dragon responsible for the deaths of Stheno and Euryale. Tiamat had tricked and used them all.

I screamed with her, in horror and sympathy for what had been done to her, for all the deaths Tiamat had caused in her life, and for what she had done to Rake. All for power.

No more. It ended now. Tiamat ended now.

Those were Medusa's thoughts—and mine. We were one.

I felt Medusa open her eyes, saw Tiamat's panic and terror, unable to stop, no time to look away.

I bore witness to the death of Tiamat, sister of Vivienne and Babylonian goddess of chaos. Her red-scaled body turned white, slamming into Medusa, the Aegis—and me.

My world went black.

37

I woke up with a wet face.

It wasn't blood. I was on the receiving end of enthusiastic Ruby kisses.

I groaned and rolled over. I hurt pretty much everywhere, but at least I hadn't been squashed by falling chunks of Tiamat.

I was still mostly under the Aegis, which was now covered by a blanket. Medusa's eyes were closed again. I didn't need to see it. I felt it.

"Hey, partner," Ian rumbled from somewhere above me.

I blinked my eyes open. I think I knew how a turtle must feel after being clipped by a car.

"Hey, yourself."

I pushed myself out from under the Aegis and got a look at the back side. Any other shield would've been crushed beyond recognition. The Aegis didn't have a single dent.

Medusa had destroyed Tiamat and saved me.

I gazed blearily at the debris around us. The white stone that Tiamat had become was turning to powder and blowing away. Carlos and Quinn had been avenged.

My thoughts were still as groggy and slow as the rest of me. Didn't someone else need saving?

"Rake!" I gasped and sat straight up—at least I tried. I mostly floundered around on the ground. I waved an arm in Ian's general direction. "Help me up!"

He did, but entirely too slowly for my liking. "Easy, you've only been out about two minutes. You've got time."

In the next instant, Calvin was doing his infantry medic thing and shining one of those little pin lights in my eyes.

"I don't have a concussion. We need to go."

"I'll be the judge of that. Hold still."

Then it hit me. "You're alive."

"Well, I should hope so."

Roy snorted from nearby. "Like a locked door and pile of rocks is gonna stop us. We're all still alive and kicking."

I pushed Calvin away—or tried. I was starting to panic. "We need to get the Aegis to Rake. The boat's too slow. How are we—"

Ian put his hands on my shoulders and turned me around.

There was Vivienne Sagadraco in all her majestic draconic glory. A one-story version of her dragon form instead of three.

She was safe.

"And saddled," said her amused voice in my mind. *"I can have us there in a few minutes."*

Mortimer Winters emerged from under one of Ms. Sagadraco's massive wings. "I conjured a saddle for you and a harness for the Aegis. You'll land on the Regency's helicopter pad. Communications are still down, so I contracted Gethen telepathically. He'll be waiting. Vivienne's wearing one of Dr. Tarbert's disks, so no one will see you."

Ian lifted me into the saddle and he and Sandra fastened the leg harnesses. Fortunately, I'd done this before. I'd flown with Rake on a goblin sentry dragon at what our commandos had taken to calling the Battle of Bannerman Island. Rake had done the piloting then. Ms. Sagadraco could pilot herself just fine. All I had to do was hold on.

And not throw up on the boss.

Vivienne Sagadraco's takeoff was as smooth as an elevator.

I appreciated her consideration.

Once we were level with Lady Liberty's waist, I got a clear view of the damage.

The entire torch balcony, including the torch was tilted precariously to one side. The statue's wrist looked bent. Her internal frame was steel, so she had taken one heck of an impact.

"Our new allies from the Chrysler Building were quite enthusiastic," the boss said in my mind. *"They saved my life. I want to properly thank them. I'll also need to have Alain send more money to repair the torch."*

"And the visitors' center," I added. *"Stheno wrecked the place...and we, uh, kinda helped."*

"That's quite all right, Makenna. We all do what we must."

The sun was halfway above the horizon.

Please, please let us get there in time.

I was still looking at the Statue of Liberty when I saw it, or thought I saw it. Maybe I did have a concussion.

Lady Liberty had just winked at me.

Well, Ord had said statues over twenty years old were sentient. I'd talked to a bronze owl. Why couldn't a copper lady wink at me?

Stunned, I gave her a little finger wave.

Maybe that was how the Chrysler eagles had known they were needed. Had Lady Liberty alerted the gargoyle council that she had a psychotic dragon and even crazier gorgon in her basement? Plus, an evil mage had turned said basement into a pocket dimension. If all that had been going on directly under my feet, I sure would've noticed.

The great lady had called, and the big guns responded.

Lady Liberty's lips curled ever so slightly at the corners, like Mona Lisa, another lady with a secret.

Maybe Lady Liberty's bent wrist wasn't entirely the Chrysler eagles' doing.

Yesterday afternoon, we'd landed on the Regor Regency's roof in a helicopter. This time I was coming in on a dragon.

Gethen was waiting.

The goblin couldn't see us, but he sure felt it as Ms. Sagadraco landed with powerful beats of her wings. He had to brace himself against the open doorway.

Once I'd extracted myself from the saddle, I unbuckled the harness holding the Aegis and dismounted. When I was no longer touching Ms. Sagadraco, the disk no longer kept me invisible. To Gethen, it must have looked like I popped out of thin air. The boss morphed back into her human form and turned off the disk.

Gethen's eyes were steady on mine. "I knew you would come back."

We went inside.

Sophia Galanis and Helena Thanos still knelt by Rake's side in the exact same place. They hadn't moved in over twelve hours.

Tears of gratitude welled up in my eyes.

Rake was now wearing his robes instead of having them draped over him like a blanket.

He was perfect. If Sleeping Beauty or Snow White had been a prince, this is how they would've looked. We were also at the top of a tower, and I'd helped slay one dragon and flown here on another.

I was desperate for a fairy-tale ending to this nightmare.

"I dressed him at his request," Gethen said from my side. "He said his protective runes are more powerful when the robes are worn correctly."

Rake had once told me that if goblins were going to die in battle, they wanted to leave behind a good-looking corpse. He'd also said that being immortalized in stone had its appeal. Unless someone was clumsy and obliterated the masterpiece. He didn't wish to be reduced to dust.

Sophia and Helena stood.

"Stheno and Tiamat are dead," Ms. Sagadraco told them. "Euryale fought Stheno to give us time to catch my sister before she could use the Aegis. Stheno killed her. I am sorry."

Sophia nodded solemnly and held out her hands for the

Aegis. I gave it to her, and she removed the blanket covering Medusa's face, gazing into her friend's eyes for the first time in over seven thousand years.

"My dear, sweet Medusa," Sophia whispered. She took the Aegis to the edge of the circle and knelt once more. She spoke softly to her friend in what must have been ancient Greek. Then she listened. After what seemed like an eternity, Sophia let out a ragged breath and her shoulders sagged.

Was it too late? It was too late.

Sophia gestured for me to join them.

I hesitated, then obeyed, my steps leaden.

"Medusa has spoken to you without words. You have seen her heart and she has shared her suffering with you. You have cried with her."

I nodded once, crying again now.

"She knows your heart, as well. She will heal Rake, but it must be with your help. She has told me I cannot heal him because I do not love him. Do you?"

I'd been willing to die so the Aegis could be brought back here to heal Rake.

"Yes."

"There can be no doubts. You would give your life for his."

"Yes."

Sophia Galanis held the Aegis out to me.

"Take it. Look at her and heal him."

Now came the doubt. Not whether I loved Rake, but that I could heal him.

"I don't know what to do."

Sophia put her warm hand on mine. "Medusa will tell you

what needs to be done, but you must look at her of your own free will and without fear."

I forced myself to breathe, slowly, evenly. I had seen Medusa's love for her sisters. I had felt her suffering. She had never harmed a living soul. It had taken a goddess at the height of her power to turn Medusa into what she was. Athena was no longer here. Neither were Stheno or Tiamat. I was here, and Medusa wanted to help me.

Gethen lowered the protective circle around Rake.

I took the Aegis, knelt next to Rake, turned the shield toward me, and looked upon the face of Medusa.

I didn't see a screaming face covered in liquid metal. I saw Medusa as she had once been, young, beautiful, innocent, with blue eyes that shone in wonder at the world. Eyes that a vengeful Athena had turned into the ultimate weapon.

A single tear fell from one glorious eye, trailing down a flawless cheek.

"Take it," Medusa said in my mind. *"Touch it to the eyes of your beloved."*

I did.

I wiped away the tear of the greatest gorgon and smoothed it on Rake's closed eyes.

My love and Medusa's tears.

I carefully set the Aegis aside, and bent and kissed Rake's lips. They grew warm.

Rake opened his eyes.

My body heaved with a grateful sob. "Hey, baby," I managed.

He breathed in and out against my face, warm and alive. I gently touched his face and kissed him again.

Rake gave me a sleepy smile. It was the most beautiful thing I'd ever seen—at least as much as I could see through eyes filled with tears. A couple of them fell on his face.

"You're raining on me," he murmured.

"Live with it."

His dark eyes brightened. "I will," he said solemnly.

I made a decision, *the* decision. "I will" was the same as "I do," wasn't it?

"Do you still want to get married? To me?" I clarified.

"Of course. You're not just doing this because I almost—"

"No. Almost losing you made me realize just how much I love you. Life is too short, and too uncertain not to have the one you love."

His gaze searched my face. "To have?"

I smiled. "And to hold. The sooner, the better. Rake Danescu, will you marry me?"

Rake reached up and took my hands in his. His were warm and steady. Mine were shaking a little. Rake slowly kissed each of them, one after the other. Then he went back for seconds.

My smile broadened into a grin. "That's great, but I need verbal consent."

"Yes. Yes, I will marry you."

I sat up with what had to be the goofiest grin ever. "We're engaged." Then I went back to kissing Rake. "Guess who left a trail of breadcrumbs that helped us find the Aegis?" I asked him. "Though I shouldn't ask, because you'll never guess."

"Marek."

"Wrong. Isidor."

"What?!"

"We wouldn't have found the Aegis in time if it hadn't been for him." Then I told Rake how Isidor had helped us.

Rake laughed, loudly and full of life. "Isidor Silvanus saved my life. He is so going to hate that."

I turned to Medusa to thank her, but the Aegis wasn't there. Sophia was holding it, and Helena stood next to her, their eyes wide with shock. Behind them, Gethen and Ms. Sagadraco were likewise amazed.

My body tried to panic again, but it was just too tired. "What's wrong?"

"She's gone," Sophia said. The gorgon turned the Aegis toward us.

The center of the shield had been set with Medusa's head. It was now smooth metal, mirror bright—and empty.

"After you healed Rake, Medusa smiled and her face began to fade," Helena said.

"Perhaps healing Rake healed her, freed her," Sophia said. "Medusa had never been given the opportunity to heal, only kill."

The Aegis was now just a shield.

I hoped that somewhere, somehow, Medusa and her sisters were together again and at peace.

38

Three days later
Herald Square Park

The sun was out, the sky was blue, and the people sitting at the café tables around us were relaxed and happy.

So were we.

Rake was healed, but still taking it easy. Gethen and I were sticking close to ensure he did as his doctor—the Regency's goblin healer Dr. Gerald Jules—had ordered. In the unlikely event Rake escaped me and Gethen, his security team had him surrounded. They were here with us, out of sight but on the job. Rake insisted all the fuss was completely unnecessary, but I knew he really didn't mind.

Ian was here, as was Vivienne Sagadraco, but she'd insisted

we sit down while she popped into Macy's to pick up an order. If a fire-breathing dragon wanted to shop by herself, you let her.

The two of them had just come from the Chrysler Building. Ms. Sagadraco, as a philanthropist well known for financing historical building restoration, had called to arrange a tour, specifically inquiring about the eagle gargoyles. She'd been told there was a structural issue with two of the eagles. Cracks had inexplicably developed where the eagles attached to the building. They had been inspected less than two weeks ago, and the cracks hadn't been there.

Frankly, I was surprised that dislodging themselves to come to our rescue and wedging themselves back into their settings hadn't caused more than a few cracks.

Ms. Sagadraco had immediately offered to pay for the restoration, which got her and Ian a visit to the sixty-first floor to see the damage—and the chance to thank the eagles personally, which had been her intention all along. Ian had asked questions about the building to distract their tour guide while the boss expressed her gratitude.

Due to the damage to the Statue of Liberty and its visitors' center, the island would remain closed for the foreseeable future. The doors to the pedestal and crown hadn't been the only ones fused shut. The same had happened to the security room. When the guards had managed to free themselves, they saw the damage. What had happened to the visitors' center was a mystery, but the damage to Lady Liberty's wrist and torch was consistent with a small plane collision. One plane, possibly two, had been spotted just before dawn. All local airports had been closed due to the blackout, so the search was on for a small plane with commensurate damage.

I shaded my eyes to look up at the two owls perched atop the James Gordon Bennett memorial. I'd already spoken telepathically with Bartholomew and Beatrix to thank them for working with the city's gargoyle council to secure the help of the Chrysler eagles. Yes, Lady Liberty had played a large role, but it'd been a true ensemble effort. I'd told them that Ms. Sagadraco wanted to personally thank them and Wentworth.

"Have you told your family about the engagement yet?" Ian asked me.

"In another couple of days." I wasn't wearing an engagement ring yet because neither Rake nor I were ready for the media feeding frenzy that was sure to ensue. The stone for the ring was still safe in the locket on its chain around my neck. Rake and I were wearing just enough of a glamour to allow us to be out in a public park.

Rake grinned. "Told you we should've done this in Vegas."

"And our families would've killed us."

He shrugged. "Mine would just be thrilled to know I'm capable of making a commitment."

"How involved are we going to allow them to be?" I asked.

"As little as possible. I love my mother and sisters, but giving them *carte blanche*? No, just no. *We* will control this wedding."

I reached over and took his hand. "Agreed. In spades. Our families can throw us one party each, but the wedding will be ours."

"Where do you want to have it?"

"The same place you want to have it. Here. At your hotel. I'm sure your staff will do a splendid job."

"We are known for our society weddings."

"Then that's settled. How about the date? When I tell my family, they'll want to know. Yours will, too."

"How about when we know, we'll tell them. I'll have Genvieve pull the hotel event calendar to see what weekends have already been booked. Picking a date should be fairly simple."

We stopped and looked at each other.

We both knew we could claim control over our families all we wanted to. Claiming was one thing. Enforcing it was something else entirely.

I sighed. "This is going to be a complete three-ring circus, isn't it?"

"We can only hope it goes *that* well."

"Vegas is gonna look so good before this is over."

Rake had a thousand-yard stare as he nodded. "Yes. Yes, it is."

Vivienne Sagadraco approached our table carrying a small-ish Macy's bag. The men stood and Ian held a chair for her. She'd requested one facing the James Gordon Bennett monument.

"One moment, please," the boss told us. She gazed at the top of the monument, where the brother and sister owl proudly surveyed and guarded the park. I couldn't hear their conversation, and I was fine with that. It was personal and private. After a few minutes, I could just make out what I assumed was Bartholomew and Beatrix accepting her gratitude with solemn nods of their bronze heads, their eyes briefly glowing green. If anyone else noticed, they'd have chalked it up to a trick of the midday sun.

The owls resumed their vigil and Ms. Sagadraco turned to Rake.

"Marek Reigory is attempting to buy his way into my good graces," she said.

Rake huffed a laugh. "I'm not surprised. What's his offer?"

"He has proposed being my 'inside man' in the cabal."

"That would be useful. Just don't trust him."

Now it was Vivienne Sagadraco's turn to laugh. "About as far as I could throw him with this body. But I am considering it. In the meantime, Mortimer has seen to it that Mr. Reigory will remain precisely where we have put him until I make a decision. He is very comfortable and equally secure."

"Wise. And if you decide the risk is too great, you could always put Marek in the same room with Phaeon Silvanus. Normally, I'd put my money on Marek in that bout, but Phaeon is a crafty devil. It's possible neither would survive the encounter."

"Should I find incarcerating both too dangerous for my people, I may consider your advice," Ms. Sagadraco told him. "On a more positive note, I thought you might like to know Dr. Tarbert is working on a block of sorts for you against Marek. That way, if I do decide to employ his services, and Viktor Kain incinerates him, you will not go up in a puff of smoke. Or if Phaeon eliminates him."

"I do have a birthday coming up," Rake said. "That would be a welcome gift. Is the good doctor enjoying his new job?"

"Very much so. With Tiamat dead, he can invent to his heart's content, secure in the knowledge that his inventions will be used for good, not evil."

"Have you heard from Helena yet?" I asked her.

"I have. They've arrived on Milos. The sisterhood has a small estate there. Sophia and Zyta believe it's time to bring the sisterhood into the light. They will be headquartered there for the time being. If they outgrow the estate, they have more than adequate resources to purchase whatever they need. Zyta said that Euryale knew the risks of leaving Greece and was tired of living, though in her case, it was merely existing. Her suffering is over, as are Stheno's and Medusa's. They are free, as is the sisterhood. They no longer are tied to the caves and caring for Euryale and Stheno. Helena will be staying with them for a week or so, then returning home. Sophia will remain for now."

The women had taken the empty Aegis with them. Usually, you suffer and then die. Medusa had died and then suffered. She had never healed from what was done to her. I only hoped she was now at rest.

Ms. Sagadraco was looking over my shoulder, smiling. "Ian, would you find another chair? I'm expecting someone, and he's just arrived."

I turned around to see, and when I did, it was all I could do not to squeal.

Dad. Cernunnos.

Minus the antlers and armor.

I didn't squeal, I kept myself from running and jumping into his arms, but I did get myself a humongous hug. It was a good thing I was glamoured or the press would've had a field day with that one. Steady girlfriend of billionaire caught in clinch with hot, blond mystery man.

He was wearing jeans, running shoes and a hoodie like

hundreds of thirty-somethings in the city. Except he only looked young. My father was over five hundred years old.

He put his hands on my shoulders, bent and kissed my forehead, then gazed down at me with his bright green eyes. "I understand you tried to call me. I apologize for not being available. I'm sorry again that I can't stay long now."

"I really didn't want you to answer."

"Why?"

"I was afraid you'd come here to help and get hurt."

"Hurt?" He blinked. "Excuse me?"

Ian spoke up. "I've tried, sir. I think it's a lost cause."

Cernunnos smiled and extended his hand to my partner. "You must be Ian."

Ian stood and shook my dad's hand. "Yes, sir. It's an honor to meet you. I've been wanting to thank you for Janus."

"Believe me, lad, it was my pleasure."

We all sat. It was beyond wonderful to just sit and talk to my dad with the man I was going to marry, surrounded by my SPI family.

I think Rake was having similar thoughts. Though he looked a little distressed.

Oops. I caught his eye and winced. "Sorry."

Rake ran a hand over his face. "Quite all right, darling. Extenuating circumstances."

Dad looked from Rake to me and back again. "Is there something I should know?"

I started to respond, but Rake held up a hand.

I held up a hand of my own. "Hey, *I* asked *you*."

"This time."

"Yes, it's my first and only time proposing. I want to tell."

Rake gestured that I should go right ahead. "Happy wife, happy life."

I gave Dad what had to be a goofy grin. "We're engaged."

"I'd guessed that." He glanced down at my hand, then at Rake. "Where's the ring?"

My future groom sighed. "I know, sir. About that..."

We proceeded to tell him about our last couple of days.

"Vivienne told me some of this," my father said. "She contacted me for two reasons. One, to ask if I could come here today to put your fears to rest concerning my whereabouts. As you can see, I'm whole and well. Two, to inquire about the gorgon sisters, but in particular, Medusa." He glanced at the sky. "I imagine you can't see many stars from this place."

"Next to none," I told him.

"When you are away from the city, look for the constellation known as Perseus." He gave us a small smile. "The star representing Medusa is no longer there. She is free, as are her sisters. You have all done exceedingly well."

I stared in disbelief. "The whole star's gone?"

Ian and Rake had their phones out. The race to Google was on.

Ian's eyes went a little wide. "Found it. Dated yesterday." He skimmed through the article. "Algol, the demon star, represents the head of the gorgon Medusa in the constellation Perseus... It's a variable star or eclipsing binary star, meaning it waxes and wanes in brightness, representing the eye of Medusa... It brightens and dims in an exact two-day, twenty-hour, and forty-nine-minute cycle. Three days ago, it dimmed, then seemingly disappeared... Astronomers are baffled."

We were all silent.

"Medusa is at peace," Cernunnos said softly. "She is together again with her sisters, and in death, Stheno has been healed from her madness."

When the Celtic god of death, repository of the knowledge of all Masters of the Wild Hunt since the beginning of life on this world, told you someone was at rest, you believed him.

Vivienne Sagadraco didn't ask about her sister, so I wasn't about to. Maybe she had asked my father when she'd contacted him about coming here. But there was one thing about her I had to ask.

"With Tiamat gone, what about the cabal?" I asked her. "What about Viktor Kain?"

"There are many adversaries, Makenna. When one is defeated, another will arise to take their place. In the case of the cabal, it will probably be Viktor."

"So, the cabal continues, and no one ever wins?"

"Like the direction of the wind, the definition of what it means to win changes. We must celebrate the times fate shifts in our favor, as it did three days ago—and learn from our failures when it does not. My relationship with Tiamat was very similar to that of Euryale and Stheno. One sister was consumed with hate and revenge. The other refused to go down that path. She continued to love, to give, and to live. Ultimately, Euryale gave her life for her love of Medusa."

Vivienne Sagadraco fell silent, possibly thinking of Tiamat and hoping that her sister who had hated so many for so long, was also finally at peace.

I think Vivienne was, and I was glad for her.

At some point, the Macy's bag had fallen over, and part of its contents had spilled out.

I couldn't believe what I saw. Wait until the guys in the bullpen heard about this. "Is that what I think it is?"

Ms. Sagadraco picked up the bag and put it on the table. "Replacement plush dragon toys for Ruby. I bought her one to play with in my office. It's gone missing, so I bought her two more." The boss pulled the bright blue stuffie out of the bag. "I was glad to see they had another exactly like the one that was lost." She gave the toy an admiring look. "I think it rather resembles me." The edge of a sly smile appeared, and her all-knowing eyes gleamed with mischief. "Wouldn't you say so, Agents Fraser and Byrne?"

ABOUT THE AUTHOR

Lisa Shearin is the *New York Times* and *USA Today* bestselling author of the SPI Files novels, an urban fantasy series best described as *Men in Black* with supernaturals instead of aliens; the Raine Benares novels, a comedic fantasy adventure series; and the Aurora Donati paranormal thriller series.

Lisa is a greyhound mom, avid tea drinker, vintage teapot and teacup collector, grower of orchids and bonsai, and fountain pen and crochet addict. She lives on a small farm in North Carolina with her husband, a small pack of spoiled-rotten retired racing greyhounds, and enough deer, birds, and woodland creatures to fill a Disney movie.

Website: lisashearin.com
Facebook: facebook.com/LisaShearinAuthor
Twitter: @LisaShearin

Printed in the USA
CPSIA information can be obtained
at www.ICGtesting.com
LVHW042012191023
761584LV00010B/407